Gisela Elsner was born in Nuremberg in 1937. She was educated in Vienna, Munich and several other West German cities, studying philosophy, literature and drama. Her first novel, *Die Riesenwerge (The Giant Dwarfs)*, was published in 1964 to considerable critical acclaim. It won the Formentor Novel Prize, was translated into fourteen languages and at the time of its British publication was hailed by the *Times Literary Supplement* as 'extremely comical . . . a tour de force maintained with extraordinary skill'. Her eight other novels, including *Offside*, have been equally well received both for their comic brilliance and trenchant social observation. Gisela Elsner has lived in Italy, France and England, and now resides in Munich.

Offside

Gisela Elsner
Translated from the German
by Anthea Bell

Published by VIRAGO PRESS Limited 1985
41 William IV Street, London WC2N 4DB

First published in West Germany by Rowohlt Verlag GmbH, 1982

Copyright © 1982 by Rowohlt Verlag GmbH, Hamburg
Translation copyright © Anthea Bell 1985

British Library Cataloguing in Publication Data

Elsner, Gisela
  Offside.
  I. Title   II. Abseits, *English*
  833'.914[F]   PT2665.L67
  ISBN 0-86068-530-6
  ISBN 0-86068-535-7 Pbk

Typeset by Clerkenwell Graphics
and printed in Great Britain by
Anchor Brendon, Tiptree, Essex

Although Lerchenau had literally risen from the ground within the shortest possible time at the beginning of the sixties, it could still be seen, some two decades later, that the planners and developers of this part of the city in the south of M had by no means taken their task lightly. Far from it: their endeavours at the time had amounted to a campaign against the monotony endemic, almost without exception, to residential building in this country in the post-war era. Concentrating mainly on providing diversity and non-uniformity, or rather what is commonly described as variety of street layout, they had seen their way to taking a good many risks where harmony was concerned. Thus, the various housing blocks, particularly on the borders of Lerchenau, were not just of remarkably different heights. They were also all painted, and not always too happily, different shades of colour. There was a bright yellow block, for instance, which caught the eye in as unfortunate a manner as did a glaring sky-blue block of a shade which was, to put it mildly, distinctly dubious, especially on cloudless summer days.

Yet one could hadly call the place too colourful. The grass areas between the blocks, which had always, incidentally, kept any part of Lerchenau from bearing even a remote resemblance to a stony desert, largely neutralized even the most doubtful of shades. Obviously relying on Nature herself to provide diversity here, the planners and developers had made all the grass areas absolutely identical in shape. They were all planted with birch trees. At the front of each grass area, by the footpath that led to the doors of the apartment

1

buildings, grew privet hedging planted out as a square and concealing the dustbins of its own building inside it. In the middle of each grass area stood a sand-box, a dark green climbing frame, a dark green swing and a dark green seat, as well as one of the numerous dark green litter bins distributed all around Lerchenau, where even the children used them. And at the back of each grass area, rammed into the ground, there was a framework which was positively besieged by the housewives: a quite ingenious, tree-like metal framework with washing lines rigged between its branching arms and washing hanging from them even on wet days. The housewives of Lerchenau unanimously desisted from the use of this tree-like metal framework only on Sundays and holidays. Even at Christmas no one hesitated to hang out and take down washing on the roofed and over-narrow balconies, or in the basements which likewise were not nearly big enough to take everything that seemed to need washing in this part of town. The women of Lerchenau never stopped bewailing the lack of other facilities for hanging out wet clothes. It made for conflict. It led not just to vehement differences of opinion beside the metal frameworks, where every last centimetre of washing line was always fully occupied, and down in the basements; it caused actual hostilities.

Apart from that, the planners and designers of this quarter had taken its inhabitants' needs into account in a way that left little to be desired. The two shopping streets, one to the south and one to the north of Lerchenau, which were never really busy, contained the usual savings bank branches and self-service shops, and more besides. Lerchenau had, for instance, three boutiques, two shops selling jeans, a sauna and a delicatessen, which had recently delivered a whole lobster to a bachelor accountant as soon as he ordered it. Lerchenau had the extremely popular shop of Herr Aubele, the wine merchant, where you could stand around an empty barrel and have a free tasting of various wines before buying. Lerchenau had an English hairdressing saloon as well as two ordinary hairdressers. And Lerchenau had, in all, four restaurants: the Pizzeria Boccaccio, the Balkan Grill, the Acropolis and, for the most recherché tastes, a bistro called Le Bou-Bou, which was fully booked almost every evening.

In short, Lerchenau might not have a wealth of attractions to offer such as those to be found in, say, Malching, the artists' quarter and night-life district of the city. Nor, despite its extremely clean and often deserted streets, mostly named after famous composers, could it compete in distinction with such superior residential areas as Gundershausen or Ebensee. But the inhabitants of Kröblitz, Frettach, Rottstädt or Zittau would have been happy to be able to pay the kind of rents asked in Lerchenau, not to mention the prices fetched there ever since the early sixties by owner-occupied properties.

For Lerchenau was undoubtedly one of the better parts of M. Nothing could alter that, not even the illustrated article on architecture and town planning which had recently come out in one of the province's biggest magazines, moving most of the people of Lerchenau to indignation that still kept flaring up, particularly in the self-service shops. For reasons they could not fathom, this article had described Lerchenau bluntly as a sterile housing ghetto. Moreover, its author had said he found the prevalent atmosphere here nothing short of depressing, and he attributed the above-average sales of antidepressants in the pharmacies of Lerchenau to this supposedly depressing atmosphere. In the same context, he even mentioned the three cases of suicide which had, incontestably, occurred in Lerchenau during the year.

The article had been illustrated by several photographs, some large and some small, of various housing developments in various cities, all of which had risen from the ruins of the post-war era. These photographs included a full-page colour picture taken in Lerchenau, and showing the glaring sky-blue housing block in the Gluckgasse, mentioned above, in a detailed manner which the people living in that block considered an invasion of their privacy.

The person who felt his privacy most invaded by the full-page colour picture was a relatively young man called Besslein, Ernst Besslein, to be exact, who had just emptied his rubbish bucket into one of the dustbins and was now making his way with precise and measured tread, like someone who knows all eyes are upon him, back to the sky-blue building in the middle of the block, where he and his wife had a three- roomed apartment. Thanks to the little orange tree and the little azalea which stood in pentagonal earthenware pots in the living-room window, and the two deckchairs with their green and purple floral pattern on the balcony, it was so easy to identify this apartment that Ernst Besslein had been alternately cast into fury and desperation: desperation that had first made him remove the little orange tree and the little azalea from the window and put the deckchairs with the green and purple floral pattern away in the basement, and fury that had then made him put the houseplants and the deckchairs ostentatiously back in their places. Nor was that all: he had even stayed off work sick for a day, fearing his colleagues' mockery, although they did not seem to know what had happened and thus could not guess how exposed he had felt ever since the aforesaid illustrated article appeared. On this day off work, he had written thirteen letters in all to the magazine editor, starting off very angry, then becoming icily ironic, and in the end positively dripping with contempt. He had read the last and, he thought, most successful of these letters, beginning with the words *You have been so extraordinarily kind as to photograph my apartment,* out loud to his wife, his parents and several of the other occupants of the building. He had even stamped it and put it in his briefcase. But he had not posted it. In the last resort, his fear of exposing himself even more by sending it was considerably greater than his original fury.

This fear, which had a great influence on all Ernst Besslein's decisions and had often prevented him from assuming the rewarding role of hero, showed even in the way he looked. For Ernst Besslein, naturally a rather inconspicuous man of medium height to start with, already developing a small paunch and displaying a certain stiffness of the hips when he walked, had himself gone to great pains to make sure there was nothing noticeable about him. His hair, light brown and not particularly abundant, could not be described as either eccentrically long or eccentrically short. It just covered his ears and neck, in a discreetly fashionable style, and was only partly combed down over his forehead. The carefully trimmed and brushed moustache on his narrow upper lip was discreetly fashionable in style too. He habitually twisted his upper lip slightly, believing that this gave him a certain look of superiority. Apart from the moustache and the twisted lip, his face was notable chiefly for his metal-framed glasses, also in the correct fashion, with slightly tinted lenses which made his rather small, grey-green eyes look more grey than green. And last but not least, his ochre synthetic fibre suit was correctly fashionable too. It was a single-breasted suit with relatively narrow trouser legs, and showed at a glance how inexpensive it must have been, in spite of the toning ochre waistcoat under the jacket. For the trouser legs were a little too short, the waistcoat stood out rather far from the wearer's chest and the jacket creased. As soon as it was smoothed down behind, creases would inevitably appear in front, and as soon as it was smoothed down in front, creases would inevitably reappear behind. Ernst Besslein, who still thought with satisfaction that the suit, which was indeed very cheap, had been a good buy, was perfectly well aware of this.

All the same, he had smoothed his jacket down several times on the short journey to the dustbin and now he smoothed it down again one last time, first behind and then in front, feeling that all eyes were upon him (for no reason at all, since at the moment not a living soul was watching), before he entered the sky-blue apartment building in the middle of the sky-blue housing block at the end of the Gluckgasse.

✳

The Bessleins' apartment might indeed be just seventy square metres in size, like most of the three-roomed apartments in Lerchenau. And like most of the three-roomed apartments in Lerchenau, it consisted of a fairly large living room with dining area and a narrow, roofed-over balcony, a medium-sized bedroom, a small kitchen, a bathroom with turquoise tiling and a bath tub which was much too short, and – for about the last week – a nursery. But apart from its dimensions and its decidedly unimaginative use of space, it had little in common with most of the other apartments in this district. Or at least, none of the other apartments anywhere around was fitted out and furnished in so uncompromisingly modern a style as the apartment rented by the Bessleins.

You noticed the boldness with which Ernst Besslein and his wife had reflected the spirit of the times in the design of their home the moment you stepped into the extremely narrow corridor. Not only was it painted a pale and chilly grey but the uneven surface of the rough-textured wallpaper underneath the paint made it look like a coat of plaster. The corridor was lit by two spotlights which directed their glaring beams at the ceiling. They were placed to the left and the right of a piece of chunky wooden lattice-work full of knotholes and studded with black nails, their heads the size of saucers. A sturdy coathanger hung from each nail.

Otherwise, the most striking items in this corridor were the white plates the Bessleins had screwed to the doors as soon as they moved in, two years ago, just for a joke. There was a plate on the front door bearing the legend "Emergency Exit". There was a plate on the bedroom door bearing the legend "No Voyeurs". A plate with the words "Please Do Not Disturb During Sittings" showed you the way to the lavatory, and, finally, the living-room door bore a notice considerably larger than the other plates informing the Bessleins' guests before they entered the room, which was indeed practically fit for an exhibition, that it was forbidden to spit on the floor.

In fact the living room, lacking any kind of homely touch, rather resembled an airline office. It was furnished all in black and white. For instance, the seats of the armchairs, which were shaped like concave hemispheres, were white, while the square bases to which these seats were fastened with large and supposedly decorative screws were black. The coffee table, consisting of four adjacent cubic units, was white. The standard lamp, on the other hand, was black. It was shaped like an upside-down letter L with a spotlight on the end of it, its glaringly bright beam turned on a picture hanging over the black and white striped sofa. This painting was an abstract in oils, full of pretzel-shaped squiggles and entitled *Dying Demonstrator*, and had been given to Ernst Besslein for his thirtieth birthday by the artist, a distant relation of his, called Meichelbeck: Fred Meichelbeck, to be precise.

The bedroom was adorned by another abstract in oils, full of pretzel-shaped squiggles and entitled *Unemployed Youth*, given to the Bessleins as a wedding present by the artist Fred Meichelbeck, who was considered leftist, not least because of the names he gave his paintings. Apart from a wardrobe, two chairs that really belonged in the living room and two box-shaped, apricot-coloured bedside tables, the bedroom contained nothing but an apricot-coloured double bed resembling a large rubber dinghy. It was inflatable, and the advantage of it was that if you needed the space it occupied for something else you could let the air out, roll the whole bed up and put it away in the wardrobe.

However, you would have looked in vain for such a practical piece of furniture in the nursery. Indeed, this nursery was the only room in the apartment that made a distinctly nondescript impression. The Bessleins had stored all the furniture that did not suit the style of either living room or bedroom here. The room contained the walnut piano given to Lilo Besslein by her parents for her First Communion. It contained the far from sturdy pine desk at which Ernst Besslein had written his thesis. And it contained the antique bureau Lilo Besslein had inherited from a childless great-aunt. Piles of baby clothes and nappies were now visible through the glass panes in the bureau doors. A bath towel, a brush and a box of powder lay on the desk, which was to be used as a changing table. Apart from these items, there was nothing to show that the room was a nursery except for a white cot, occupied by Ernst Besslein himself as a child, and five soft toys: a hedgehog, an owl, a crocodile, a giraffe and a dachshund.

Ernst Besslein had bought the five soft toys only that day, and when he got home, late in the afternoon, he arranged and rearranged them on the various pieces of furniture in all sorts of different ways until he thought the effect reasonably satisfactory. However, coming into the nursery again just now, he was disappointed to see that in spite of their size the soft toys did hardly anything to give the room more character. He even got the impression that it looked more nondescript than ever. Frowning, he inspected the dachshund and the crocodile on the piano, the hedgehog and the owl on the bureau, and the giraffe on the desk. He thought they all looked as much out of place where they were standing as the towel, the brush and the box of powder looked on the desk, or the piles of baby clothes and nappies behind the glass panes in the bureau doors. However, he refrained from any further alteration to the disposition of the soft toys and the arrangement of the furniture, which he and his wife had moved from one wall to another time and again over the past week, trying everything in every possible part of the room. There's obviously nothing to be done about it, he said to himself, and he left the nursery with a shrug of his shoulders, but still feeling guilty.

That day, Ernst Besslein, who secretly hoped for a son, had become the father of a baby daughter.

*

Dr Gutt's gynaecological hospital was on the western outskirts of the city of M, and stood on an island in the middle of an artificial lake, upon which the convalescing patients could be rowed by members of the hospital staff on fine days. The only access to the hospital was over an arched pedestrian bridge; only ambulances and vehicles driven by doctors and delivery men might be driven across it. The hospital itself was a bright yellow two-storey building surrounded by grounds containing tall trees and a great many benches. There was a miniature golf course near the left wing where mothers who had had their babies used to amuse themselves in the afternoon. There was a cafeteria in the right wing, with a sun terrace going down to the banks of the lake. Several lethargic, overfed swans were always to be found at the end of it, waiting for the mothers to come and feed them. Piped music played cheerful tunes all day long in the cafeteria, at a volume of sound that drowned out the cries of women in labour in the delivery rooms overhead. However, you could often hear those cries from the corridors or reception area: apart from the constant arrival of ambulances, they were among the few indications that this building, frequently taken by day trippers for a hotel and restaurant, actually was a gynaecological hospital.

9

Almost all other clues had been done away with. Thus, the typical hospital smell of disinfectant was overlaid throughout the building by a lilac fragrance, if a rather overpowering one, sprayed around the place every morning by the foreign cleaning women. Thus, the nurses wore fetching lime-green cotton overalls instead of white caps and uniforms. They tied their hair back with lime-green ribbons. And the patients, who mostly wore velvet, silk, brocade or lace dressing gowns as they walked up and down the corridors with a noticeably shuffling gait or assembled outside the boutique in Reception, which displayed whole hospital wardrobes in its windows, looked more like an opera audience at a first night.

There was a hairdresser's in Reception as well as the boutique, and a beauty shop and a florist's, which Ernst Besslein was just leaving with a bunch of roses. He felt rather out of place in these surroundings, though he could not quite say why. So he hurried to the lift at the far end of Reception as fast as possible, and went up to the first floor and his wife's room. Quite a loud sound of voices was coming from the room. Ernst Besslein knocked, and opened the door without waiting for an answer. To his surprise, he saw that his mother and father-in-law the Ohlbaums had arrived from N, as well as his own parents. All holding champagne glasses, they were surrounding his wife, who was sitting on the edge of the bed with her hair freshly done, her face freshly made up, wearing a new pink lounging suit and looking at several not particularly elegant nightdresses which her mother had obviously brought her. Ernst Besslein first embraced his parents, then greeted his in-laws, and finally kissed his wife.

You're looking marvellous, he said.

I went to the hairdresser this morning, and after I'd had my hair done I bought this lounging suit, said his wife. You wouldn't believe what the patients here spend on dressing gowns and nighties and pyjamas.

I hardly dared go out in the corridor, she added.

It's a very pretty outfit, said Ernst Besslein, who was having some difficulty in concealing his annoyance at the extra expense. The mere fact that his wife was in a single room was costing him a lot; his medical insurance only covered a third-class room.

And I saw such a lovely pink dressing gown in the boutique, a perfect match for this lounging suit, his wife went on, and she smiled roguishly at her father, who was tall and broad-shouldered and, despite his paunch and his unmistakable double chin, looked a much finer figure of a man than Max Besslein, half a head shorter, who had lost his right eye and his right arm in the war.

The two mothers were utterly different as well. Frau Ohlbaum was small and plump. She was wearing a curly, mid-brown wig with blonde highlights in it, and her full breasts came bursting out of her corsets. Like all her clothes, her knitted turquoise dress was just a little too tight. At the moment, her rather coarse but not unattractive face was even more flushed than usual, because of the champagne. Her arched, carefully plucked, thin eyebrows were elongated with grey eyebrow pencil. She was wearing pale blue eye-shadow on the lids of her pale blue eyes, which were slightly too small. Her lips were painted, and she wore a great deal of jewellery, first because she liked to, and second to show what the wife of a director of the Seitz Works could afford. A pair of white-gold earrings, each set with three small diamonds, dangled from her ears. A white-gold necklace with five larger diamonds hung around her short, broad neck. A diamond brooch was pinned to her knitted turquoise dress. There were three white-gold bracelets on her short, strong arms, and besides her wedding ring, no fewer than four white-gold rings set with diamonds on her equally short, strong fingers.

Ernst Besslein's mother, Frau Wilma Besslein, looked completely colourless in comparison. She was wearing a plain, grey suit, its jacket too big for her narrow shoulders,

11

although the skirt was stretched tight over her waist, which had spread unbecomingly. Her broad, flat walking shoes made her feet look even larger and her legs even thinner than they were anyway. She had stuck a comb into her hair, which was far from thick and already going grey in front. As usual, she had refrained so completely from any attempt to improve her looks that you could only suppose she did it for reasons of conscience.

All I had was a plain, towelling dressing gown when Ernst was born, she now remarked. But you can't imagine how happy I was.

Aren't you happy, she inquired of her daughter-in-law, in unmistakably sharp tones. Her daughter-in-law was obviously hurt by the question.

Yes, of course I am, she said, and she put the bunch of roses her husband had brought her down on the bedside table so carelessly that it gave him a slight pang.

We don't go making a great show of it when we're happy, not in our family, remarked Frau Ohlbaum, who couldn't stand Wilma Besslein and her prim manner, before turning to her husband and pointing out that their daughter needed a dressing gown.

Oh, I can do without the dressing gown, said Lilo Besslein, whose face had assumed a sulky expression.

But her father, used to reacting promptly to his wife's hints and wishes, would have none of that.

You go and buy it, my dear, he said, and let me know what it cost.

The nurses look after you much better if you've got pretty things to wear, said Frau Ohlbaum, and she poured the remains of the champagne one of the nurses had placed in a cooler into her own glass, without asking if anybody else wanted some.

They look after the baby better too, if the mother's got pretty things to wear, she added.

And what are you two going to call the baby, asked Max Besslein, who was being extremely reticent and unlike his usual self today.

12

Lilo's decided to call her Olwen, said Ernst Besslein, and he cast a cautious glance at his mother-in-law. Her face suddenly went even redder.

But that's no kind of name, she cried.

It's a very unusual name, Wilma Besslein corrected her. What made you think of it, she asked her son.

Lilo found it in a novel, he said.

I still say it's no kind of a name, repeated Frau Ohlbaum, and she turned to her daughter, whose expression was now even sulkier.

Do you want to make the poor little thing miserable, she inquired. Other children will laugh at her the moment she tells them her name's Olwen. You know how cruel children can be. And there are so many pretty names. Why don't you call her Sabine, or Angelika.

Because I like Olwen better, said Lilo Besslein, who had always had trouble standing up to her mother, and she glanced at her husband in a silent plea for help.

However, he acted as if he didn't know what she was after. He had no intention of getting mixed up in a quarrel between mother and daughter. But his mother-in-law was pressing him to say where he stood on the issue.

Your child's mother may be acting irresponsibly, but you're the father, you can't just let her get away with it, she cried.

Well, Lilo likes the name, said Ernst Besslein, and he was about to add something else, but stopped short.

For at this moment one of the nurses came into the room with a tray holding a pot of coffee and a slice of cake. As she was putting the tray down on the bedside table and picking up the bunch of roses, Wilma Besslein asked if they could see the baby.

Yes, of course, said the nurse. I'll take you to the nursery straight away.

Just let me put these roses in a vase, she added, leaving the room.

No one said anything for some minutes after she had closed the door behind her. Ernst Besslein realized that his mother-in-law had by no means calmed down. Indeed, the veins on her temples were now swelling and her eyes bulging from their sockets. She was looking daggers at her daughter, who seemed to be near tears.

So you're absolutely set on calling her Olwen, are you, she inquired.

Well, after all, she's my baby, not yours, replied Lilo Besslein as the nurse came back into the room and put the vase of roses down on the table, beside the wine cooler.

Would you come with me, please, she said, addressing herself chiefly to Wilma Besslein, who followed her, along with her husband and son. Paul Ohlbaum merely made as if to follow too, but stopped after he had taken a couple of steps towards the door, for his wife was staying put.

Don't you want to go with her, he asked.

I don't want to see this little Olwen, she said, and she opened her turquoise handbag, took out a mirror and a lipstick, and began touching up her lips. All of a sudden she was calmness itself.

Embarrassed, Paul Ohlbaum looked from her to his daughter, who now began to sob weakly.

I'll never forgive you for this, she hissed at her mother.

Oh, let's go. I'm not staying here to be insulted, said her mother, and she put her mirror and lipstick back in the handbag and went to the door, which was still open.

As she left the room, Paul Ohlbaum stayed put for a moment, irresolute, rubbing his hands in embarrassment without appearing to notice it. Then he took a hesitant step towards the bed after all, obviously meaning to say goodbye to his daughter. Simultaneously, however, he seemed to be alarmed by the notion that this might send his wife into another temper, for no sooner had he taken that one step than he turned abruptly on his heel and left the room too.

When her parents had gone, Lilo Besslein began sobbing harder than ever. Her tears, however, were tears of rage and not grief. She had clenched her fists. Her face was all distorted. The black lines she had elaborately traced around her pretty blue eyes dissolved, and black rivulets ran down her cheeks.

Her husband and her dismayed parents-in-law found her like this when they came into the room. Ernst Besslein, whose relationship with his parents was a very much better one than Lilo Besslein's with hers, asked what had happened. But his wife had no intention of answering his question. She cast him a venomous glance.

Kept safely out of everything as usual, didn't you, she said, wiping her face on the sheet. You're such a coward, oh, you're just so wet and feeble. I'm sorry I ever had a baby of yours at all.

Yes, I am, I'm sorry I did, she repeated, to the astonishment of her parents-in-law.

How can you say such a thing, cried Wilma Besslein, putting an arm around her son's shoulders. He was looking extremely crestfallen.

This maternal gesture infuriated Lilo Besslein even more.

Oh, just look at the pair of you, it's really silly. Mother and son, talk about togetherness, she cried, while Wilma Besslein, face wooden, let her arm drop again.

I think we'd better go, she said, propelling her husband towards the door.

Ernst Besslein followed his parents without a backward glance at his wife, who began to sob again. He was mortally offended by her calling him cowardly, wet and feeble. He walked down the corridor to the lift with his parents in silence. He went down to the ground floor with them in silence. When they reached Reception, Wilma Besslein suggested a visit to the cafeteria. Ernst Besslein and his father agreed. As they headed for the cafeteria, Wilma Besslein made sure her son was in the middle of the three of them. Once they were in the cafeteria, overcrowded at this time of day with mothers who had given birth and pregnant women waiting for labour to begin, she went on mothering him in a way he thought touching. Although he really needed to lose several

15

pounds in weight, she saw that his father ordered him two slices of gateau. She gave him a taste of her cheesecake. He gave her a taste of his gateau. His father gave him a taste of his fruit tart. He gave his father a taste of his gateau. His mother gave his father a taste of her cheesecake, and his father gave his mother a taste of his fruit tart. This kind of thing was usual with the Besslains, whose family life was harmonious in the extreme, unlike that of the Ohlbaums.

Ernst Besslein enjoyed being on his own with his parents again. Exposed as he was to his wife's constant criticism, the fact that they never found fault with him did him good. His mother asked, sympathetically, if his wife often nagged him like that. He could have told her that Lilo frequently called him much worse than cowardly, wet and feeble. But he shook his head in a melancholy way and suggested talking about something else.

However, his mother was not ready to change the subject yet.

Lilo doesn't seem at all happy, she said.

She struck me as radiantly happy yesterday, said Ernst Besslein.

Didn't she want the baby, inquired his father.

She was horrified to find she was pregnant at first, said Ernst Besslein. But she's been looking forward to it these last few months, all the same.

Still, she just said, loud and clear, she was sorry she'd ever had a baby of yours, remarked his mother.

We'll see how she feels tomorrow, said Ernst Besslein, who was having difficulty in concealing his dejection. He ate the rest of his gateau in silence, brooding over his wife's changeable moods. He had suffered from them ever since they were married, almost three years ago. He had hoped the birth of the baby would make his wife more stable, but she seemed even less stable than before. He wondered if she really were sorry she'd had his baby. He told himself she probably just said so in a moment of temper. He thought of her shrill screams in labour the day before. He felt he would like to go back up and see her again. He felt he would like to be conciliatory and make up the quarrel. But he was afraid of being soft and so losing face.

She's probably sorry she went on like that by now, he said, speaking mainly to his mother, who sat staring at her empty plate, lost in thought, while his father paid the bill. He would have liked to sit there with his parents for a little longer, but his father was suddenly in a hurry to leave. Ever since his retirement, he had displayed a kind of hectic activity for no good reason. He rose and made for the door of the cafeteria, without looking to see if his wife and son were following, and then waited impatiently for them. Wilma Besslein made sure her son was in the middle of the three of them again as they went down the corridor. Passing the lift, she asked whether he wanted to go back up and see his wife. Ernst Besslein merely shook his head. He escorted his parents to their car, embraced them, and stood waving goodbye until they had disappeared from sight. Then he went to his own car, which was standing nearby. He opened the door, put his safety belt on and started the engine.

I'm going to get drunk this evening, he told himself before he drove off towards Lerchenau.

*

Meanwhile Lilo Besslein, having calmed down, was busy making up her eyes again. It was some time since she had dared to face the world without any eye make-up. She opened a small jar of silvery pale blue eye-shadow, ran her forefinger over the creamy substance, and applied it first to her right eyelid, then to her left eyelid. Next she opened a little bottle of liquid eye-liner, dipped a fine brush into the black fluid, leaned right over the wash-basin until she was close to the mirror, and drew two black lines, first along the rim of her upper right eyelid, then, after dipping the brush back in the black fluid, along the rim of her upper left eyelid, each line extending

17

some three of four millimetres beyond the outer corner of the eye. When she had drawn both lines she inspected them expertly to see if they were the same. She then dipped the brush back into the black fluid again and drew two more lines, first along the rim of her lower right eyelid, then along the rim of her lower left eyelid, these two lines meeting the upper lines a little way from the corners of her eyes and forming acute angles with them. She checked that both these lines were the same too, thickened first the line along the lower right eyelid and then the line along the lower left eyelid with another stroke of the brush, and then painted over those areas of pale skin still showing between the outer corners of her eyes and the acute angles formed by the meeting of the lines along the upper and lower eyelids. Yet again, she checked to see if the two black areas at the corners of her eyes matched. With another brush-stroke she extended the left-hand corner, which struck her as a little bit smaller than the right-hand corner, and looked at herself in the mirror once more. This time she was satisfied with the result of her labours. She put the brush down on the glass shelf under the mirror, which also held her moisturizer, her night cream, her cleansing milk, her facial tonic, her make-up and her eye make-up remover. She put the tops on the little bottle of liquid eye-liner and the little jar of silvery pale blue eye-shadow, picked up a case which held, among other things, several brushes and eyebrow pencils and a pencil sharpener, and took out a metal container about the length of a ballpoint pen. She unscrewed this container, pulled out a round brush loaded with mascara, and began applying it to her lashes. Whenever two lashes stuck together she picked up a needle which she kept in the case as well and used it to part them before re-applying the brush. Eventually, she pushed the brush back into its container, put it in the case, and took out one of the eyebrow pencils, which she used to lengthen her carefully plucked eyebrows. Once again she checked to see that both lines matched. Then she opened her little bottle of make-up, let a few drops fall on the back of her hand, and began distributing them around her face. When she had done that, she combed her curly, mahogany-coloured fringe over her forehead, and earnestly examined her entire face. She told herself she looked pretty now, and smiled at her reflection for some minutes, before switching off the light over the mirror and leaving the bathroom.

When she got back to her bed she stood there for a moment, irresolute, and glanced at the novel on the bedside table. She had brought it with her for hospital reading, but she didn't want to read. She felt her stomach. To her vexation, it was not flat yet. She felt her breasts, which were noticeably enlarged. Not for the first time since the birth of her baby daughter she was overcome by anxiety about her figure, and wondered if her pregnancy might have done it permanent damage. Sighing, she lay flat on the bed and did the exercises taught her that morning by one of Dr Gutt's assistants, dark-haired, dark-eyed, wonderfully virile-looking Dr Borelli. As she did them she tried conjuring up the image of Dr Borelli. She fancied him more than she fancied her husband. She wondered if she had made the same kind of impression on him. But thoughts of him soon vanished. The exercises called for all her attention. She got out of breath. She felt herself begin to sweat. However, she went on doing exercises until one of the nurses brought her baby daughter into the room.

She had not been thinking about the baby at all, but she immediately switched to the role of happy young mother.

There's my girl at last, she cried, stretching out her arms for the baby, who suddenly began to cry quietly.

Now, now, what are you crying for when I'm bringing you to your Mummy, the nurse asked the baby.

Oh, who's a little lady, then, she added. A real little lady. Little ladies mustn't cry, though, must they.

I expect this little lady's hungry, said Lilo Besslein.

Hungry are you, little lady, she asked the baby, opening the top of her pink lounging suit. She soaked a cotton wool ball in spirit and began using it to clean the nipple of her left breast. When she had finished, the nurse laid the baby in her arms. Lilo Besslein put her nipple in the baby's mouth, and she immediately began sucking. The nurse stood beside the bed for a moment, with a doting smile on her face, and then left the room.

So you're already a real little lady, are you, then, Lilo Besslein inquired. She had read a book which said one should talk to babies from the start.

Oh yes, you're a real little lady, you are, she said, looking unenthusiastically at her daughter, who had two large bumps at the back of her head, the aftermath of birth. Her eyes were slits, and pale blue like all new babies' eyes. Her nose looked rather squashed. Her ears stood out slightly and had distinctly long lobes. Thin, dark brown hair, about a centimetre long, covered her head. The fontanelle above her forehead rose and fell with her pulse-beat. Her only attractive features, Lilo Besslein thought, were her tiny little hands, now clenched into fists. Carefully, she opened one of the two fists and put her forefinger into the baby's little hand, which instantly closed around it.

Holding my finger tight, are you, she asked the baby.

Oh yes, you're holding it ever so, ever so tight, she said, without taking her eyes off the baby. She wondered if she loved her. She tried to work out her own feelings. Apart from a faint sense of anxiety, however, she felt nothing. She had carried her daughter for nine months, yet the baby seemed strange. She might just as well have been any other mother's new baby. Lilo Besslein observed the greedy way the baby sucked at her breast with a certain distaste. She saw traces of white milk at the corners of her mouth. Suddenly the baby stopped sucking. She turned her head aside, and the nipple slipped out of her mouth. She began crying quietly again. Rather worried, Lilo Besslein directed her nipple to the baby's mouth once more. The baby sucked once or twice before letting it slip out.

Now then, why have you stopped drinking, she asked the baby. She cupped her left breast in her hand and squeezed it quite hard. To her surprise, she found there was no milk left in it. She did up the top of her lounging suit, laid a clean nappy over her shoulder, and held the baby so that they were breast to breast and the baby's head reached above her own shoulder.

Who's going to do a nice little burp, then, she asked the baby.

This little lady's going to do a dear little, nice little burp, she said, rubbing away at the baby's back with her hand. The baby burped violently, bringing up a gush of milk, which soaked the shoulder of the new pink lounging suit as well as the nappy.

Irritated, Lilo Besslein put her baby daughter down on the bed and inspected the damage. The slightly acid, milky smell nauseated her. She went into the bathroom, took off the top of the lounging suit and washed the soiled patch in the basin. While she was hanging it up over the bath, the baby began whimpering again. Feeling that too much was being expected of her, she hurried back to her bed and glanced at the baby, who had just brought up another gush of milk. The whitish, faintly acid liquid clung to her chin and her little pink jacket. Her face was red. Her mouth was wide open, showing her toothless gums. Her arms and legs were flailing up and down.

Lilo Besslein stood there by the bed for a moment, totally at a loss. For the first time, she felt she just wasn't up to the responsibility she would have to take for her child. She was sorry her mother and her mother-in-law were no longer here. She felt tears rising again, and the one thing that stopped her shedding them was the fact that she had only just re-done her eyes. Finally she rang for the nurse. Since the nurse did not appear at once, she put on a pyjama jacket and a dressing gown and set off in haste for the nurses' room. Half-way there, she suddenly felt afraid the baby might have fallen off the bed. She rushed back to the room, where her small daughter was lying on the bed and yelling for dear life. As she approached the bed, the nurse appeared in the doorway and looked inquiringly at Lilo Besslein. Much agitated, Lilo Besslein explained that she didn't know what to do.

She brought up a whole lot of milk, twice, she said.

Well, that's nothing to worry about, said the nurse.

But she hasn't had enough milk anyway, said Lilo Besslein.

And why is she crying like that, she inquired.

Oh, you just want to pick her up, said the nurse, and she went over to the bed, picked the baby up, and carried her up and down the room. The baby stopped crying at once. Lilo Besslein burst into hysterical laughter. The nurse handed her the baby.

You'll have to learn to cope on your own, she said before she left the room.

Lilo Besslein walked up and down her room with the baby. She didn't know what to say to her. She suddenly felt it was silly, asking the baby questions and then answering them herself. Whenever she got to the window she looked down at the grounds. At this time of day, the patients out there were mainly expectant mothers waiting for labour to start and older women who had come in for gynaecological operations. The new mothers were all in their rooms with their babies. Lilo Besslein reckoned she had to look after her daughter for another quarter of an hour. The time seemed to creep by. She told herself this wouldn't do; here she was, already feeling bored with her child. She thought of the weeks, months and years she would have to spend in that child's company. She wondered

22

why she couldn't feel as happy as everyone expected. Her unhappiness seemed like bad manners. She would never have dared mention it to anyone. She sat down on the edge of the bed and looked at the baby. To her dismay, the baby began yelling for dear life again. She instantly stood up and resumed walking up and down the room. But the baby would not stop yelling. She didn't know what to do. She was on the point of ringing for the nurse again, and all that held her back was the fear of displaying her weakness. She tried, and failed, to ignore the baby's crying. It did worse than irritate her: it infuriated her. She would have liked to smack the baby's face. She gritted her teeth so hard that they grated together. Simultaneously, she remembered her horror when she saw the positive result of her pregnancy test, some eight months ago. She remembered getting hold of the addresses of hospitals which did abortions. She remembered her conversations with her husband, her girlfriends in N and her parents, who had all persuaded her to have the baby. She remembered how she had eventually become reconciled to having a baby, how she even looked forward to it during the latter months of her pregnancy. She wondered why she wasn't as happy now as she had been told she would be. She felt as if her husband, her girlfriends and her parents had tricked her. She sat down on the bed again and looked at the baby, who was still yelling for dear life. She wondered why she felt no bond between them. Then her conscience suddenly pricked her, hard. She gently wiped the tears from the baby's cheeks with her hand, and then rocked her in her arms. But the baby went on crying until the nurse came in and took her, whereupon she stopped. Lilo Besslein burst into hysterical laughter again. The nurse gave her a rather odd look before she left the room.

When she had closed the door behind her, Lilo Besslein went into the bathroom. She took down the trousers of her lounging suit and her pants, threw the blood-soaked sanitary towel she was wearing underneath them into the bin behind the lavatory, and sat on the lavatory seat. When she passed water her perineum stung so much where Dr Gutt had cut it during labour that she moaned softly. Standing up, she saw a pool of blood in the lavatory pan. She flushed the lavatory, a rather worried expression on her face. Then she went to the wash-basin, soaked some cotton wool in warm water, and carefully wiped away the blood between her legs. As she did so, fresh drops of blood fell from her genital area on to the cotton wool, dyeing it scarlet. For a moment she felt as if all her blood were draining away, and her face looked worried again. She quickly put a new sanitary towel between her legs, pulled up her pants and the trousers of her lounging suit, and went back into the bedroom. She lay down on the bed. She tried to think of something pleasant. She failed. And once again uncontrollable fear swept over her: fear that she would not be up to the demands the baby was making on her.

✳

A week later she and the baby were discharged from hospital. Ernst Besslein, who came to fetch them in his car, was surprised by her sudden aura of confidence. Though he suspected this confidence was due to the effects of the anti-depressant tranquillizer Dr Gutt had prescribed her, he was glad to see her so carefree. She didn't even seem to be worrying about the state of the apartment. Indeed, as he parked the car in the Gluckgasse she said it was good to be home. He got out of the car, locked the door, came round to the other side and let her hand him out the baby, who had been asleep thoughout the drive. Now the baby opened her eyes, and he felt as if she were looking around her.

What a clever little thing she is, he said, before giving the baby back to his wife, who had now got out of the car herself. He took her case out of the boot, then put an arm around her shoulders, and they walked up the path together. Their neighbour Frau Deininger, a plumpish woman of about forty, married to a civil servant, was on her way down the path carrying a rubbish bucket. When she reached them, she put the bucket down and tip-toed closer to look at the baby. Much to the Besseleins' satisfaction, she seemed enraptured.

Oh, isn't she sweet, she cried, almost screeched. Just look at those little eyes and that little nose and that little mouth and those little fingers. Ooh, she's good enough to eat.

What are you calling her, then, she inquired.

Olwen, said Lilo Besslein, slightly irritated because Frau Deininger had come rather closer to her small daughter than she really liked.

Well, to be honest, that's a name I never heard before, said Frau Deininger.

And we've decided not to have her christened, said Ernst Besslein. Not only did he think this a very bold step but he expected to make a great sensation by announcing it. He observed Frau Deininger closely, but to his disappointment she seemed quite unmoved by the information.

Quite right too, was all she said before picking her rubbish bucket up again, wishing the Besseleins all the best in her near-screech, and setting off on her way to the dustbin.

Not much sensibility there, remarked Ernst Besslein, as he and his wife walked towards the sky-blue building in the middle of the sky-blue housing block.

She wasn't at all surprised to hear we're not having Olwen christened, he added.

But his wife did not reply to either remark. Her mind seemed to be on other things. She went through the main door of the building and climbed the six steps to the door of their own apartment in silence. There was a strained expression on her face as she waited for her husband to open the apartment door. She was afraid she was going to find the place hopelessly untidy. No sooner was she inside, however, than she realized it was in a state of painful neatness, and moreover, her husband had obviously dusted the furniture very recently and seemed to have gone over all the carpets with the vacuum cleaner. Lilo Besslein couldn't spot any fluff at all on them. He had a small surprise waiting for her in each room, too. There was a bunch of roses on the white coffee table in the living room, with a handwritten card leant up against it saying *Welcome Home*. There was a little box of sweets on the apricot-coloured bedside table in the bedroom. There was a big jar of night cream on the glass shelf under the bathroom mirror, and a bottle of champagne in a cooler in the kitchen.

Lilo Besslein, who had not been expecting such a welcome, felt both touched and abashed. She kissed her husband on the mouth, much less skilfully than usual, and then carried the baby into the nursery, where she found the soft toys bought by Ernst Besslein, as previously mentioned, on the day of her daughter's birth. Although she thought all these soft toys were in extremely poor taste, she was overcome by mingled emotion and shame again.

He's a good man, he really is, she told herself, as she put the baby down on the blanket spread over the desk and took off her woolly cap and her little woolly jacket. She smiled at Ernst Besslein, who was standing awkwardly in the doorway in his ill-fitting ochre synthetic fibre suit and telling her, in his slightly grating voice, how he didn't intend to give little Olwen a conventional girl's upbringing.

He was going to buy her a lorry and a digger truck and an electric train set, he said. He was going to play football with her and teach her to climb trees, he said. He was going to be perfectly frank with her in sexual

matters too, he said; he was going to let her see him
naked from the very start, he was going to share the
bathtub with her, and he was going to tell her how
babies were born as soon as she was old enough to
understand.

He was getting quite carried away, emphasizing his
remarks with chopping motions of his hand. Lilo
Besslein, who was busy taking off the baby's wet
nappies, got the impression that he regarded himself as
an educational pioneer in the matter of his daughter's
upbringing. She glanced surreptitiously at him as he
stood there in the nursery doorway, feet turned out,
with his little paunch bulging under his ochre waistcoat
and the roll of fat over his hips which never would go
away, in spite of all his sporting activities. And not for
the first time, she found it hard to take him seriously.
She compared him with the lovers she had had before
him. She wondered whether she would have been
happier with dark-haired, dark-eyed Udo Comenius, a
law student; she had broken with him just before they
would have got engaged. She thought of Alexander
Florence, a medical student from a prosperous family
background. She actually had got engaged to him,
rather ostentatiously, five years ago, and then he had
thrown her over for someone else. Ernst Besslein had
just been a sort of stopgap to her at the start, and then
she went on going out with him for lack of other
invitations. She had been attracted mainly by the
persistence with which he courted her. It was this
persistence, displayed at a time when the best circles of
society in N were smiling pityingly at her – a girl whose
fiancé had jilted her – and her desire to get away from
home, or rather away from the influence of her overbearing mother, that had finally made her agree to
marry him. The marriage did her no good socially;
indeed, she had gone down in the world slightly. Unlike
the parents of Alexander Florence, who owned a
surgical instruments factory, a villa, a big holiday home

beside Lake Garda and several apartment buildings, Ernst Besslein's parents had acquired no more than a small house in one of the better parts of N, in spite of habits of strict thrift bordering on parismony such as their son displayed too. Max Besslein had been just an engineer at the Seitz Works before he retired, whereas Paul Ohlbaum was a director of the firm. Ernst Besslein, who had always been a model of filial obedience and never, even as a teenager, had any differences of opinion with his parents, followed in his father's footsteps without stopping to think about it much. He had no particular inclinations, so he studied engineering like his father. And like his father, he applied for a position at the Seitz Works. Professionally speaking, the only difference was that Ernst Besslein was employed at the Seitz Works branch in M, while his father had been employed at the Seitz Works branch in N. Ernst Besslein did his job without asking himself if he enjoyed it. Early in their marriage, he had often told his wife at supper, in his characteristically long-winded style, about little incidents that had happened at work that day. After a while, however, he realized that she was only half listening, or not listening at all. Since then he had kept quiet about his professional life, and indeed Lilo Besslein took no interest in it. She knew the Seitz Works made machinery for manufacturing filter cigarettes, and that was enough for her. Once a year, when the firm had a party to which wives were invited, she went with her husband and was bored to death. Now and then they went to the firm's tennis club on Saturday afternoons. Now and then they were invited to coffee or to supper by his colleagues Dülfer, Einsele and Urzinger. Now and then they invited his colleagues Dülfer, Einsele and Urzinger, along with their wives, to coffee or to supper with them. On these occasions Lilo Besslein showed what a good housewife she was. She would spend the whole of the previous day in the kitchen, busy baking tarts and cakes, or preparing exotic salads and marinating choice cuts of meat. She would lay the table with the Rosenthal china her parents had given her when she got engaged to Alexander Florence. She took the Rosenthal glasses out of the adjustable wall unit reaching almost to the ceiling beside the dining area of the living room, along with the silver-plated cutlery and the silver-plated candlesticks, which, like most of her crockery, cutlery and linen, had also been given to her by her parents when she got engaged to Alexander Florence. She laid all these things on the dining table which, when fully extended, fitted in the living room only if you put the two black and white armchairs in the bedroom and moved the white coffee table over to the sofa.

Although she had been living in this apartment for two years, Lilo Besslein still suffered from its lack of space. She had grown up in a villa with a big garden, complete with swimming pool. She wished she had a bigger and better-proportioned apartment. Early in their marriage her husband had opened a savings agreement with a building society, but saving for your own apartment turned out to be a very dubious proposition, with the prices of owner-occupied properties rising annually. There could be no question of moving to a larger and thus more expensive rented place; the Bessleins were already paying a rent of seven hundred and forty marks. Before her daughter was born, Lilo Besslein had worked part time as assistant in a pharmacy in order to have some money of her own over and beyond her meagre housekeeping allowance to spend on new clothes, cosmetics and hair-dos, and so that she could treat her husband to a meal out in a good restaurant in Malching, the artists' quarter of the city. There were no extra earnings now, and she realized she couldn't give in to her frequent desire for a spending spree any more. But she had still blown the last of her bank account on the expensive pink dressing gown in the boutique at Dr Gutt's hospital, as well as buying the pink lounging suit. She deeply regretted the purchase of the dressing gown now, and dared not mention it to her husband, who was watching as she changed the baby's nappy, positively eager to learn how to do it himself.

When she had changed the nappy she handed him little Olwen and went into the kitchen to prepare a feed. She had decided to stop breast-feeding her daughter three days before. Her swollen breasts and her awareness that her body was still at another living creature's service had bothered her so much that she consulted Dr Gutt, and he prescribed something to stop the milk. Although her conscience pricked her, she had felt much better in herself ever since. Ernst Besslein watched her make the bottle; he wanted to know how to do that too. When she had checked its temperature she gave it to him and, beaming happily, he carried his baby daughter into the living room, sat down on a chair in the dining area and put the honey-coloured teat into her mouth.

When the baby had finished her bottle he propped her up and waited for her to burp. Then he gave her back to his wife and went to get his cine-camera. It was just two in the afternoon, and the living room was flooded with sunlight. Some children from the sky-blue block were playing a noisy game of football on the grass outside the window, between the little orange tree and the little azalea, and he filmed her for about a minute. Then he stood in front of the window, holding the baby, and got his wife to film him for about a minute too. Finally they put the baby down in her cot, where she instantly fell asleep, and filmed her lying there for about a minute.

I'll film her being bathed and changed tomorrow, Ernst Besslein said, and just then the telephone began to ring. It was his brother-in-law Eugen Rittmeier, back from a week's visit to Thailand with his wife, ringing to congratulate him on the birth of his daughter. He asked when they could come and see the baby. Ernst Besslein, having made sure his wife didn't mind, invited them straight round for coffee. As soon as he had put the phone down it rang again. This time the caller was Fred Meichelbeck the artist, his distant relation. Fred Meichelbeck said he was going to give him and his wife a watercolour to mark the occasion of their daughter's birth. Ernst Besslein invited him to coffee too. This cast his wife into a state of agitation that rather surprised him. She asked him, anxiously, if it was obvious that she was still five pounds overweight. She asked him how she was looking. She asked him what she should wear. Finally, she asked him to go out and buy some cakes, and disappeared into the bathroom to apply a face mask. Then, with the white mask on her face, she hurried into the bedroom and inspected all her clothes in the wardrobe. She decided to wear a black and gold striped blouse and black jeans with narrow gold braid down the side seams. The jeans were such a tight fit that she had to lie flat on the floor and hold her breath to get the zip done up and fasten the waistband. She stood up again, groaning, felt the mask, which had hardened on her face by now, and went into the living room. She moved the two black and white armchairs aside, pulled the dining table out, put its extension leaf in place and laid it for coffee. Then she went back into the bathroom to remove the mask from her face with a damp cotton wool ball.

When Ernst Besslein got back with a carrier bag full of cakes and put his head in at the bathroom door, she was busy making her eyes up. He knew better than to disturb her at this task, and withdrew his head again at once. He went into the kitchen, unpacked the cakes, hastily devoured a slice of gateau and arranged the remaining slices of tart and cake on a cake plate. Then he carried the two black and white armchairs out of the living room and into the bedroom, took one of the bedroom chairs into the living room, and placed it at

31

the table. Finally he sat down on the sofa and opened the sports section of the national daily paper he took. However, he found it hard to concentrate on it today. He kept thinking of his wife and baby. He was glad they were both home. He was glad everything was almost back/to normal now. His wife's absence had felt like a state of emergency, and he didn't like states of emergency. He was only thirty-two, but he set great store by a quiet life. While his wife was in hospital he had not once gone off the rails; he hadn't even put his resolution of getting drunk into practice. He thought of the champagne he had put in the cooler to chill. He would have liked to drink a glass of it with his wife before their guests arrived, and was just asking himself what she could be doing in the bathroom all this time when she came into the living room, with the slightly stiff smile she always wore when she had just done her face. She asked him if she'd pass. He looked at her standing there in her high-heeled shoes, which made her long legs look even longer, in her skin-tight jeans, which fitted her round buttocks snugly, with her curly mahogany hair emphasizing her pale complexion, and her large, black-rimmed eyes, shaded by long lashes.

You look very pretty, he said, although he liked her far better without make-up, and he rose and took a step towards her, meaning to kiss her. But she fended him off with both hands, afraid he might smudge her make-up, and went straight into the kitchen to start the coffee machine.

The coffee was just running through the filter when the doorbell rang three times. Ernst Besslein opened the door and greeted the Rittmeiers with great heartiness, as usual.

Hello, you old rascal, he cried in what was practically a bellow.

Hello, you old devil, you, his brother-in-law bellowed back. He had obviously overdone the sunbathing during his week in Thailand, for his face, neck and hands were bright red. With a touch of malicious pleasure, Ernst Besslein noticed that the skin was already beginning to peel on the bridge of his nose and his forehead. His sister Gitta's face, neck and arms were even redder. The intense sunlight had given her little wrinkles at the corners of her eyes. She too greeted Ernst Besslein, whom she called Ernesto, in what was practically a bellow, before she turned to Lilo Besslein, who was anxiously pointing out that the baby was asleep, and gave her a large bunch of roses and a packet of disposable nappies.

Although Lilo Besslein had expected the Rittmeiers, who ran a flourishing estate agency, to produce a rather more generous present to mark her daughter's birth, she expressed immense delight. They went into the living room and sat straight down at the table since the armchairs were in the bedroom. Ernst Besslein got the champagne glasses out of the wall unit and the bottle of champagne he had really meant to drink alone with his wife out of the kitchen, and opened it with much ostentation. They drank to the baby's health. Gitta Rittmeier, in particular, insisted on seeing her, so they rose from the table again and tip-toed into the bedroom, where Ernst Besslein's sister hung over the cot with an enraptured expression on her face for several minutes, giving the impression that she just couldn't see enough of the baby. To Ernst Besslein's annoyance, however, his brother-in-law merely glanced briefly at the child and then went straight back to the living room.

As they sat down at the table again, Ernst Besslein explained, portentously, that he was not having his little daughter christened. And once again he was disappointed to find that neither his brother-in-law nor his sister seemed in the least surprised, let alone shocked.

Yes, quite right, said Eugen Rittmeier, obviously bored, before pointing to the fifth place laid at table and asking who else was coming.

Fred Meichelbeck. He's never punctual, said Ernst Besslein, casting a sharp glance at his brother-in-law, who did not especially like the artist. He's giving us a watercolour to mark the baby's birth, he added. He absolutely insists.

Well, at least he'll be rid of another of those pictures; he's been sitting on them God knows how many years, remarked Eugen Rittmeier, much to Lilo Besslein's indignation.

One of these days his pictures may be very much sought after on the art market, she said, and then abruptly fell silent.

For at this moment the doorbell rang.

Ernst Besslein went to open the door and welcome the artist who, unlike the rest of his guests, was not infected by his mode of greeting and did not raise his voice to a near-bellow. Then he took him into the living room, where Lilo Besslein came to meet him with her rather stiff smile. With exaggerated courtesy, Fred Meichelbeck bowed so deeply to her that she couldn't help laughing. Then he asked Ernst Besslein if it was all right to kiss his wife, just for once, and without waiting for an answer kissed Lilo Besslein rather boldly full on the mouth – much to her annoyance, she blushed – before handing her the roll of cardboard containing the watercolour and a small bunch of overblown white roses which, he claimed, he had just stolen.

That's what made me late, he said, and skipped over to the dining table to greet the Rittmeiers, with the fascinated eyes of Ernst Besslein's sister Gitta as well as of Lilo Besslein upon him.

Fred Meichelbeck was a slight, narrow-shouldered man who looked as if he was of medium height only by dint of wearing built-up heels. Even his very elegant, light grey flannel suit, which he must have bought with one of the fees he earned by writing critical essays on art for various radio stations, did not conceal the fact that he was exceptionally thin. He had not sold any pictures for years, so these critical essays kept his head above water. Apart from his thinness, the most striking thing about him was the faint resemblance he bore to Trotsky. Fred Meichelbeck, who was also a quarter Jewish, cultivated this resemblance to the best of his ability. His curly, prematurely grey hair rose above a slightly receding forehead. He wore rimless glasses reminiscent of Trotsky's pince-nez, and a grey goatee like Trotsky's covered his receding chin. He also had a prominent nose, with extremely large nostrils and little grey hairs sprouting from them. There were deep lines on his forehead and around his eyes and mouth already, although he was only forty-five. They gave his thin and almost bloodless face a look of asceticism. It was probably this ascetic expression which inclined most women to like Fred Meichelbeck – indeed, to chase him with a view to having one of those affairs for which Meichelbeck was famous in artistic circles in Malching: more famous than he was for his art. Thanks to his ascetic exterior, he seduced married women as well as girls twenty or twenty-five years younger than himself, and owing to the incautious way he went about Malching with them or boasted of his affairs to third parties, he had already been involved in a number of divorce cases. In general, he did not break entirely with the various ladies he seduced once they stopped going to bed together. He was adept at getting an erotic affair to shade off into friendship, and so his mistresses, past and present, would meet in his attractive studio apartment in the centre of Malching, gossip about their relationships with him without any bitterness, and sometimes even make friends. There were frequently so many women in Meichelbeck's apartment that his men friends described it as a regular harem. His ladies knew he drank a lot and never had regular meals, so they used to bring him presents of whisky, cognac and wine, or of ham, French cheeses, honeydew melons and French bread, and in return he advised them on their current love lives. He also quite obviously enjoyed having an audience of them as he sat in a wicker chair to prime his canvases or moved nimbly about, now standing and now kneeling, to apply the black, pretzel-shaped squiggles typical of his style to a canvas or a sheet of paper. Canvases up to two metres square and covered with black, pretzel-shaped squiggles hung side by side all over his apartment walls. They stood stacked by the walls of his studio, and he had more stacks of pictures stored in the loft and basement of the building. His dealer in M and his dealer in Lyons kept the rest of his productions stacked in their own basements. Neither had sold a single picture of his for over ten years; they were both waiting for the day when abstract art was in fashion again. Occasionally Fred Meichelbeck got angry with himself for his remarkable lack of success and so began sporadically painting extremely uncouth works of representational art, and they would urge him to stick to his own style although neither had bought a picture from him for years. They even refused to accept any more of his works on commission. Every few years they would get his old pictures out and have a show of them, attended mainly by Meichelbeck's women friends. The press took no notice of his exhibitions. Fred Meichelbeck got his revenge for the general neglect of his artistic work in his critical essays, in which he inveighed now bitterly, now contemptuously against the country's prominent art critics and his more successful colleagues. Apart from this, he went on filling his rooms with more pictures. He had produced a great many of them, but you could not describe him as industrious. He usually slept until eleven or twelve in the morning; when he finally got up he would make himself a cup or so of instant coffee laced with cognac, pick up the telephone and chat to his many women friends and his few men friends until afternoon. Then he dressed, left the apartment building, and spent the afternoon in one or other of the two best-known artists' bars in Malching, the Daisy or the Ba-Ba-Lu, where he met his acquaintances and women friends. It was not until evening that the urge to work would sometimes seize him, and then he painted at high speed, often surrounded by a female audience, putting his black, pretzel-shaped squiggles on canvas or paper. An oil painting took him no more than two hours to complete, and he had spent just half an hour on the watercolour Lilo Besslein was now removing from its cardboard tube. She slowly unrolled it.

The watercolour had a bright red background and, like all Fred Meichelbeck's work, it was positively swarming with black, pretzel-shaped squiggles, mostly intersecting or at least touching. The swarm thinned out towards the sides of the picture, where there were only a few isolated pretzel-shaped squiggles on the bright red background.

Lilo Besslein gazed at the watercolour, fascinated, before showing it to her husband and the Rittmeiers, who did not seem able to make anything of it at all. You could tell their eyes were wandering over the black squiggles only out of politeness. Finally Eugen Rittmeier asked what the watercolour was called.

Exploiter In Action, said the artist who, as previously mentioned, was considered leftist, in particular on account of the titles he gave his pictures. Eugen Rittmeier was obviously bewildered.

Exploiter In Action, he repeated, with a forced laugh.

I thought exploitation had died out in this country nowadays, he added, irritating Lilo Besslein, who used to give vent to very radical opinions in front of the artist.

Just look at Reinhardt von Allershausen, she said. He owns the Seitz Works. He's the very model of an exploiter.

I'm one of his employees, and I don't feel exploited, remarked Ernst Besslein, whose views were decidedly conservative.

You are exploited, dear, all the same, said his wife. Think what the directors earn compared to you.

Well, they have to take more responsibility than I do, said Ernst Besslein, to the amusement of Fred Meichelbeck, who had been lighting a cigarette.

I wouldn't mind taking responsibility for just about anything if they offered me that kind of money, he said, laughing, and he carelessly flicked ash onto the plate in front of him just as Lilo Besslein was about to put a slice of cake on it. She went to get him another plate, and he apologized profusely as she put it down on the table. However, she wouldn't hear of his apologizing.

No, no, I'm the one who ought to apologize, she said. I didn't give you an ashtray. She did not want Fred Meichelbeck, who had a great reputation for shocking the conventionally minded, to think her bourgeois. As it was, when she was with him she always felt rather ashamed of living in such thoroughly bourgeois surroundings and leading such a thoroughly bourgeois life. And she suspected that Fred Meichelbeck did not take her husband at all seriously. In fact, she was afraid he didn't take her particularly seriously either. She wondered why he kept on visiting them. She wondered if she herself was the reason for his visits. She couldn't be sure. She thought of the full-blown white roses he had stolen for her. She thought of the way he had kissed her on the mouth when he arrived.

Would you like some cognac in your coffee, she asked, pouring him a cup.

You divine my most secret desires, he replied, looking so deep into her eyes that she blushed again, to her annoyance. She turned quickly away and got the cognac bottle out of the built-in bar in the white wall unit. When she turned to the table again, she found that Fred Meichelbeck was still staring at her.

Why are you looking at me like that, she asked, putting the bottle of cognac down in front of him.

But Fred Meichelbeck merely smiled before turning to

Ernst Besslein, who poured cognac first into Fred Meichelbeck's coffee and then into his own.

Your wife's looking lovelier than ever, he said. Would you let me paint her portrait.

The fact is, I'm planning a whole series of portraits, he added.

Well, that's entirely up to Lilo, said Ernst Besslein, looking inquiringly at his wife.

I'm going to be rather tied to home now, what with the baby, she said.

You could come and sit for me in the evenings, though, when Ernst's back from work, said Fred Meichelbeck.

That's right; I'm learning how to change the baby and make her bottle, said Ernst Besslein.

Oh, aren't you feeding her yourself, asked Gitta Rittmeier, and she looked at Lilo Besslein in surprise.

No, breast-feeding made me feel like an animal, she said, to the horror of her sister-in-law and the amusement of Fred Meichelbeck.

It really is rather a revolting process, he remarked.

It's the most natural thing in the world, said Eugen Rittmeier, adding cognac to his own coffee.

Yes, well, it's precisely the most natural things in the world that can be the most revolting, said the artist. I mean, just look at a woman in advanced pregnancy. That's a disgusting sight, I must say.

I really hated the way I looked in the last months of my pregnancy, said Lilo Besslein.

I looked awful, didn't I, she asked her husband.

I thought you looked marvellous when you were pregnant, he said. He was obviously going to say something else, but he stopped short.

For at this moment the baby began to cry. To their guests' amusement, the Bessleins both rushed off to the nursery in agitation and hung over the cot. Lilo Besslein saw at a glance that the baby had brought up some milk again. She picked her up, wiped her mouth

39

and chin, gave her a clean jacket and then carried her into the living room, so that Fred Meichelbeck could see her too.

The artist seemed far from enraptured by the sight of the baby.

They all look like old men, he told Lilo Besslein, who had not expected quite such a crushing comment, and at first she did not know what to say. She didn't particularly like the baby's appearance herself, and her daughter still had those large bumps at the back of her head, acquired during the birth.

I've got used to the way she looks, she remarked.

Why, she's a lovely baby, she's a perfect poppet, cried Gitta Rittmeier, and she rose and went over to the child.

Who's a dear little poppet, she asked the baby, taking the small hands that were flailing rapidly back and forth.

Oh, you're a poppet, a real little poppet, she told the baby. Fred Meichelbeck's face assumed a scornful expression, and he looked at his watch without bothering to conceal his boredom. This did not escape Lilo Besslein, who took the baby back to the nursery and put her down in her cot. No sooner was she back in the living room, however, than the baby began crying again.

Could you go and see to her for once, she asked her husband. He hurried out of the room directly, and she sat down. She was afraid Fred Meichelbeck wouldn't fancy her in a maternal role. When her husband came back into the living room carrying the baby, she did not even turn to look. Instead, she tried bringing the conversation round to art, but her husband and her sister-in-law wrecked her efforts by talking to the baby, both at once and at the tops of their voices. After a brief intermission, the baby began yelling again. Fred Meichelbeck glanced at his watch once more. Lilo Besslein got the impression that he could hardly stand

40

the baby's yells; she didn't like them much, either. He was drumming his fingers restlessly on the table and occasionally running them through his curly grey hair. Eventually he took a deep pull on his half-smoked cigarette and stubbed it out on his plate. Then he stood up, saying he must be going, he had another appointment. He said goodbye to the Rittmeiers and Ernst Besslein, who was sorry he was leaving so early. Lilo Besslein showed him to the front door of the building, where he kissed her on the mouth again.

I'll ring you about that portrait, he said, and once more he looked so deep into her eyes that she was annoyed to find herself blushing. Then he hurried away, taking the steps two at a time.

✳

Contrary to Lilo Besslein's expectations, Fred Meichelbeck did not ring either next week or the week after that. At first her heart beat fast whenever she heard the telephone ring, but it was never anyone calling her except her parents, her parents-in-law, the Rittmeiers or her husband's colleagues' wives. By now she felt sure Fred Meichelbeck, for some reason or other, had given up any idea of painting her portrait. She didn't know whether to feel glad or sorry. On the one hand, she was afraid she wouldn't be up to the artist's standards, since he was supposed to be so experienced erotically; on the other, she very much wanted something to happen to her to make a change in the monotony of her existence and lift her out of her depression.

Ever since her daughter's birth her life had been so dull that on a weekday she sometimes didn't know if it was only Wednesday, or if she had got to Thursday or Friday yet. Every morning, a great desire just to stay there in bed and leave her husband to cope with the baby and the chores came over her. Every morning she fought it off. As soon as the baby began crying, which

41

was generally about six in the morning, she got up and went to the bathroom, where the first thing she did was to take one of the anti-depressant tranquilliser capsules prescribed by Dr Gutt. Then she made the baby's bottle, changed her and gave her her feed. Once the baby's wind had come up, she put her down in her cot again and set about getting breakfast, whether or not the child was crying. While she did this, her husband took his shower. Breakfast was often ready before he had finished shaving, and she would sit at the table in the dining area with nothing to do, waiting for him to put in an appearance. When he did come into the living room carrying the newspaper, she would notice that his grey-green eyes, rather small to begin with, looked even smaller in the morning, and she would shrink slightly, with faint revulsion, when he automatically leaned over to give her a kiss. He never noticed her flinching. He yawned more than he talked at breakfast. His eyes watered, and he often had to take his glasses off to wipe them. Lilo Besslein tried not to feel distaste for the way in which he spread himself several slices of bread, in spite of his incipient paunch and the roll of fat over his hips. But she could never quite ignore it. She couldn't help watching as he spread butter thickly on his bread, put two slices of ham on it, placed a sliced hard-boiled egg on top of that, spread mustard on the slices of egg and finally topped the egg and mustard with slices of pickled cucumber. And every morning she tried not to feel distaste for the way he ate, but she could never manage to ignore that either. She couldn't help watching as he held the newspaper in his left hand, opened his mouth so wide that the gold fillings near the corners of his mouth showed, and used his right hand to stuff the bread with its triple-decker topping into that mouth, so energetically that bits of egg or cucumber kept falling on the tablecloth or the carpet.

As soon as he had left the apartment she went back to bed and closed her eyes, though she couldn't drop off

to sleep again, to make the wearisome day ahead of her
shorter. She finally got up at nine, at the latest, and ran
herself a hot bath. She stayed in the bath until nine-
thirty. The she dried herself, rubbed oil into her body,
and got dressed. She went to the letterbox, not
expecting anything, and there was seldom any mail for
her. She opened her husband's mail, which he had said
she could do, and skimmed through it without much
interest; it usually consisted of nothing but printed
matter. At ten she bathed the baby and gave her
another feed. Then she cleared the breakfast table,
washed the dishes, dusted the living room and the
bedroom, watered the little orange tree and the little
azalea, and finally ran the vacuum cleaner over the
carpets on the floors of the bedroom, the living room,
the nursery and the corridor. At noon she took another
tranquillizer capsule, and then began to make herself
up. She had taken to spending almost two hours a day
in front of the mirror recently, and the longer she spent
painting her face, dabbing stuff on it, rubbing it in and
wiping it off, the less she liked the look of herself. By
about two in the afternoon, when it was time to change
and feed the baby again and take her out for a walk, her
make-up might be immaculate but she felt so dissatisfied
with her appearance that she was most reluctant to be
seen outside the apartment. At this point, and going
against medical advice, she would take another tranquillizer capsule. When it took effect she could venture
out into the street with the baby and the pram. She did
not debate whether to walk to the shopping street in the
south of Lerchenau or the shopping street in the north
of Lerchenau: she automatically made for the shopping
street in the south of Lerchenau because besides its two
self-service stores, it had a jeans shop and three
boutiques. She looked at the displays in the windows of
the jeans shop and the three boutiques every day,
although they were changed only once a fortnight.
Sometimes an irresistible wish to buy something would

come over her, and then she went into one of the boutiques and spent the housekeeping money on clothes which she had to hide from her husband in the evening. But generally she contented herself, these days, with looking in the windows before she went to the self-service store to buy food for supper and next day. Then she set off for home.

She did not go straight back to the Gluckgasse, but went a long way round to give the baby plenty of fresh air. However, she was usually home again by three in the afternoon. There was not much left to do there. She sometimes put dirty clothes in the washing machine, sometimes she ironed, sometimes she knitted, sometimes she phoned her husband's colleagues' wives, sometimes she played records and drank Martini after Martini, sitting on the black and white striped sofa, looking at the grass area planted with birch trees outside the living-room window and waiting for it to be time to lay the table for supper.

Some four weeks after her daughter's birth, while she was listening to records and drinking Martini and looking at the grass area outside the living-room window, where children from the sky-blue housing block were noisily playing football, Fred Meichelbeck rang her, quite unexpectedly. He wanted to know when he could paint her. She reeled off a whole string of prior engagements she said she had to meet first. In the end they agreed on a date: Wednesday evening of the following week. Lilo Besslein found herself contending with highly contradictory feelings and considerations during the next six days, between this telephone call and the date they had made. Sometimes she felt she was looking forward to seeing Fred Meichelbeck, at other times she nearly cancelled the whole thing. She watched her husband even more closely than usual. Sometimes she was sure she loved him, sometimes he struck her as a fool, not worth loving. When he slept with her for the first time since the baby's birth, however, she showed tenderness that briefly set him wondering why. Next morning she picked a quarrel with him over nothing in particular, and made sure they did not make it up properly before her date on the Wednesday.

When Wednesday finally arrived she dialled Fred Meichelbeck's number several times to tell him she wasn't coming after all, but as soon as he picked the phone up at his end she put it down again at hers without saying anything. She spent almost four hours in front of the bathroom mirror. She tried on all her trousers, blouses and shirts, and eventually decided to wear white jeans and a white shirt. She took several tranquillizer capsules in the course of the day, and drank several Martinis that afternoon. The Martinis made her feel ready for anything, and she waited impatiently for her husband to come home. As soon as he was back she set off.

She drove a long way round, so as not to reach Fred Meichelbeck's apartment early, but she still got to the building where he lived ten minutes ahead of time. Determined not to show any weaknesses, she waited in her parked car for a little while, smoking a cigarette, before she got out and rang the bell. The building had no lift, and she had to climb up five floors. When she reached the top of the stairs, panting, she found Fred Meichelbeck standing in his doorway in a paint-spattered shirt and an equally paint-spattered pair of trousers. He kissed her on the mouth again, and then led her into the living room, where she was rather taken aback to find two young women, one of whom introduced herself as Rosi and the other as Buzzi. Both of them inspected Lilo Besslein with unconcealed curiosity. She had much ado to hide her disappointment, and noticed that they were both very attractive. The one who called herself Rosi had a distinctly Mediterranean look, with expressive dark eyes and abundant dark hair. The other girl, who said her name

45

was Buzzi, had big blue eyes and long fair hair. Both claimed that Fred Meichelbeck had told them a lot about her.

We only stayed to see what you look like, said Buzzi, with a forthrightness that confused Lilo Besslein more than ever.

We're just going, though, said Rosi, as she reached for the bottle of cognac standing on the table and poured some into her glass.

Fred's painted both our portraits already, said Buzzi, and she smiled at Fred Meichelbeck, who had sat down with his sketch pad in one of the wicker chairs.

All my portraits are declarations of love made to beautiful women, he said, addressing himself chiefly to Lilo Besslein, who didn't know what to say to that. She would have liked a cognac too, but she felt shy about asking Fred Meichelbeck for one. He looked intently at her and then began his first sketch.

You can talk while I draw you, don't worry, he said, and he tore the first sheet off his pad, crumpled it up and tossed it carelessly on the floor before starting on the next one.

I don't know what to talk about, said Lilo Besslein. She looked helplessly at Rosi and Buzzi, who were obviously beginning to feel bored.

Well, better be going, said Buzzi, and she rose and shook hands with Lilo Besslein, who suddenly wished she would stay.

Rosi, having rapidly tipped the rest of her cognac down her throat, got up too.

She was glad to know Lilo Besslein was up here, she said graciously, wishing her goodbye.

Fred Meichelbeck saw both young women to the door, where Lilo Besslein could hear them all talking for a while. She heard Rosi and Buzzi giggling softly, too, and she felt less confident than ever. Firmly, she picked up the bottle of cognac and poured some into Rosi's empty glass. By the time Fred Meichelbeck came back into the room she too had emptied the glass, and she poured herself some more.

Maybe we'd better go straight to the studio, said Fred Meichelbeck, putting a record on. It was music with a Latin American rhythm. Humming quietly, he carried one of the wicker chairs into the studio, and Lilo Besslein followed him with the cognac bottle and the glass.

The studio was in a state of indescribable confusion. Its floor was littered with crumpled newspapers, paint rags, cigarette ends, bits of charcoal, empty paint tins and broken brushes. Paint was spattered not just over the walls but on the panes of the big window too. Canvases, mostly very large ones, stood stacked up everywhere. Fred Meichelbeck had no space left for painting except part of the wall by the door. He propped a clean white canvas up against this wall, and once more scrutinized Lilo Besslein so intently that she didn't know where to look.

Now, tell me about yourself, he said at last.

Lilo Besslein asked what he wanted to know.

Well, tell me what you do all day long, said Fred Meichelbeck.

I'm kept busy doing chores and looking after the baby, said Lilo Besslein.

Doesn't sound very exciting, remarked Fred Meichelbeck.

It isn't very exciting either, said Lilo Besslein.

Fred Meichelbeck asked how the baby was.

Sleeping and drinking and making dirty nappies, said Lilo Besslein.

You don't seem to be a very happy mother, said Fred Meichelbeck, and he sketched the outline of a head on the canvas in charcoal.

I can't stand a woman who acts the happy mother, he added.

I'm not actually an *un*happy mother, said Lilo Besslein. I'm just rather disappointed because everyone said I'd be blissfully happy, and I'm not.

You're quite enchanting, said Fred Meichelbeck, and he knelt down in front of the wicker chair where Lilo Besslein was sitting and kissed first her knee, then her wrist and then her arm, before he turned back to his canvas, obviously aroused, picked up the charcoal and sketched in two indeterminate eyes, one indeterminate nose and one indeterminate mouth.

Can't paint your portrait till I know you better, he said at last, and he took a couple of steps towards her, bent down and kissed her lingeringly on the lips.

As she felt his tongue in her mouth, and his hands groped for her breasts and slid between her thighs, Lilo Besslein was feverishly debating whether to sleep with him. However, he gave her no time to think it over. He took her hand and led her into his bedroom, beyond the studio. Once there he flung her on the double bed in the middle of the room and kissed her passionately again, but he could not dispel her misgivings.

I'm not on the Pill, she said. This obviously brought him down to earth.

He sat up at once and looked inquiringly at her.

Right, then I'll just pop out and get something, he said, briefly kissing her on the lips again before he left the bedroom.

In a moment Lilo Besslein heard him close the front door. She sat on the edge of the bed, wondering whether to stay here or go back into the living room. She really wanted to drive home. She thought of her husband, looking after the baby, and felt severe pangs of conscience. All at once she got up and went into the studio, where she found the cognac bottle and poured more cognac into her glass. She tossed it straight back and returned to the bedroom with the bottle and the glass. As soon as she got there she thought it might really be better to wait for Fred Meichelbeck's return in the living room. She went through the studio, carrying the cognac bottle and the glass, and sat down in the living room on the divan which did duty for a sofa beside the scratched coffee table. She poured more cognac into the glass and tossed it back again. She realized she was beginning to get tipsy. In spite of her tipsiness, however, she no longer had the faintest desire to go to bed with Fred Meichelbeck. She wondered if he'd be able to understand that. She told herself his vanity would most likely be wounded. She poured herself yet another cognac, drank it, and went to the lavatory, which was in the bathroom.

Fred Meichelbeck got back as she was coming out of the bathroom. He took her hand again, led her back to the bedroom and flung her on the bed. And as he kissed her, and his hands groped for her breasts and slid between her thighs, Lilo Besslein pretended to be tremendously excited. He unzipped her jeans, and she began to undress at once, surreptitiously watching Fred Meichelbeck, who was undressing too. With faint revulsion, she noticed how white and thin his body was. He had an adolescent's narrow shoulders and thin, hairless arms. His buttocks were gaunt. He was broader on the hips than the shoulders, and thin as he was there was no overlooking the fact that he had a small paunch.

I hate these things, he remarked, pulling a condom over his penis and throwing himself on Lilo Besslein again. Yet again she was surprised to find how little he weighed.

Having the reputation of a Don Juan to sustain, he tried all sorts of positions with her, without getting her really excited. She gasped and moaned and finally faked an orgasm. She was actually relieved when he rolled to one side and lit a cigarette. She asked for one too, and they lay side by side smoking in silence. Then Lilo Besslein got up and went to the bathroom, where she washed and inspected her make-up.

When she got back to the bedroom Fred Meichelbeck was already dressing. Lilo Besslein picked up her own clothes and dressed too. Then they both went into the studio, where Fred Meichelbeck wiped the charcoal sketch off his canvas with a rag. He asked Lilo Besslein to sit down in the wicker chair again, but she was afraid her husband might be getting impatient.

I'll come back another day, she said.

Fred Meichelbeck saw her to the door, and suddenly hugged and kissed her in a way that actually did excite her.

Promise you will, he said.

I swear I will, said Lilo Besslein, smiling and raising those fingers used in the taking of an oath, before she went downstairs.

She knew she had had too much to drink, and so drove back to Lerchenau very carefully indeed. Luckily, there was not much traffic at this time of day. On the way home she wondered what to tell her husband about the portrait, and whether anything about her showed she had been up to something. She cast one glance into the mirror when she reached the Gluckgasse, and then got out of the car and walked up the path to the front door of the sky-blue apartment building.

Although it was bedtime, she found her husband on the living-room sofa, reading the paper and drinking beer. He had obviously drunk a good deal of beer. His face was flushed, and his eyes looked even smaller than usual. Seeing him sitting there like that, her conscience suddenly felt clear. She told him about Rosi and Buzzi. Then she mentioned the portrait, saying Fred had begun to paint it. He was very keen to see it.

Did Fred Meichelbeck make a pass at you, he asked, so suddenly that she nearly lost her composure.

He treated me like a lady, she said, before she went into the bathroom to take her make-up off.

It was the first time she had ever cheated on her husband.

*

Lilo Besslein went to see Fred Meichelbeck once or

twice a week, but the portrait was making slow progress, since she spent most of the time in the artist's double bed. Then again, visits from his friends of both sexes often kept Fred Meichelbeck from working on the picture. Lilo Besslein was eager to get acquainted with his circle of friends herself. It included, among others, actresses playing in experimental theatres, girls who were graphic artists or songwriters or painters or photographic models, and men who had not yet found fame as artists and writers. Most of them were both Bohemian and left-wing. Indeed, one of Fred Meichelbeck's friends was a Communist. If you didn't happen to be discussing the latest amorous affairs of Malching's artistic society in Fred Meichelbeck's living room or studio, you talked politics. Lilo Besslein had taken to reading the newspaper, quite often, so that she could join in. She signed several petitions, such as one protesting against apartheid. She also got accustomed to chain-smoking. She was smoking up to forty cigarettes a day. She smoked at home, and in Fred Meichelbeck's apartment, and even in the street. She engaged her husband in discussions of bourgeois notions of morality, or government policies. These discussions generally degenerated into quarrels, in the course of which both Besslein hurled insults at each other. However, the way his wife was spending the housekeeping money upset Ernst Besslein even more than the opinions she had recently adopted. She kept using it to buy new clothes, almost at random, and no longer hid them from him; then she had to ask him for more money several times a month. She did not actually neglect the housework or the baby, but she kept complaining of all the work both of them made for her. She began thinking of finding a child-minder for the baby so that she could go back to working part time in a pharmacy. For one thing, she felt she would like to have some money of her own to spend, and for another, she wanted easy access to tranquillizers. She was still taking several capsules a day.

51

Once or twice she had tried to go without them, but very soon she had been so troubled by anxiety feelings that she reached for the box of blue and white capsules again. She was going to three different doctors to get prescriptions for tranquillizers now, and she took four capsules a day instead of two, ignoring the directions. On days when she had a date with Fred Meichelbeck she took five or six, for though she was not really in love with him she suffered from violent jealousy of many of his women friends. There was Larissa Pretzfeld, for instance, a photographic model who did secretarial work too. She was half a head taller than Fred Meichelbeck, and notorious for the number of her abortions. She displayed a tendency to confide in Lilo Besslein which irritated the latter intensely. There was Brigitte Henneberg, for instance, a voluptuous blonde who sometimes visited the apartment with her husband, an unsuccessful writer. She would stare at Lilo Besslein and treat her with something like hostility. There was Katharina Wüko, for instance, daughter of a director of the Seitz Works and an architecture student. She took every chance she got of showing that she didn't take Lilo Besslein seriously. And last but not least there was Beate Dötzel the actress, a fragile girl with rather short legs. Fred Meichelbeck used to help her learn her parts. She was condescending to Lilo Besslein, and frequently gave her to understand that she, Beate Dötzel, could wind Fred Meichelbeck round her little finger.

Lilo Besslein tried to discover which of these four Fred Meichelbeck was sleeping with. Sometimes she was sure it must be Beate Dötzel. Sometimes she would plump for Larissa Pretzfeld, sometimes for Brigitte Henneberg. But then again, she couldn't discount Katharina Wüko, or Rosi and Buzzi. She felt like driving to Fred Meichelbeck's apartment every day, just to find out which of these ladies was visiting. She rang him daily during the week to question him, more or less skilfully. At weekends, when she couldn't ring because her husband was at home, she would make up her mind to have it out with him. But whenever an opportunity of doing so offered, she let it pass, feeling afraid of looking foolish. She did all she could to run his friends down instead. She told him Beate Dötzel's legs were too short, she told him Larissa Pretzfeld was too tall, she told him Brigitte Henneberg really ought to lose some weight, she told him Katharina Wüko was flat-chested. Fred Meichelbeck only laughed. Not jealous of them, are you, he asked her.

Another thing that bothered Lilo Besslein was her inability to pin him down. He was noncommittal, even in bed. He didn't say he loved her, he didn't even say he liked her. Talkative as he was in the usual way, he never uttered a word during intercourse. They might have been doing gymnastic exercises together. But Lilo Besslein kept going back to him. She sometimes said no, to make it more exciting, but to her disappointment Fred Meichelbeck didn't seem to mind that either. He never pressed her, simply took her into the studio and went on with the portrait, which had not looked very much like her from the start, and was getting even less so the more he worked on it. When Lilo Besslein saw him kneeling or crouching or standing in front of it, painting over whole areas of the face, she often wondered if the picture would ever be finished.

Her husband was clamouring to see it, and she put him off as best she might. He obviously did not like her going to Fred Meichelbeck's once or twice a week. He made no outright objections, but he got his revenge in his own way by spending a couple of evenings a week out himself. He regularly spent one evening drinking with his colleagues Dülfer, Einsele and Urzinger, and the other evening playing tennis with Dülfer, Einsele or Urzinger at the Seitz Works club. On her evenings at home alone Lilo Besslein phoned Fred Meichelbeck, who usually had visitors and so, to her vexation, was very short with her on the telephone. She phoned her mother, who had now reconciled herself to having a granddaughter called Olwen. She phoned a school friend in N, and she phoned Frau Dülfer, Frau Einsele and Frau Urzinger, although she was not particularly fond of any of them. As she made her phone calls she drank Martini after Martini. When she couldn't think of anyone else to ring, she switched the television on and waited for her husband to come home, which he usually did considerably the worse for wear. He would get her to give him a headache tablet and then went straight to bed while she was still in the bathroom. By the time she came into the bedroom he would be fast asleep, and she wondered why she had bothered to wait up for him.

On the three evenings they did spend together, Fridays, Saturdays and Sundays, they quarrelled more often than not. Domestic peace or strife generally depended on the television programme. If it was a good one, they spent the evening sitting amicably side by side on the sofa. If it left something to be desired, all attempts at quiet conversation led straight to an argument.

In fact it was becoming harder for the Bessleins to get through the whole of their Saturdays and Sundays. Before their daughter was born they used to lie in bed till noon at weekends, then go to eat out in Malching, and finally stroll around the shopping streets in the city centre. But since the birth of the baby they had had to get up at six in the morning even on Saturday and Sunday, so that those days were intolerably protracted. While it was still summer they could put the top of the pram on the back seat of the car and go out with the baby to bathe in a nearby lake, and spend Saturday afternoons and Sunday afternoons in a beer garden. But it was too cold for sitting out of doors now, and the Bessleins could not think of anything to do but take the pram out in the often deserted streets of Lerchenau on Saturday and Sunday afternoons. Lilo Besslein found these walks so depressing that she sometimes stayed at home. Even the anti-depressant tranquillizers didn't stop her feeling depressed at weekends. When she was not actually busy seeing to the baby or making breakfast, lunch or supper, she sat around with nothing to do, waiting for something to happen that would make a difference to her life. But no such thing ever did happen. And the less anything happened to her, the less able she was to cope with those small events that did relieve the monotony of her existence. These, apart from her visits to Fred Meichelbeck, comprised invitations from her husband's colleagues, whom she liked as little as she liked their wives. Evenings with the Dülfers, the Einseles and the Urzingers always followed the same pattern, but every time she was about to set out to visit them Lilo Besslein suffered from fits of nervous coughing and from nausea which actually made her vomit at times. She often felt so sick that her husband had to say they couldn't come at the last minute. She could not help it: or rather, she could have gone to a doctor for help, but she was ashamed to tell any doctor about her nervous cough and her nausea. She felt ashamed in front of her husband, too. She tried to fight her anxiety feelings. She told herself that absolutely nothing could happen to her, so long as she was polite to the Dülfers, the Einseles and the Urzingers. Yet when the Dülfers asked her and her husband to supper again, her anxiety came back. She couldn't understand it. As soon as she was ready to go out she was racked by the nervous coughing that went with her nausea, and she threw up in the lavatory pan while her husband stood in the bathroom doorway, looking helpless. He suggested one of her tranquillizer capsules. Lilo Besslein took two, and within ten minutes the cough and the nausea were getting better. Ernst Besslein carefully picked the sleeping baby up out of her cot, put her in the top of the pram, and they drove off to the Dülfers, who owned their apartment on the

55

southern outskirts of the city of M.

Although it was eight in the evening by now, the Dülfers had not put their children to bed yet. They had three little girls of one, two and three, and they were firmly convinced that they were doing their guests a favour by letting them see their small daughters. The three little girls, so tired that they were getting silly with it, romped all over the apartment wearing the pretty pyjamas Irene Dülfer had probably put them into especially for her guests' sake. The floor of the whole place was littered with toys. The Einseles and Urzingers, who had arrived earlier than the Bessleins, were sitting on the sofa, which had a lime-green cover, watching these juvenile antics with strained smiles. They had children too, and did not dote on infants as whole-heartedly as Irene Dülfer, who was already pregnant again. Karl Urzinger, a tall, broad man whose calm Lilo Besslein found as irritating as Heinz Einsele's obvious restlessness, kept trying to start a conversation on some subject other than the Dülfers' three children, but neither the children nor Irene Dülfer would give him a chance. The smallest girl was crawling about at the guests' feet, upsetting glasses Jürgen Dülfer had just filled with sherry. She kept grabbing cigarette packets off the coffee table, and howled with fury when they were taken away from her. The middle girl asked her mother to read her a story. Shrill-voiced, Irene Dülfer read out loud: moo, says the cow, cock-a-doodle-doo, says the rooster. The eldest girl wanted to demonstrate the exercises she had learnt at dancing class. By means of hints and gestures, Irene Dülfer actually got her guests to the point of watching, in silence, while her daughter clumsily aped the exercises she had been taught.

The Dülfers did not put their children to bed until nine o'clock, when both parents said prayers with their daughters, gave them their bedtime sweeties, kissed them, put out the light and shut the bedroom door. However, as soon as the adults were sitting down in front of a fondue set, two plates of raw pieces of beef and a tray of dishes containing all sorts of sauces, the two eldest girls appeared in the living room again. The Dülfers did not send them back to bed, but sat them on their laps.

How much longer are you going to stay up, then, Irene Dülfer asked her eldest daughter, whose name was Marina.

As long as you, said Marina, and the Dülfers' guests, busy spearing pieces of meat on their fondue forks and dipping them into the simmering oil, dutifully laughed. The child smiled coyly.

Don't want to go to sleep at all, said the second daughter, whose name was Sandra.

If you don't get any sleep you won't grow, said Ernst Besslein, to the annoyance of Irene Dülfer, who immediately protested.

You shouldn't scare her, she said, gently stroking the child's head. Sandra had thin blonde hair and was distinctly overweight.

Of course you'll grow, darling, even if you don't get any sleep, she added.

I'll grow, cried the child, tossing her head flirtatiously.

Do you always let them stay up so late, inquired Lilo Besslein, disinclined to fall for the image of maternal bliss so prominently presented to her by Irene Dülfer.

Yes, we let them come in here if they can't sleep, said Irene Dülfer. They're only young once, after all.

But they're worn out, said Lotte Urzinger, look at their eyes, they're just little slits.

I don't believe in forcing them to do anything. People were always forcing me to do things when I was a child, said Irene Dülfer, and she popped a piece of fried steak into her daughter's mouth. To the obvious horror of the Einseles, who clearly did not feel like expressing their views on the Dülfers' methods of child-rearing, the little girl spat it out on the plate again.

That's the way to go about raising little despots,

remarked Karl Urzinger, and he glanced first at the Einseles and then at the Bessleins, who both nodded.

After all, said Ernst Besslein, the children were going to have to do things they didn't want to later on.

The sooner they realize they can't have everything their own way, the better for them, he added.

Jürgen Dülfer asked what he, Ernst Besslein, would forbid his own daughter to do.

Well, I wouldn't have let her come back into the living room after I'd put her to bed, for instance, said Ernst Besslein, and he glanced at his wife inquiringly, as if expecting her to support him.

She merely shrugged her shoulders. She might be a mother herself these days, but she was not particularly interested in child-rearing theories. She was now as bored as she had been scared before they left home. Surreptitiously, she watched Irene Dülfer, who was now trying to make her eldest daughter understand that grown-ups sometimes liked to be on their own. She told herself she could never have been as patient as that. She saw Irene Dülfer's pale, tired face. She saw the dark rings under her eyes and the little wrinkles at their corners. She wondered why Irene Dülfer wanted so many children. She wondered how she managed to forget all about herself and exist only for the children. She didn't know whether to admire or despise her for it. She tried to understand Irene Dülfer, but it was no use. Irene Dülfer was a mystery to her. She watched her now, rising to her feet, heavy with pregnancy, to take the two children back to bed.

Daddy come too, said little Sandra.

So Jürgen Dülfer left the table too, and went off with his wife and the two children.

That's the way to go about raising little despots all right, repeated Karl Urzinger, and he speared a piece of meat on his fondue fork and dipped it in the simmering oil.

For several minutes the other guests too were busy

cooking their own pieces of meat, silently waiting until they were brown and crisp, whereupon they took their fondue forks our of the hot oil and dipped the meat in one or other of the savoury sauces Irene Dülfer had made. At last the Dülfers came back into the living room.

I think it'll be all right now, Jürgen Dülfer was just saying, when the Besslein's baby daughter suddenly began to cry. Ernst Besslein had put her in the Dülfers' bedroom when they arrived.

It's ten o'clock, time for her feed. She's speaking up, and quite right too, said Ernst Besslein, already rising to his feet.

However, Lilo Besslein told him to stay where he was. She went into the kitchen with Irene Dülfer to put the baby's bottle in a pan of hot water. When it was the right temperature, she and Irene Dülfer went into the bedroom, took the baby out of the top of the pram, and changed her nappy on the Dülfers' double bed. The baby smiled at them.

Oh, isn't she sweet, isn't she a darling, cried Irene Dülfer, as Lilo Besslein gave her small daughter her bottle. You absolutely must bring her into the living room afterwards.

And is she soon going to have a little brother or a little sister, she inquired, with a hopeful look on her face.

We thought we'd give ourselves a little time first, said Lilo Besslein, although she did not, in fact, intend to have any more children at all. But that was something she dared not tell anyone. She was afraid people would react as if she were breaking the rules of good conduct.

Well, you don't want to leave it too long, said Irene Dülfer, before leaving the bedroom to attend to her other guests.

As the baby rapidly emptied her bottle, Lilo Besslein wondered whether she actually should take her into the living room. She decided not to. She suspected that the Einseles and Urzingers had already had quite enough of children, what with the Dülfers' three. She burped the baby, caressed the back of her head, and then put her back in the top of the pram.

Irene Dülfer protested loudly when she returned to the living room without the baby. Ernst Besslein immediately got up and went to fetch his daughter. She had dropped off to sleep at once, but now her eyes were wide open again as she lay in her father's arms looking at the Dülfers and their guests, who all, if rather dutifully, proclaimed her to be sweet, a poppet, entrancing, and the spitting image of her father. He eventually took her back to the bedroom, where she instantly began to howl.

Lilo Besslein left it a few minutes, to see if she was going to calm down again, and when she didn't she set off for the bedroom herself. She found her husband kneeling beside the top of the pram, talking to the yelling infant.

She'd gone straight off to sleep, but you just had to show her off, she snapped, before picking the baby up out of the pram and walking her up and down the bedroom.

Well, she's nothing to be ashamed of, said Ernst Besslein.

Oh, and is that supposed to mean I was ashamed of her, snapped Lilo Besslein. She was fast asleep, and you're so ridiculously proud of being a father you went and woke her up. Now she's going to scream the place down. Nothing if not persistent. She gets it from you.

You go back and I'll stay here, she added.

Ernst Besslein said no, why didn't she go back.

I'll soon get the baby calmed down, he said.

Oh yes, and have everyone saying I'm a bad mother, said his wife.

If you don't leave me alone with her this minute you'll be sorry, she added, and this remark actually did induce him to leave the bedroom.

She paced up and down the room for some time, holding the baby. Then she sat down on the edge of the bed. No sooner was she sitting down, however, than the baby began screaming again. She stood up and went on walking her up and down. She would have liked to be eating fondue. She would have liked a glass of wine. Not for the first time since the birth of her baby, she felt hard done by. Suddenly she had not the slightest wish to go on pacing up and down the Dülfers' bedroom.

I'm not having you spoil my entire evening, she said, and she put the baby down in the top of the pram. The baby began howling again. This time the noise infuriated Lilo Besslein so much that she switched off the bedside lamp and went back to the living room.

You're not leaving her to cry, are you, inquired Irene Dülfer. She looked in concern at Lilo Besslein, who was sitting down at the table again.

There's nothing the matter with her, she's just bored, said Lilo Besslein, and she speared a piece of meat on her fondue fork and dipped it in the simmering oil. She tried to ignore the baby's crying. It seemed to be upsetting the others, and not just her husband, for they all listened for several minutes.

Poor little thing, said Jürgen Dülfer, makes you feel quite sorry for her.

Children never cry without a reason for it, said his wife. Maybe she's got a tummy pain, or she's scared of being in a strange room, she added, and she looked reproachfully at Lilo Besslein, who had a set expression on her face.

Do you often leave her to cry like that, Irma Einsele asked her.

Good heavens, what an idea. The moment she so much as murmurs we come running, replied Ernst Besslein, on his wife's behalf. Then he rose to his feet, gesturing apologetically in her direction.

61

I can't bear to sit and hear her crying her heart out, he said, leaving the living room. Immediately afterwards the crying stopped.

And that's the way to go about raising little despots too, remarked Lilo Besslein, chiefly addressing Karl Urzinger, for she hoped that he at least would be on her side. But Karl Urzinger was not on her side. All present seemed to be united in their opinion of her, without actually having to express it out loud. They were also united in their opinion of her husband.

It's quite touching, the way Ernst looks after that baby, said Lotte Urzinger.

Well, he doesn't have her all day long, like I do, said Lilo Besslein, feeling increasingly sour.

Lots of fathers don't do a thing for their children, even in the evenings, said Irene Dülfer, and it looked as if she were about to add something, but she suddenly stopped short. For in the bedroom, Ernst Besslein had begun to sing.

Oh, he's singing her to sleep, she cried, isn't that sweet. And she looked reproachfully at Lilo Besslein. Lilo Besslein considered her husband to be showing off so much in acting the part of devoted father that she wouldn't deign to say what she thought of it. She wasn't for a moment sorry she had left the baby to cry. All of a sudden she didn't mind in the least whether the Dülfers, the Einseles and the Urzingers thought her a bad mother. Of course, she could still have risen from the table and gone back into the bedroom herself, but she had no intention of giving way to the subliminal pressure being brought to bear on her, particularly by Irene Dülfer. Nor had she any intention of taking part in the conversation, which was still concerned with parents and children and how to bring the latter up. As she silently speared pieces of meat and dipped them into the simmering oil, in between times rapidly emptying her glass, which Jürgen Dülfer immediately refilled, her resentment of her husband increased. She could still hear him singing in the bedroom. She determined to make him pay for his behaviour. I'll have something to say to him about that, and this very evening too, she said to herself, and she tossed back the wine in her glass and lit a cigarette, although the others had not finished eating yet. The Dülfers, in particular, registered the hasty emptying of her glass and the way she lit the cigarette with thoughtful glances. Jürgen Dülfer instantly rose and filled her glass again. Irene Dülfer went to find an ashtray.

You don't smoke in the same room as the baby, do you, she asked Lilo Besslein.

Yes, I even smoke out in the street, she said.

You know, said Irene Dülfer, you really ought to remember you're making the baby smoke too.

A little bit more smoke won't make much difference, what with all the pollution in the atmosphere these days, said Lilo Besslein, and she continued to smoke in silence.

They began discussing ways of giving up smoking. Heinz Einsele had given up six months ago. Karl Urzinger had given up two whole years ago. They all agreed that the essential factor in giving up was tremendous will-power. At last Ernst Besslein came back into the living room. He told them all the baby had gone to sleep, and he smiled at his wife as he sat down at the table. His wife did not smile back. She glared at him instead, and tapped her watch with her forefinger, indicating that she would like to leave before long.

Oh, surely you don't want to go yet, inquired Irene Dülfer. The gesture had not escaped her notice.

We have to get up at six in the morning, said Lilo Besslein, giving her husband, who would obviously have liked to stay a little longer, a savage kick under the table.

We all have to get up at six in the morning, said

Lotte Urzinger. That's how it is when you have children.

I'd give anything to have my sleep out, just for once, said Heinz Einsele.

But the sacrifices one has to make are worth every bit of it, said Irene Dülfer.

Don't you agree, she inquired hopefully of Lilo Besslein, who now rose to her feet.

Let's hope so, was all she remarked, and while her husband, too, rose and went to fetch the baby in the top of her pram she said goodbye to the Einseles and Urzingers, who seemed surprised by their abrupt departure. The Dülfers, who went to the front door with them, were quite obviously offended. At that moment, however, Lilo Besslein couldn't have cared less. She felt she could not stay in the room with such narrow-minded people one moment longer. She breathed more freely when she was out in the open. She watched her husband open the car door and put the top of the pram on the back seat, without helping him as usual. Shivering, she got into the car herself and closed the door as quietly as she could so as not to wake the infant. For the baby's sake, too, she did not say anything cross about her husband's behaviour on their way back to Lerchenau. Even when they had reached their apartment, and the baby was back in her cot, she initially kept her comments to herself. She simply took her sheets, pillows and quilt out of the bedroom and into the living room and made a bed up on the black and white striped sofa. Baffled, Ernst Besslein watched her movements. Finally he asked what the matter was.

I'm not sleeping in the same bed as the sort of fool who sings his baby to sleep, said Lilo Besslein.

So what if I did sing her to sleep, said Ernst Besslein. You can't seriously be holding that against me.

You were trying to show me up as a rotten mother,

cried Lilo Besslein, you and your paternal devotion. I left her to cry, and you had to go in and sing to her. Of course, that impressed everyone no end. There were you, the perfect father, and there was I being treated as an unnatural mother.

You do exactly what those squares expect you to do, she added.

The Dülfers aren't squares, said Ernst Besslein.

Oh, aren't they just squares. The fact is, you don't notice because you're such a square yourself, cried Lilo Besslein, and she rushed into the bathroom and took four tranquillizer capsules. Then she went back to the living room. Her husband, really offended now at being called a square, had left it. She very much wanted to tell him she despised him, she wished she was divorced from him, she was sorry she ever married him. But she controlled herself, feeling silence would be more effective. She opened the living-room window a crack, switched off the standard lamp, lay down on the sofa and pulled the quilt right up to her chin, as she always did when she was feeling forlorn. She wondered if Fred Meichelbeck might be able to help her improve things, but no sooner did the notion occur to her than it struck her as absurd.

He's not the right man for me either, she told herself, and she decided to take things into her own hands.

*

Over the next few weeks, Lilo Besslein studied the Situations Vacant section in the newspaper as soon as her husband had left the apartment. When she thought an advertisement looked attractive, she gave her next-door neighbour the key to the apartment so that she could look in on the baby now and then, and went off to present herself at the pharmacy advertising te job. She had no luck to start with. Other applicants were preferred. She began by applying only for jobs in pharmacies in the city centre or Malching; she felt she would at least like to turn her back on Lerchenau during working hours. As time went by, however, her requirements became more modest, and when she saw an advertisement one morning for a job in a Lerchenau pharmacy she hastily dressed, gave Frau Deininger the key to the apartment, and set off for the pharmacy in question, which was in the shopping street to the north of Lerchenau.

She had sometimes got her tranquillizers there, but the pharmacist, Frau Högemann, gave no indication of knowing her by sight. Two assistants went on serving customers while Frau Högemann took her into the night-duty room, looked at her papers, and then asked why she had not been working for the last seven months. Lilo Besslein said she had had a baby, and Frau Högemann seemed to think this an acceptable reason. She told Lilo Besslein the post would be vacant in some four weeks' time, on the first of December; she said the salary was one thousand two hundred marks, and she asked if she would be able to work Tuesdays, Thursdays and Saturdays. When Lilo Besslein said yes, Frau Högemann said she would like a day or so to think it over, and asked her to ring the day after next.

Leaving the pharmacy again, Lilo Besslein was not sure whether to hope she got the job or not. On first meeting, she did not particularly like or dislike Frau Högemann, a small, slim woman of about forty. Given the choice, she would have preferred a pharmacy which was not entirely staffed by women, and she would still have liked to work in a pharmacy in the city centre or Malching. Just now, in early November, Lerchenau struck her as even bleaker than usual. The birch trees planted everywhere had lost their leaves some time ago. The grass areas in between the buildings were cheerless and deserted. The streets of Lerchenau were deserted too. It took her a quarter of an hour to get home, but the only person she met was

66

an old lady walking her dachshund.

Back in the apartment, she found Frau Deininger walking up and down with the crying baby. She took the baby and apologized for giving her neighbour so much trouble. Frau Deininger asked how the job interview had gone, and said she really ought to think it over again; did she really want to hand the baby over to a child-minder so soon, asked Frau Deininger.

This is exactly the age when children need their mother most, she added.

But there was no changing Lilo Besslein's mind. She had heard more than enough of that argument already. Her mother had said children needed their mother at this age. Her mother-in-law had said so too. And her husband said so whenever she mentioned her efforts to find a job. She suspected that he hoped those efforts would come to nothing. He couldn't understand her wish to be at least a little independent of him. He did not actually put difficulties in her way, but he gave her no support at all. Her triumph was all the greater when she did get the job in the Lerchenau pharmacy. She immediately bought five white overalls and put a small ad in the paper for a child-minder on three days a week. Several women rang in answer to her advertisement, but they all lived too far from Lerchenau except for one, a woman called Frau Finsinger, who lived in the Frettach district bordering on Lerchenau. Lilo Besslein made an appointment to go and see her the next afternoon.

She had looked at the city street map before setting out, to see where Frau Finsinger lived, but she still got so well and truly lost that she arrived half an hour late. She quickly took the top of the pram containing her small daughter out of the car, and cast a brief glance at the building where the Finsingers lived. It was an old one, and did not seem to be in particularly good repair. Large areas of plaster were crumbling away; some of the windows were thick with dirt; the staircase, which had once been painted bright yellow, could have done with another coat of paint. On her way up to the first floor, Lilo Besslein also noticed a penetrating smell of garlic.

Frau Finsinger was waiting for her on the first floor, holding her own baby. She was about thirty, tall and fat, with lank, greasy hair and a rather shrill voice.

She introduced herself as Anni Finsinger before she asked Lilo Besslein in. Lilo Besslein followed her down the corridor with mixed feelings. There were toys scattered all over the floor of it, and confusion also reigned in the living room, where a little boy of about two and a little girl who was probably the same age were playing with a train. Half-eaten apples, banana skins and biscuits lay all over the place in this room, as well as toys. All the chairs had been knocked over, and Frau Finsinger had to pick two of them up before they could sit down.

This was how the place looked every day, but she'd got used to it, she remarked, before explaining that only the baby she was holding and the little boy were her own children.

I'm looking after the little girl for her mother, she said. She drops her off in the morning and picks her up again in the evening.

That would be four children for you to look after, counting my little girl, said Lilo Besslein. Wouldn't that be a bit much for you.

Oh no, not at all, if it was up to me I'd have half a dozen kids, said Frau Finsinger, and she bent down and put the baby she was holding on the floor. It immediately crawled over to the other two children, who had just begun to quarrel. The little girl, whose name was Marion, was yelling and pursuing the little boy, who had taken the train they had both been playing with away from her.

That's my train, shouted the little boy, whose name was Markus, and he made for his mother, howling, and stumbled over the crawling baby, who began to howl too.

Go on, let Marion play with the train too, said Frau Finsinger.

I want my Mummy, screamed little Marion. Her yells awoke Olwen, whom Lilo Besslein had put down on the floor beside her in the top of the pram. She began yelling too. Lilo Besslein burst into hysterical laughter.

I couldn't stand this sort of thing the whole time, she told Frau Finsinger who, to her amazement, sat there quite unmoved. She took the train away from her son, who instantly began rolling about on the floor in protest, and gave it to little Marion, who went off with it to the farthest corner of the room. She picked her son up off the floor and stroked his head soothingly. Finally she picked up the baby and rocked it on her lap until it stopped howling. Then she put it down on the floor again. All this made Lilo Besslein feel she certainly had the equable temperament necessary for looking after children. She could never have been so calm herself. As her own baby was still howling, she took her out of the top of the pram and walked up and down with her. In doing so, she noticed that there was dust on the furniture, and the window had obviously not been cleaned for quite some time. She wondered whether she ought to entrust her small daughter to Frau Finsinger. The baby was beginning to calm down, and Frau Finsinger came over to take a look at her. She seemed enraptured.

Could she hold the baby, she asked Lilo Besslein, who immediately handed her over. The baby smiled at Frau Finsinger, who began talking to her.

Oh, who's a friendly little thing, then, she said. There's a nice smile for me, even though you don't know me yet. We'll soon be getting to know each other ever so well, though, won't we, if your Mummy's going to have me look after you.

How much would you want a month, asked Lilo Besslein.

Without hesitation Frau Finsinger said she would want two hundred and fifty marks a month. This sum did not strike Lilo Besslein as exorbitant. All of a sudden she felt Frau Finsinger's rather unkempt appearance, and the state of her apartment, did not matter so much after all. She instantly told Frau Finsinger that she would agree to that. This, for some reason, seemed to be a relief to Frau Finsinger, who sat down at the table again, still holding the baby. Lilo Besslein sat down too, to discuss details. She told Frau Finsinger either she or her husband would bring the baby before eight in the morning, either she or her husband would fetch her after six in the evening, she would need to be changed and given her bottle at ten in the morning, two in the afternoon and six in the evening. And she told Frau Finsinger it was essential for the baby to be taken out for a walk in the afternoons; it had not escaped her eye that neither Frau Finsinger's children nor the little Marion had very heathy complexions. Frau Finsinger agreed to all this. Feeling decidedly ill at ease in the company of so many children liable to begin howling again any moment, Lilo Besslein said goodbye to Frau Finsinger, who had either forgotten or was too thrifty to offer her so much as a cup of coffee.

Driving home, she could have sung aloud for joy. After the beginning of December there would be three days a week when she need not look after the baby. As soon as she got home, however, her conscience pricked her. She thought of Frau Finsinger's untidy appearance, her lank and greasy hair, the dirty overall she had been wearing. She thought of the dust on her furniture and the big, smeared window. Instead of putting her small daughter down in her cot as usual, she spread a blanket on the carpet in the living room, put the baby on the blanket, sat down on the carpet beside her and offered the baby a coloured rattle, which the baby grasped, dropped and grasped again as soon as it was handed back to her.

Have you got the rattle, then, she asked the baby.

Oh yes, you've got the rattle-rattle-rattle, she told the baby.

Did you throw the rattle away, then, she asked the baby.

Oh yes, you've thrown the rattle-rattle-rattle away, she told the baby.

Does a little mousie want her rattle back, then, she asked the baby.

Oh yes, a little mousie-mousie wants her rattle-rattle-rattle back, she told the baby, and then stopped abruptly. She suddenly felt it was very undignified to be talking such nonsense. Putting the rattle down, she began alternately bending and stretching the baby's little legs. Then she raised and lowered her little arms several times. Then she was not sure what to do with the baby next. She left her lying on the floor and started laying the table for supper. When she had done that, she changed her small daughter's nappy, gave her a bottle and put her to bed. Then she looked at the time. Six-thirty already. Her husband should have been home by now. She wondered what was keeping him out so late. She was eager to tell him about Frau Finsinger. Sitting down at the supper table, she looked hungrily at the plate of sliced sausage standing on it. She had not eaten anything since breakfast, for she was trying to lose weight. She knew her husband very much preferred her to wait until he got home before starting supper, but she buttered a slice of bread, put a good helping of sausage on it and took a bite. No sooner had she done so than she heard her husband put his key into the apartment door. For a moment she thought of hiding the slice of bread, but she rejected the idea immediately.

There's nothing wrong about it if I start supper on my own, just for once, she told herself, and she stayed

71

where she was, took another bite of bread, and waited for her husband to appear. He opened the front door of the apartment, closed it, took his shoes off, and looked in at the living-room door with a smile. When he caught sight of the slice of bread in her hand, however, his expression swiftly changed to one of injury.

Started supper already, have you, he said in a voice that quivered slightly.

Oh, don't be so petty, cried Lilo Besslein. I haven't had anything to eat all day. I was so hungry I just couldn't wait any longer.

What do you mean, petty, inquired Ernst Besslein. All I said was, you've started supper already.

So why are you looking so injured, cried Lilo Besslein.

I am not looking injured, said Ernst Besslein, and he sat down at the table in a manner that showed he felt deeply wounded, and began to butter his own slice of bread.

Well, don't let's start quarrelling over a silly little thing like that, said Lilo Besslein, and she tried to put her hand on his, the one that was holding his knife.

Are you saying I started quarrelling, inquired Ernst Besslein, and he withdrew his hand from hers.

Lilo Besslein went on eating in silence. She wondered whether this was the right time to tell her husband she had found a child-minder for the baby. She decided to leave it till after supper.

Why don't you say anything, she asked him.

You're not saying anything either, he said. He poured some beer into his tankard and continued his silent meal.

Lilo Besslein tried not to let his behaviour upset her. She tried not to lose her temper. She knew very well that a fit of temper would quite possibly ruin not just this evening but several evenings to come. Her husband was given to nursing grievances. He would take note of every word she spoke in anger and bring it up against her next time the occasion offered. Once again, she took the hand holding his knife.

Now, do stop being cross because I started supper without you, she said.

Ernst Besslein removed his hand again and looked at her. He was still deeply wounded.

Well, you could have waited a few minutes, couldn't you, he said.

How was I to know when you'd be back, asked Lilo Besslein. This conversation was beginning to get her down. She had similar conversations with her husband quite often: conversations in which he was always trying to put her in the wrong. She felt a violent dislike of him arise in her. Unsuccessfully, she tried to repress it.

Don't you think we'd better change the subject, she said.

Ernst Besslein merely shrugged his shoulders before he began buttering another slice of bread, in silence and still wearing the same injured expression on his face. With ever-increasing dislike, Lilo Besslein watched him lay a lavish helping of ham on the bread, put a sliced hard-boiled egg on top of the ham, spread the sliced egg with mustard, and top the ham, egg and mustard with slices of pickled cucumber. It was like some kind of ritual. Suddenly she could restrain herself no longer. She felt an irresistible urge to interrupt this ritual. Swiftly, she leaned over, picked up his plate and flung it on the floor before he could react at all.

I'm not having a hidebound bastard like you spoil my whole evening, she shouted as he leaped up, stared angrily at the broken plate, the pieces of egg and pickled cucumber lying on the floor, and the slice of bread lying some way off, and then marched out of the living room, slamming the door. Lilo Besslein heard him slam the bedroom door too. All was perfectly quiet for a moment, and then the tenants of the apartment above banged on the ceiling with a broomstick.

Stupid squares, hissed Lilo Besslein. She was already

73

wishing she had not thrown the plate on the floor. She got up, went to fetch a dustpan and brush, and swept up the broken china, the sliced egg and cucumber and the bread. She took the dustpan back into the kitchen. Then she wondered what to do next, and whether to go into the bedroom and apologize to her husband. But she told herself he wouldn't respond to any attempts at reconciliation for at least two or three days. He was extremely adept at keeping a quarrel doggedly going. She quailed already at the thought of the evenings they would spend together in total silence. She took four tranquillizer capsules, sat at the supper table and waited for them to work. It suddenly struck her that this quarrel gave her the chance to go and see Fred Meichelbeck. She wondered whether to ring him first, just to be on the safe side, but she was afraid her husband might listen in. She got her coat on, put the car keys in her handbag, and left the apartment without exchanging another word with her husband. Outside the apartment door she almost fell over Frau Deininger, whose turn it was to clean the staircase this week. She was on her hands and knees, wiping the pale grey tiles over with a damp cloth. She had obviously heard the entire quarrel. Just now, however, Lilo Besslein did not much mind. She said a hasty good evening and left the building before Frau Deininger could buttonhole her. She ran down the path and got into her car. As she drove to Malching she told herself it was a great thing to have a lover: were it not for Fred Meichelbeck, she told herself, she would have spent the whole evening unsuccessfully trying to make things up with her husband. She drove faster, and as there was not much traffic about at this time of day it was only quarter of an hour before she reached the building where Fred Meichelbeck lived. To her relief, she saw lights on the fifth floor. The front door of the building had not yet been locked, and she climbed the five floors up without ringing the bell first.

Reaching the top of the stairs, she heard music in Fred Meichelbeck's apartment. She rang three times, and the music was turned off. Floorboards creaked, but nobody answered the door. She rang three more times, and put her ear to the door panel. She could hear whispering inside, followed by muffled giggles. After that all was perfectly still in the apartment. She wondered whether to knock and say who was there, but she was afraid that would only lead to worse humiliation. She told herself Fred Meichelbeck must have a woman in there, and for obvious reasons didn't want to be disturbed. She went downstairs again, feeling shaky at the knees. She was near to tears, but she fought them back. Once she reached her car she wondered whether to drive straight home. She thought of her husband's injured expression. She thought of the silence he was sure to preserve all evening. Suddenly it occurred to her that she could go to one of the Malching bars frequented by artists, the Daisy or the Ba-Ba-Lu. She decided on the Ba-Ba-Lu, only one block along from Fred Meichelbeck's apartment building. Leaving her car where it was, she set off on foot. The closer she came to the bar the more misgivings she had. She knew young women on their own did go there, but she still felt apprehensive about entering the place without an escort. She had to summon up all her resolve to open the door and walk the few steps to the bar counter, where there was a large crowd. She pushed her way past two groups of young people, who were talking excitedly and paid her no attention at all, and waited for the barmaid to come and take her order. When the barmaid had brought her rum and Coke, she turned her back on the bar counter and looked around the nearby tables, hoping to spot friends or acquaintances of Fred Meichelbeck's. However, she couldn't see a single face she knew. The people at the tables were having to converse in what was almost a shout, too, because of the loud rock music filling the room. She realized none of them was paying her any attention either. This was a relief at first, but after she had been standing by the bar for some time she began to feel less happy about it. Indeed, it was slightly annoying. Turning back to the bar, she looked at herself in the big mirror fitted behind the shelf of bottles. She told herself she obviously wasn't pretty enough for anyone here to notice her. Quickly she emptied her glass, paid, and left the bar. An immigrant worker approached her on the way back to the car. He asked if she'd like a cup of coffee with him. She shook her head and walked on faster than before. The immigrant worker followed her a little way and then turned back. So I'm good enough for an immigrant worker and that's about it, she said to herself bitterly. She felt she was near to tears again, and once again she fought them off. Once she had reached her car she glanced up at the fifth floor of Fred Meichelbeck's building. There was still light in the windows. Feeling utterly disheartened, she got into her car and drove home.

Back home, she discovered that her husband was still in the bedroom. She cleared the supper table, washed the dishes and then laid the table for breakfast next morning. After that she went into the bathroom and took two more tranquillizer capsules before she began removing her make-up. When she had taken her make-up off she looked in the mirror and suddenly hated herself. She thought her face utterly insignificant. She thought her eyes were too small, her nose too big and her lips too thick. She grimaced before she began spreading a thick layer of night cream on her face. Then she sat on the edge of the bathtub and wondered how to approach her husband. She didn't think there was any point in it, but she decided to apologize. Quietly, she opened the bedroom door and glanced at the bed. He was lying on it, full length, arms behind his head and staring at the ceiling. As he did not so much as turn his head in her direction, she knelt down beside the low bed and bent over his face, so that he had no choice but to look at her. He stared at her without any expression at all, except that his lips, thin enough to start with, had narrowed even more in bitterness.

I just wanted to say I'm sorry, she said.

He simply stared at her and did not reply.

Look, she said, can't you make an effort and forgive me straight away, just for once, and she took him by the shoulders and shook him. Then she asked what did she have to do to get him to forgive her. He simply stared at her, and still said nothing. She realized that there was no point at all in trying to make it up, for the time being. Once more she came close to losing her temper with him, and it was only thanks to the numerous tranquillizer capsules she had taken that day that she managed to control herself and keep from shouting at him again. She got up, opened the wardrobe, took out the bedclothes and threw them on the bed. Then she went back into the bathroom, undressed and washed. When she came back into the bedroom she saw that her husband had made up the bed, as usual. She got into bed, and he went through his customary routine of going to the kitchen to make the baby's bottle, waking the baby, changing her, feeding her and putting her down again, before he himself undressed and washed.

Behaving terribly correctly, just so no one can hold anything against him, Lilo Besslein told herself as he came back into the bedroom with a bottle of mineral water in one hand and a glass in the other. She watched him put the glass down on the bedside table, open the bottle of mineral water and fill the glass from it. She watched him sit down on the edge of the bed, take his watch off and place it beside the alarm clock, wind the clock, and then compare the time on the faces of both watch and clock. She watched him get

77

into bed and switch off the bedside lamp. He cleared his throat, several times. For a few minutes she waited for him to wish her good night, at least. But he just lay there, silent and motionless. Such a silence between two people lying so close together was rather alarming. She felt like shouting out loud, to break that brooding silence in the bedroom, but she stopped herself. For a moment she nearly reached out to touch his hands, which he had folded over his chest outside the bed-clothes as he always did before going to sleep. But she already knew, from experience, that he would not respond to such a gesture, and so she refrained from that as well. She felt utterly forlorn. She remembered standing outside Fred Meichelbeck's door not so long ago, she remembered the creak of the floorboards, the whispering and the muffled giggles she had heard in his apartment. The memory gave her a sharp pang. She was near to tears again, and fought them off once more. The bastard, she said to herself, well, that's it, so far as I'm concerned. I never ought to have got involved with him at all. She made herself think of other things. She thought of finding the baby a child-minder. She thought of getting the job at the pharmacy. Both, she felt, were rays of hope. She was sure going back to work would make a difference to her life. She tried to picture herself working in the pharmacy, but all the tranquillizers she had taken that day left her unable to conjure up any but the most blurred of images. She saw herself standing in the shop, serving a customer. She saw herself sitting in the laboratory, making up boric lotion and suppositories. She saw herself opening the poison cupboard in the drugs room and taking out a glass jar with a black label and something written on it in white. She got no further. Weariness overcame her. She turned on her side, and within a few minutes she fell into a deep and dreamless sleep.

*

Lilo Besslein had some trouble getting accustomed to her work at the pharmacy at first. She could not lay her hands on the medicaments straight away. She took too long adding up bills. She took too long giving customers their change. She kept forgetting to stamp prescriptions, and Frau Högemann had to remind her, and would then look thoughtfully at her. And to start with she found it hard to remember the customers' names. Frau Högemann liked her assistants to greet the customers by name: people prefer a place with the personal touch, she used to say.

But Lilo Besslein's new job presented her with quite a different sort of problem as well. She kept catching things from the customers. If they came in for a cold cure, she had a cold herself two days later. If they came in for a bronchial remedy, she had bronchitis herself two days later. If they came in for a patent medicine for flu, she had flu herself two days later. She refused to stay off work sick, however, and kept on going to the pharmacy even when she had a chill and a temperature, for fear of losing her job. She tried to cure her ailments on her days off, but she could never stay in bed for more than an hour or so because of the baby and the chores that had to be done. Then Christmas came, and she had to go to N with her husband and small daughter to spend the Christmas holiday with her parents and parents-in-law. While Ernst Besslein looked forward to seeing his own mother and father, she dreaded the thought of seeing hers. Every Christmas, regular as clockwork, they had family arguments, usually set off by something quite small. As the Besslein started off on the drive to N they were advising each other on the best way to behave, but after a while they ran into a snowstorm on the motorway and Ernst Besslein had to concentrate on his driving. They made slower progress than they had expected. To her husband's annoyance Lilo Besslein was chain-smoking, even though the baby was on the back seat in the top of the pram. She knew how keen her father was on punctuality. Then there was a traffic jam on the motorway just before they reached the exit road to N, delaying their journey even more, and they were an hour late by the time they arrived.

Lilo Besslein's parents had obviously been waiting at a window of the villa, keeping watch on the road, for they were standing in the doorway of the house, looking reproachful, as Ernst Besslein drew up. There was a fir tree standing by the door, its fairy lights already switched on. As her daughter came towards her carrying the top of the pram, Margot Ohlbaum called out to her: oh, they'd been terribly worried. Paul Ohlbaum asked her why they didn't start earlier.

We'll have to leave the presents till after dinner or the venison will dry out and the dumplings will fall to bits, he added, as Max Besslein and Wilma Besslein appeared in the spacious entrance hall behind him. Unlike the Ohlbaums, they were both wearing evening dress. Taking not the slightest initial notice of Lilo Besslein, they immediately made a beeline for the baby, who had slept all through the drive and was still asleep. Lilo Besslein indicated that it would not be a good idea to wake her up now, and took her into the living room, where there was a large Christmas tree beside the table laden with presents. She put her down on the Persian rug, still in the top of the pram, and then kissed first her parents and then her parents-in-law.

You don't look at all well, said her mother-in-law.

You look terrible, said her mother, in reproachful rather than anxious tones, before telling everyone to go and sit down at the dining table and disappearing into the kitchen to dish up the meal. Lilo Besslein helped her. Her father filled their glasses with red wine, and then carved the saddle of venison into pieces of roughly the same size, disposing the slices on separate plates. They all heaped their own plates with red cabbage, cranberry jelly and dumplings, poured gravy over the lot and began to eat. Paul Ohlbaum raised his glass. They drank to the lady of the house, who did not at first seem inclined to trust the many compliments she was paid: she wondered if the roast venison mightn't have been a little tenderer, she wondered if the gravy mightn't have been a little thicker, and if she shouldn't have let the red cabbage cook a little longer. Eventually she returned to the subject of her daughter's appearance.

I felt really alarmed when I saw you, she said. You look dreadfully pale and run down.

Don't you think she looks awful, she asked Wilma Besslein.

Wilma Besslein, along with everyone else at the table, scrutinized her daughter-in-law, who felt like running out of the room to avoid all their stares, and said she looked absolutely worn out.

Right from the first I thought working in that pharmacy wouldn't do you any good, she added, without taking her eyes off her daughter-in-law.

Well, you were wrong, if there's one thing that does do me good it's my job in the pharmacy, she said, trying to suppress her irritation. She knew very well that none of the family approved of her working. She glanced at her husband, for support, but he did not look up from his plate; he seemed to be concentrating entirely on the food.

It was a ridiculous notion of yours anyway, going back to work in a pharmacy, said her father. I mean, I wouldn't say a thing if you had to rely on your part-time earnings, like some women. But Ernst is earning well enough, and if you do need a little extra to buy yourself some clothes you've only got to ask your old father.

So why don't you, he inquired, with a questioning look at his daughter, whose expression was one of defiance.

Because I don't want to be a drone, she said. The

housework and the baby don't stretch me. I get depressed. I don't have anyone to talk to all day long except my neighbour or one of the girls at the self-service store. I can't stand it.

But you've got the baby, exclaimed her mother. The veins on her temples were swelling again, in a rather alarming manner.

The baby doesn't make up for not having an adult to talk to, said Lilo Besslein.

Then you never ought to have married and had a baby, said Wilma Besslein. An outside job just doesn't fit in with looking after a home and a baby. You suffer, and the baby suffers most of all.

How you can bring yourself to hand a six-month-old baby over to a perfect stranger I don't know, cried her mother. I never let you out of my sight when you were that age.

Mothers used to know where their responsibilities lay better than they do these days, remarked Max Besslein, helping himself to another slice of roast venison and asking his wife to cut it up for him.

And the damage to the baby will show, very early on, said Margot Ohlbaum. She'll be shy and timid. She won't know where she belongs. She won't trust you a bit because you keep on leaving her with this perfect stranger.

Oh yes, that's right, paint everything as black as you possibly can, that always was your line, cried Lilo Besslein, and she jumped up to rush out of the dining room, but her father caught her wrist.

Now, my dear, we want to spend a happy Christmas Eve together, he said.

Then we'd better change the subject, because I don't think we're going to agree on this one, said Lilo Besslein, sitting down again.

For a little while nobody said anything. Then her mother started discussing her job at the pharmacy again. Look at it realistically, she said, and it wasn't much of a job. She, Lilo, was nothing but a glorified salesgirl. She hadn't even studied pharmacology, so there was no way she was going to rise in the profession. She might think the job more rewarding than housework for the first month or so, but it was sure to seem very boring later on. She could still remember how Lilo always used to complain of the monotony of her job.

And the damage she was inflicting on the baby through her thoughtlessness wasn't irreparable yet, she could give notice any time she liked, she added, looking expectantly at her daughter.

But Lilo Besslein did not reply. She was determined not to give up her job at the pharmacy. She felt much more confident now that she had a measure of independence again, and her depression never overwhelmed her while she was at work, only on her days at home with the baby. However, she couldn't bring herself to say so in the bosom of her family. She felt that if she did risk such a comment they would all turn on her. She was sorry no one here showed the slightest understanding of her problems. As time went by the members of her family had become more and more like strangers to her, and this alienation meant she had difficulty accepting the assurance with which they treated her from force of habit. She hated having to kiss her mother and father when they met. She hated having to let them keep on discussing things that were her own business. She would much rather have spent Christmas alone with her husband and her small daughter, but ever since they were married the Besslains had gone to N annually at Christmas, and neither her parents nor her parents-in-law would have understood why it shouldn't be the same this year. For a moment she was so deep in thought that she entirely failed to notice the silence around the table. Then she glanced up, and saw that it was not just her mother still staring at her: everyone else present was looking her way too. Plainly, they were all eagerly awaiting her answer. Partly out of cowardice and partly for the sake of a quiet life, she said she'd think it over.

This, however, did not seem to satisfy her mother. The baby started crying in the living room, which did put an end to the discussion, but as soon as she had been dealt with, Margot Ohlbaum brought the conversation back to her daughter's job and the dreadful effects it would have on the baby if she stuck to it. She went on in just the same vein on Christmas Day and the day after, and by the time Lilo Besslein was driving back to M with her husband and her small daughter on the afternoon of 26 December, she was so worn down by her mother's remarks that she felt almost inclined to give in to her, as she so often had before. The one thing that stopped her was the thought of her monotonous existence before she got the job in the pharmacy. Yet the job itself was far from interesting. She stood behind the counter all day, selling medicaments, and seldom had anything to do in the laboratory. That sort of job was generally done by the other assistant, Fräulein Sabine Ickstett. Lilo Besslein got on with her very well. When there were no customers in the shop they would both go into the dispensing room for a cigarette, and like Sabine Ickstett and Frau Högemann, Lilo Besslein took advantage of these breaks in the work to dose herself with one of the many patent medicines they stocked that were supposed to prevent colds and flu. One and all, they proved useless. In defiance of the patent medicines, the three women kept catching things from the many ailing customers who called at the shop daily. They had coughs, colds, sore throats and flu all winter. Once Lilo Besslein infected her small daughter, and had to take a week off to look after her. Otherwise, however, she went to work whether she had a temperature or not. She dreaded the thought of spending all day alone in the apartment, and did not even go back there during the two hours' lunch break. She spent those two hours with Sabine Ickstett in a pizza house near the pharmacy instead. The Pizzeria Boccaccio was never crowded at this time of day. Apart from the Italian proprietor and his staff, there was seldom anyone there except a few commercial travellers who had come to Lerchenau to sell life assurance, household insurance, vacuum cleaners, washing machines or magazine subscriptions. But there was one other regular customer Lilo Besslein saw: a blond young man with a moustache, who always had a pile of books and a pile of papers on the table in front of him and sat busily reading or making notes. She had served this young man several times in the pharmacy, where the prescription he always handed in was for anti-depressants. Initially he merely gave her a brief greeting when she came into the pizzeria with Sabine Ickstett, and then buried himself in his books again, but in the course of time he became more forthcoming. At first he and the two young women exchanged a few words from their respective tables; later, he came over to their table to shake hands and sit down with them for a while. Lilo Besslein learned that he was studying for a degree in German, and would soon be taking his Finals. She learned that he lived in a commune in Lerchenau with three other students. She learned that the three students and their girlfriends always made such a racket that he couldn't work in the apartment. She learned that he spent almost all day in the pizzeria. It was his home from home, he said with a wistful smile. Finally he told them his name, Christian Blome, and Lilo Besslein and Sabine Ickstett told him their names too. Lilo Besslein definitely liked Christian Blome, with his constant air of slight melancholy. She wondered if it was herself or her friend who interested him. There was no telling which at first, from the way he behaved; he treated them both with the same civility. Sabine Ickstett seemed to have fallen in love with him. She would smile broadly at him, and blushed when he lit her cigarette. Lilo Besslein was close to falling in love with him too. She told herself he was a few years younger than she was, and hadn't even finished studying yet, but she didn't feel that was too important. She watched closely to see how he behaved to Sabine Ickstett, who could meet him on the three days she didn't work at the pharmacy herself, but she couldn't see any signs of extra intimacy between them. She realized, however, that Sabine Ickstett was watching her too, and a note of suppressed hostility crept into their relationship. But they both went on going to the Pizzeria Boccaccio, where they would find Christian Blome expecting them. He had come to welcome a break in his own work. During the two hours they spent sitting there together, they all bemoaned their troubles. Lilo Besslein talked about her quarrels with her husband. Sabine Ickstett, who was still living with her parents, talked about her disagreements with them. Christian Blome talked about the arguments he was called upon to settle between the various members of his commune. Finally Lilo Besslein would take two of her tranquillizer capsules. Sabine Ickstett, to whom she had recommended them, took one capsule of the same tranquillizer. Christian Blome took his anti-depressant. Then the two young women set off for the pharmacy and Christian Blome got down to his books again. These casual meetings followed the same pattern for two months, and Lilo Besslein was just beginning to think that neither she nor her colleague meant any more to Christian Blome than a welcome distraction at mid-day when he asked them both to his birthday party. It was to be next day.

Lilo Besslein had told her husband about Christian Blome, but he objected when she said she was going to the party. It wasn't right for her to mix socially with people who had met her in a pizzeria, he said, and he didn't like her going to parties on her own, and what was more, a student commune was no place for a respectable married woman.

If she was bored, he added, he was prepared to get a

babysitter any time and they could go out together in the evening.

But his wife did not consider this offer anything like an adequate substitute for the party at the commune. She knew in advance that if she and her husband went out together they would spend almost the whole evening sitting in a bar in Malching, face to face and in silence, watching the people at the other tables. She knew in advance that her husband, as usual, would order a beer and one of the cheapest dishes on the menu, a hint to her not to be extravagant herself. And she dreaded the thought of dancing with him in a discotheque after the meal; he danced neither well nor willingly. She assured him there was no harm at all in the birthday party, and begged him not to mind her going out to it, just for once. She promised she wouldn't stay more than two hours, or three at the most, and she would come home early. It was no good, however. Her husband still disapproved. When she came into the living room next evening, carefully dressed for the party in black and gold, he was sitting on the sofa with a glass of beer and the sports section of the paper, and he tried to put pressure on her with his silence. She talked to him for another quarter of an hour, attempting to appease him, and got nowhere at all, so she went out, although she knew she was in for another two or three days during which he would not exchange a word with her. As Christian Blome lived on the other side of Lerchenau, she drove to his apartment. She discovered that it was in one of the twelve-storey tower blocks to the north of the district. The front door of the building was not yet locked, but Lilo Besslein rang the bell before she went up to the ninth floor. Christian Blome, dressed in dark blue sweater and blue jeans as usual, met her when the lift came up and took her into the apartment, which smelt powerfully of garlic. It was a three-roomed apartment on the same plan as her own. Christian Blome had the smallest of the three rooms,

87

which contained only a table, a chair, a mattress and a bookcase crammed with clothes as well as books and journals. The other three students shared the two remaining rooms. Their three girlfriends, who were students too, often spent the night there, which meant fitting no fewer than seven people, all told, into a living area of only seventy square metres. At the moment the other two rooms were empty. Lilo Besslein could see that they too were very sparsely furnished. There were two large mattresses on the floor of each room, with a bookcase full of books and items of clothing in between them. There were hooks on the walls, with numerous other garments hanging on them, and the larger room contained a stereo system which, at the moment, was belting out rather loud rock music. A wooden crate turned upside down stood in the middle of each room and obviously did duty as a table; Lilo Besslein saw large ashtrays standing on the crates, brim-full of old cigarette ends. There were sofa cushions scattered on the floor around the two crates.

When Christian Blome had shown her the rest of the apartment he took her into the kitchen, where the three students and their girlfriends were gathered around the cold buffet supper laid out on two upturned crates pushed together. Lilo Besslein saw Sabine Ickstett standing in the background, beside a stool with a beer barrel on it, holding a paper plate upon which she was piling salad, and looking rather lost, for the students and their girlfriends, who must all have been a few years younger even than Christian Blome, were devoting themselves entirely to the consumption of supper. They did not seem particularly interested in Lilo Besslein either, and at twenty-nine she felt rather out of place among such young people. The one thing that seemed to intrigue them was the fact that Christian Blome had invited both young women to his birthday party. They glanced rapidly from Lilo Besslein to Sabine Ickstett, who now made her way past them and joined Christian

Blome, and then turned back to the assorted salads, sausage and cheeses. Indeed, they were eating so hard that Christian Blome had to push them aside to let Lilo Besslein get something to eat herself. She tried to find a salad that had no garlic in it, for fear her husband would dislike the aroma, but when she was told there was garlic in everything she heaped a paper plate with salads all the same, not wanting to be the odd one out. Christian Blome asked if she would like beer or wine, and she said wine. He took a bottle of wine and two paper cups into his room, and she and Sabine Ickstett followed him. Christian Blome moved the chair from his table over to the mattress, but before he sat down he went out of the room again to turn down the music, saying the noise was unbearable. The students and their girlfriends protested, but when he pointed out that this was his birthday party they grudgingly let him have his way.

They play that rock music day and night, he said when he was back in his room and sitting down. He'd have moved out long ago if he could have found another room, he added. They and their girlfriends lived like pigs in this place. They'd tidied up today just for once, because he particularly asked them to, seeing it was his birthday, but usually you were falling over dirty dishes, bottles, cans, books and clothes even out in the corridor. A misplaced sense of communality, moreover, meant that no one except himself made any distinction between mine and thine, so they all made use of his room the moment he was out of the building. He would often come back after working in the pizzeria all day to find Matthias and his friend Elvira, or Hannes and his friend Karin, or Carlo and his friend Ute sleeping on his mattress in each other's arms, and they considered everything else in his room common property too. They borrowed books and journals out of his bookcase without asking first, and took his clothes and even his underclothes without asking too, so he often didn't have a change of clothing. He'd tried locking his room on occasion, but they took this very ill and said he was a square, and he hadn't been able to handle that in the long run. They were nice young people at heart, he said, so naive as to be almost unworldly, and had simply taken it into their heads to practise a new kind of togetherness.

He was just adding that he himself obviously wasn't made for this sort of togetherness when one of the three girlfriends, a student called Ute, came into the room with a paper plate of food in one hand and a full paper cup in the other, and sat down on the mattress with Lilo Besslein and Sabine Ickstett. To her surprise, Lilo Besslein saw that the girl was pregnant. She looked surreptitiously at Ute's big belly, thinking there was probably going to be a baby to disturb Christian Blome too in the near future. Meanwhile the student was scrutinizing first herself and then Sabine Ickstett with frank curiosity.

We want to ask you something, she said at last, turning to Christian Blome.

Carry on, then. What is it, he asked rather brusquely.

We'd just love to know which of them's your new girlfriend, said the student. Once again she examined Lilo Besslein and Sabine Ickstett, who were much embarrassed by this question. Christian Blome seemed distinctly nettled too. However, the student obviously didn't notice.

Well, come on, don't keep us in suspense, she said. We've got a bet on it, you see, a crate of beer. The majority thinks it's you, she continued, pointing to Lilo Besslein. Much to her annoyance, Lilo Besslein blushed.

But two of us think it's you, she added, pointing to Sabine Ickstett, who had gone red in the face too. She looked to Christian Blome for aid. He had bowed his head and was rubbing both hands over his face. Finally he cleared his throat and said, with a forced laugh: well, neither of them so far.

What do you mean, so far, inquired the student blankly, sounding disappointed.

Look, I call that a very impertinent question and I'm not answering it, said Christian Blome. If you'd been listening you'd have realized we're none of us even on first-name terms yet.

How about changing that, by the way, he added, turning to Lilo Besslein and Sabine Ickstett.

They both nodded, still feeling embarrassed, and raised their paper cups to drink to Christian Blome, while the rather baffled student left the room to go back to the kitchen and report to the others. They sat there in silence for several minutes. Lilo Besslein was wondering if Christian Blome found it hard to choose between her and Sabine Ickstett. She felt it was grotesque, the three of them still sitting here together. She wondered why he had asked them both to his birthday party anyway, and then told herself he only ever met her in Sabine Ickstett's company and didn't want to hurt the feelings of either of them. All the same, she thought it was clumsy of him. For instance, she thought, he could have rung her up and made a date for just the two of them to meet. Then she wondered about his remark to the effect that neither young woman was his girlfriend so far. She thought it implied that he did have intentions of that nature. She told herself he had his eye on one of them all right, either herself or Sabine Ickstett. She glanced surreptitiously at Sabine Ickstett, who had got herself up in great style for the occasion. She told herself Sabine Ickstett looked really good with her long, bleached hair and her brown eyes. She also told herself Sabine Ickstett was a more suitable girlfriend for Christian Blome than she was, being much the same age and unmarried. As if he guessed her thoughts, Christian Blome suddenly asked after her baby daughter.

Just beginning to crawl, she said.

Why don't you bring her to the pizzeria some day

when you're not working, Christian Blome suggested.

Lilo Besslein said she would, though she wasn't sure what Christian Blome had in mind. She wondered whether he meant he'd like to see her without Sabine Ickstett some time. Once again she glanced at her friend. The suggestion seemed to have dismayed her. She was sitting on the mattress in silence, her lips pressed together, her jaw working. In a moment or so she got up and left the room, saying she was still hungry. When she had gone, Christian Blome smiled at Lilo Besslein and asked if she'd like to dance. Lilo Besslein said yes, and they went into the room with the stereo. They danced together, in a most unfashionable way. Christian Blome actually put an arm around Lilo Besslein's waist, and she put her hand on his shoulder, and they held hands too. Lilo Besslein enjoyed dancing with Christian Blome very much. He was tall and strong, but extremely supple. While they were dancing the other members of the commune came into the room and began to dance as well, leaving Sabine Ickstett standing alone in the doorway, holding a heaped paper plate in one hand and a paper cup in the other, wearing a sickly smile and taking great pains to look cheerful.

Now you must dance with Sabine, said Lilo Besslein when they had just danced past the doorway yet again.

I suppose I'd better, replied Christian Blome, much to her relief, for she thought the remark implied that he would be dancing with Sabine Ickstett only as a social duty. Feeling suddenly overjoyed, she took her hand off his shoulder and pushed him gently towards her friend, who immediately put her paper plate and cup down on the crate in the middle of the room. As the two of them danced, Lilo Besslein sat down on one of the two mattresses and watched. She saw that Christian Blome had not put his arm around her friend's waist; instead, they were dancing separately. Once again she felt momentarily overjoyed, but then she told herself she was reading too much into such little details. She began to feel more doubtful. Going into the kitchen, she took two tranquillizer capsules, and then looked at the time. It was ten-thirty; she ought to drive home now if she was going to keep her promise to her husband, but she dared not leave Christian Blome alone with Sabine Ickstett, so she went back into the room with the stereo. She saw Christian Blome still dancing with Sabine Ickstett, who was now looking extremely happy. He had taken her raised hand, and she was twirling round and round. Lilo Besslein thought she danced very well indeed. She thought she had a perfect figure. She told herself, again, that her colleague was a more suitable girlfriend for Christian Blome than she was. She sat down on one of the two mattresses and watched the others dancing. The pregnant Ute seemed to find it too much of an effort, for she suddenly stopped, put her hands to her belly, and then lay down on the mattress beside Lilo Besslein.

Don't you feel well, Lilo Besslein asked her.

The student sat up, her manner becoming rather portentous. Listen, I want to ask you a question, she whispered to Lilo Besslein.

What is it, asked Lilo Besslein.

Are you in love with Christian, whispered the student.

What a question to ask, whispered Lilo Besslein.

Oh, so you are in love with him, are you, asked the student.

Well, don't go telling everyone, whispered Lilo Besslein.

I won't say a word, said the student, and she watched Christian Blome and Sabine Ickstett for a moment. They were still dancing together.

Is your friend in love with Christian too, she asked Lilo Besslein.

Yes, I think she is, she said. Very much so.

Wow, how exciting, said the student, and then stopped short, for Christian Blome and Sabine Ickstett were coming over to the mattress. Sabine Ickstett sat down, breathless, saying she felt quite dizzy. Christian Blome remained on his feet and asked Lilo Besslein if she'd like to dance again. She stood up, nodding, and he put his arm around her waist again and drew her close. As they danced together Lilo Besslein saw that Ute was now talking to Sabine Ickstett, and Sabine Ickstett was looking very embarrassed again. She noticed the student and Sabine Ickstett watching her, too, and felt sorry she had spoken so freely to Ute. Nor did Christian Blome fail to notice the eyes of the two young women on the mattress following him, for as they danced he guided Lilo Besslein first out of the room and into the corridor, and then down the corridor and into his own room.

Your friend seems rather jealous of you, he said, when they had reached the room.

There's no reason why she should be, said Lilo Besslein.

Shall I give her one, inquired Christian Blome, bringing his face close to Lilo Besslein's.

What do you mean, she asked, although she had a pretty good idea what Christian Blome meant.

He suddenly stopped dancing in the middle of the room, drew her towards him and kissed her. For a moment Lilo Besslein felt a wonderful sense of satisfaction; then doubts crept back into her mind. She was naturally suspicious in any case, and her experiences with Fred Meichelbeck had made her more so. Turning her head aside, she asked Christian Blome if he was planning to kiss Sabine Ickstett too.

What on earth makes you think that, he asked, and then burst out laughing.

Oh, so you're jealous too, he cried, and he kissed her again. Then he told her there was absolutely nothing to feel jealous about. He said he'd only ever met her together with Sabine Ickstett, so he just hadn't known how to make a date with her on her own without giving offence to her friend.

She's a nice girl, Sabine, but I'm not interested in her that way, he added, and then he drew her down towards the mattress. They both sat down on it before they kissed again.

They were in each other's arms when Ute appeared in the doorway, said she was sorry to disturb them, and told them Sabine had just left.

She remarked that Sabine Ickstett had seemed to be near tears.

Christian Blome said he was sorry about that.

Personally, she thought it was brutal of him, said the student. First raising the poor girl's hopes, and then disappearing into his room with somebody else.

He hadn't done anything to raise Sabine's hopes, said Christian Blome, and he turned to Lilo Besslein and asked if she thought he'd been raising her friend's hopes.

No, she replied, casting a glance at her watch and rising to her feet, any hopes of Sabine's had been of her own making.

And she'd have to go, she added, to Christian Blome's dismay. He obviously hadn't expected her to leave just yet, and asked her to stay a little longer. He said he couldn't bear to part with her so soon. But Lilo Besslein was adamant. She was afraid her husband might still be awake, waiting up for her to come in. She had never been to a party on her own since she was married, and that was three years ago. Taking no notice of Christian Blome's pleading, she made for the door of the apartment, where she put out her hand to say goodbye. But he insisted on going down to her car with her, so they both went down to the ground floor in the lift, and kissed again before they left the building. When Lilo Besslein got to the car she tried saying goodbye to Christian Blome a second time, but he insisted on keeping her company on the drive home.

And then he'd go back on foot, he said.

Honestly, what a big baby you are, said Lilo Besslein, and she opened the car door for him and then got in herself.

During her short drive home, they discussed their next meeting. Christian Blome was very keen to make a date for next day, in his room. It was not one of Lilo Besslein's working days, and she pointed out that she would have to bring her baby daughter. Christian Blome said he didn't mind that in the least.

If we want to get rid of the baby we can just hand her over to Ute, he said, she's mad about babies. Lilo Besslein agreed, and promised to come and visit him next day, in the afternoon, but her mind was not entirely on the matter. The closer she came to the sky-blue housing block where she lived, the uneasier she felt. She was afraid some of the other tenants might see her with Christian Blome, late as it was, and when she parked the car in the Gluckgasse and he tried to embrace her again, she quickly pushed him away.

It was too risky here, she told him, and she asked him to get out now and go away, fast. He did as she said, while she locked the car and ran up the path to the door of her building, suddenly panic-stricken. One glance showed her there were no lights on in her own apartment. She unlocked the door of the building, went up the six steps to the apartment door on tip-toe, and took off her shoes before she unlocked it. She stood in the corridor for a moment, listening. Hearing no sound, she slipped into the bathroom. She removed her make-up, washed her face and undressed. She took two tranquillizer capsules. Then she switched off the light and groped her way down the corridor in the dark. Reaching the bedroom door, she stopped and listened once again, but there was still no sound to be heard. She opened the door, tip-toed over to the bed, lay down and covered herself up. Then she lay quiet, listening again. To her dismay, she realized that her husband must be awake. She could tell from the sound of his breathing. He lay there quite still beside her, and never said a word. As before, she felt it was not just unendurable but positively eerie, the two of them lying there side by side in silence. The atmosphere was so oppressive that she wanted to scream, but she repressed the urge. She wondered what she could say to end the silence, but she couldn't think of anything suitable. Finally she decided to ask her husband if he was still awake. She turned towards him, she opened her mouth, but she could not utter a word of this simple sentence. Nor could she reach out her hand to caress his face. She lay on her back again and tried to ignore him. She thought of Christian Blome and the passionate way he had kissed her. She thought how he had insisted on coming home with her. She couldn't help smiling. It was hard for her to take him altogether seriously, and she could not really have said what she expected of an affair with him. It isn't going to make any real difference to my stupid mucked-up life, she told herself, and then turned on her side, trying to keep the sense of hopelessness that suddenly arose in her within bounds.

*

After this, Christian Blome and Lilo Besslein took to meeting regularly in the commune's apartment on those three weekdays when she was not at work in the pharmacy. Lilo Besslein would hand her daughter over to one of the girl students, and then disappear into Christian Blome's room with him for an hour or so. When they had made love they brought the baby in and played with her together until it was time for Lilo Besslein to leave. She always got home an hour before her husband, and had the table properly laid for supper by the time he entered the apartment. On the days she was at work, she met Christian Blome in the Pizzeria Boccaccio during her lunch break. Despite repeated invitations, Sabine Ickstett no longer joined them. She had taken to treating Lilo Besslein with overt hostility now. At work she watched her like a hawk, and as soon as she made a mistake serving a customer she made sure everyone knew about it. She was so spiteful to Lilo Besslein, indeed, that Frau Högemann had to warn her to restrain herself several times. Frau Högemann set great store by keeping the atmosphere at work harmonious. Lilo Besslein suffered from her colleague's hostility, and armed herself against it by taking even more tranquilliser capsules than usual on those days she went to work in the pharmacy. As a result, her reflexes were temporarily slowed down, and she kept being troubled by a curious absence of mind, though it lasted for such short periods that it quite escaped the notice of Sabine Ickstett, Frau Högemann and the customers. Christian Blome, however, did notice these attacks of absentness, and he asked Lilo Besslein what the matter was. She admitted she was still taking tranquillizers, but she did not tell him how large a dose she was swallowing daily. For by now she was taking twelve or sometimes fourteen or fifteen capsules a day. Whenever she tried to reduce the dosage, anxiety feelings overwhelmed her again, and she began to shake all over. Her condition frequently alarmed her. She realized she couldn't go on like this indefinitely. But she was afraid to tell anyone about it; she dared not even tell Christian Blome her secret, and in any case she was not being honest with him in that she made him give her a detailed account of everything he did or did not do, but avoided telling him the facts about her relationship with her husband. Christian Blome was jealous of her husband. He told her she mustn't sleep with him any more, and she promised him she wasn't, but when her husband slipped over to her side of the bed at night, once a week, she never said no. For one thing, she had a guilty conscience about her affair with Christian

Blome, and for another, she was afraid of hurting his feelings. In spite of those plans for the future which Christian Blome was constantly making she had no intention of leaving her husband for him. There was no kind of security at all in the life her lover had to offer her; he had even failed his exams. Thanks to her husband's job, she did have security. It meant a life that bored her to death, but she didn't think she could do without it. She was on the point of telling Christian Blome so, several times, but whenever she got an opportunity to broach the subject she let it pass; she was afraid of spoiling the relationship for good. She did not stop him looking for a job that would bring in enough for him to support her and the baby, or looking for an apartment for the three of them. She observed his efforts, feeling both touched and alarmed, and when they came to nothing she was immensely relieved. She felt bad about raising false hopes, and even worse, it struck her that she was behaving wretchedly. She could see that one day he would confront her with facts that would force her to show where she stood, and she already knew that if she refused to go and live with him she would lose him. She was already wondering how she would get over that. She was unable to love him more than she loved herself, but she was very fond of him; on those afternoons she spent with him she really came to life, and the sense of being loved gave her confidence. It helped her to cope with her life much better than before. It helped her to make light of her quarrels with her husband. At first she used to tell Christian Blome about these quarrels, mostly caused by some trifle, but she had taken to keeping quiet about them, for she discovered that as soon as she mentioned her marital troubles he increased his endeavours to find a job and an apartment. He had been choosy about jobs at first, trying to get one in a publishing firm, but once he discovered that he had no chance of that without passing his Finals, he kept telling Lilo Besslein that he would just get a job on a building site. Knowing he could get that kind of job any time early in the summer, he set about searching for an apartment all the more intensively. One afternoon, beaming with delight, he welcomed Lilo Besslein and told her, much to her dismay, that he had found a charming attic apartment in Malching. They could go and see this apartment straight away, he suggested.

He'd made an appointment with the present tenants, he added.

Lilo Besslein saw nothing for it but to agree, so they took the lift down to the ground floor and got into her car. She had brought the baby along, as usual, and they put her in the child seat her husband had fixed in the back. On the way to Malching, she asked Christian Blome how much the attic apartment cost. He said the rent was seven hundred and twenty marks a month, with about another hundred and twenty in incidental outgoings.

But, asked Lilo Besslein, how was he going to afford such a high rent.

Oh, he said, with irritating confidence, they could easily do it if he went to work on a building site and she carried on with her job at the pharmacy.

You haven't got a job yet, though, and if you do and then lose it we'll be out on the street, she said.

If that happens I'll just look for a new job, Christian Blome said, and he put an arm around her shoulders and begged her not to worry so much. After all, he went on, they'd only have to live in comparative insecurity for a year, because next year he would pass his Finals, and then he was sure to get steady work.

We may be a real married couple by then, he added.

Lilo Besslein, feeling more and more apprehensive, did not say anything to that. She could see she was going to have to disappoint him bitterly, and the realization hurt her as much as if she herself were to suffer a severe disappointment. She turned her head to him for a moment as he directed her through the streets of Malching, and looked at him surreptitiously. He was only four years younger than she was, but he struck her as not just very immature: she suddenly felt he was actually in need of protection. I'm too old and hard for him, she was telling herself, when he asked her to stop the car.

He pointed proudly to an unobtrusive building painted pale yellow, with black doors and window frames. It was an old place, in very good repair. Two large brass plates by the main entrance informed you that it contained a doctor's surgery and an accountant's office, and according to the name plates fitted inside the lift, another doctor had his private residence in the building. As they went up to the fifth floor Christian Blome, who was carrying the child, asked Lilo Besslein what she thought of it.

Much to his satisfaction, she said it was very nice. He was overjoyed; he pulled her close to him and assured her she wouldn't be any worse off with him than she was with her husband. Then the lift stopped. They came out on the landing and rang the doorbell opposite the lift. A dark-haired, balding, bearded man opened the door, shook hands with Lilo Besslein and said his name was Edgar Klose. Christian Blome introduced Lilo Besslein as his wife and the little girl he was carrying as his daughter, and they entered a rather dark but roomy hall containing a pretty cupboard in the rustic style and two bookcases full of books reaching to the ceiling. Instead of showing them the apartment, Edgar Klose stayed in the hall and told them to look around at their leisure. They went into the first room, a pleasant room of medium size with a sloping window wall and containing a large desk and two more ceiling-height bookcases. As Lilo Besslein looked around and went over to the window, Christian Blome said that if she agreed he'd make this their bedroom.

101

We'll have a double bed and a rustic cupboard in it and that's all, he said, looking at her expectantly. But she said nothing. She was wondering how he thought he was going to pay for the double bed and the cupboard. In silence, she left the first room and went on to the second. It, too, was bright and pleasant, and rather larger than the first. The Kloses were obvioulsy using it as a bed-sitting room, for it contained two divan beds, four armchairs, a coffee table and two more bookcases. As Lilo Besslein looked around, Christian Blome, getting increasingly excited, told her that if she agreed he'd make this their living room.

We'll have a sofa in it, four armchairs, a coffee table and two bookcases, he said, and he looked expectantly at her again. This time she did ask how he was planning to pay for so much furniture.

Oh, we'll get it bit by bit, he replied, and then propelled her in the direction of the third room, which was considerably smaller than the other two, and said this would be the nursery.

I'll paper it, there are wallpapers with designs of toys and animals, he added. Lilo Besslein had already turned her back on the room and was making for the kitchen. She was near tears. She didn't know how to dissuade him from actually renting this apartment without hurting his feelings. He obviously thought the financial side of the whole thing a minor consideration. He followed her into the kitchen, a really roomy one, and told her he would make it a kitchen-cum-dining room.

We'll have a big table in here and six chairs, so we can ask friends in for a meal now and then, he said, and he was obviously about to add something else, but he stopped abruptly. For here Lilo Besslein burst into tears. Much alarmed, he asked why she was crying, and she said because the apartment was far too expensive.

Oh, he said, he'd find the money all right, and he looked so determined that she suddenly couldn't help laughing. For a moment there was nothing she wanted more than to live with him and her little girl in this apartment, which was indeed a charming place. Then she thought of all the risks of leading such a life with him, and put the idea right out of her head again. For the sake of appearances she looked at the bathroom which, like the rest of the apartment, was all they could have asked for. Then she went back into the hall. Herr Klose was still standing there, and had lit a pipe.

What a lot of books you have, she said.

I'm a writer and my wife's a bookseller, said Herr Klose. He added that there was another writer living in the building.

Nobody disturbs you here, he continued, addressing himself mainly to Christian Blome, nobody goes poking their nose into other people's business. Christian Blome was looking very happy again. In high spirits, he kissed and tickled the little girl, whom he was still carrying. Watching him, Lilo Besslein felt terrible, as if she were on the point of stabbing him in the back.

She asked Herr Klose if anyone else was interested in the apartment.

Quite a lot of people had been to view it, he said, but most of them thought it was too expensive.

It was too expensive, too, said Lilo Besslein, and she indicated to Christian Blome, who was still looking enthusiastically around the apartment, that she wanted to go. They said goodbye to Herr Klose and took the lift down to the ground floor. When they reached the car Christian Blome suggested a coffee somewhere.

We could go to the Daisy or the Ba-Ba-Lu, he said.

But Lilo Besslein said no; she was afraid of meeting Fred Meichelbeck there. They decided to drive to a less well-known café, one mostly frequented by students. The café was over-full, and they had to share a table with three students discussing some legal problem in rather loud voices. They both had coffee and cheesecake, and Lilo Besslein ordered a strawberry tart for the child. When the waitress brought their order, Christian Blome fed the little girl. He was still so enthusiastic about the apartment that Lilo Besslein didn't know how to stop him taking it. He was saying they'd be living together in about four weeks' time. He promised to help her clean the apartment. He promised to do the cooking at least twice a week. In between times he kissed and tickled her small daughter, who by now rather preferred him to her mother. As soon as she saw him she would crow with glee and hold out her arms to him.

He'd make an ideal father for her, Lilo Besslein told herself, watching him feed the child. Now he was talking about the next steps to be taken over renting the apartment. He said he'd go and see his parents that evening, and ask them to lend him the necessary sum for the agent's fee and the three months' advance rent required as a deposit. He said he'd go and look for a job on a building site tomorrow, and get a certificate of employment from the construction firm, and take this certificate of employment to show the agent.

Once he had the certificate of employment, he said, there'd be nothing to stop him signing the contract to rent the apartment.

Lilo Besslein listened in silence. Once or twice she was on the point of confessing that she felt living with him in these circumstances was too much of a risk for her, but yet again she couldn't bring herself to do it. She just hoped that when his parents heard he was planning to move in with a married woman and her child they'd refuse to lend him the money he needed. She hoped he would not find a job on a building site and thus wouldn't get a certificate of employment. She hoped somebody else would snap the apartment up. In fact, she hoped they could go on just as before. Finally he interrupted her train of thought by asking why she was so quiet.

Because you keep on talking, she said, glancing at her watch. To her alarm, she saw it was already half past four, and her husband came home from work at half past five. She told Christian Blome she must get home as fast as she could. He called the waitress and asked for the bill for all three of them, but when it came he didn't have the money to pay it, so Lilo Besslein slipped him a twenty-mark note and told him to keep the change. She knew he was always short of cash at the end of the month; she had given him twenty or fifty marks several times before.

You'll get it back, he said as they left the café. He carried the little girl over to the car and put her in her child seat in the back. Suddenly feeling very nervous, Lilo Besslein had trouble getting the car out of its parking slot, and then she got caught up in a traffic jam to the south of Malching. She drummed her fingertips on the steering wheel in agitation. Christian Blome tried, vainly, to calm her down.

His lordship will just have to wait a little longer for his supper than usual, that's all, he said, viciously.

I can't stand it, you going on about him like that, said Lilo Besslein. Much to her relief, she was moving a little more freely now. However, she did not reach Lerchenau until nearly five. She dropped Christian Blome off at the top of the shopping street in the north of the district. He leaned over to kiss her goodbye before he got out of the car, but she pushed him away, afraid somebody might see them, and as soon as he had closed the car door she drove off without even waving. She finally reached home at ten past five, put the baby down on the living-room carpet and rushed into the kitchen to start frying the two kebabs she had, fortunately, prepared at mid-day ready for cooking. While they were sizzling in the pan she hastily laid the supper table. After that she took two tranquillizer capsules and then made her daughter's bottle. She was just giving the child the bottle when her husband unlocked the front door of the apartment. He put his head into the living room, pursing up his lips, and asked if he was going to get a nice kiss; he always did this when he came home in a good mood. She went over to him, pursing her own lips, and kissed him briefly and noisily. Then he came all the way into the room, right hand hidden behind his back.

Oh, have you brought me something, she asked, knowing exactly what he had brought her, for whenever he planned to sleep with her he always brought home a medium-sized bunch of red roses. She pretended to be curious, however, tugging at his right arm until the hand holding the bunch of roses came into view.

Oh, roses, oh, how sweet of you, she said, and put her own pursed lips to his again for another brief and noisy kiss, before she went off to find a vase.

Meanwhile he turned his attention to the little girl, who was still drinking her bottle. He knelt down on the carpet, picked her up and sat down on the sofa with her. Then he asked her it it was a nice bottle.

Oh yes, what a nice bottle it is, he said.

He asked her if she'd been out walkies with her Mummy.

Oh yes, who's been out walkies with her Mummy, then, he said.

At this point Lilo Besslein came back into the room with the vase of flowers in one hand and a dish holding the two kebabs in the other. She asked him to sit down at the table, and he immediately did so. During supper he asked her what she had been doing all day, and she fed him a series of outright lies. She did not mind lying to him in the least; indeed, the contempt she had felt for him since she really got to know Christian Blome made lying easier. Sometimes it actually gave her a kind of satisfaction to deceive him, for she secretly held his lack of suspicion about Christian Blome against him. She saw it not as an indication of his faith in her but as a sign of indifference, and she thought nothing at all of his bringing her a bunch of roses this evening. She knew that the purchase of a bunch of roses once a week had become pure routine to him.

And had anything interesting happened at work, she inquired for the sake of appearances, having finished her kebab.

He seemed glad of this question; he leaned back in his chair and told her, in his rather grating voice, about a token two-hour strike at the Works that day over the breakdown of wage negotiations.

The workers' wage demands would scuttle the economy yet, he added, and looked challengingly at her.

She did not contradict him, however. Now that she had stopped seeing Fred Meichelbeck and his friends, her interest in politics and economics had died right down again. She no longer read the newspaper, and when her husband switched the television set on to watch the news she generally went out to the kitchen. She had enough trouble in coping with herself and her own life; she hadn't any energy left over to concern herself with anything outside her private domain.

Had her husband had enough, she asked him, before she rose and began to clear the table. As usual, he didn't help her; he thought clearing the table was one of her duties, and she did not object. While she washed the dishes she heard that grating voice of his, talking to the child, and she told herself that at least he was a good father. When he came home in the evening he always paid much more attention to the baby than he did to her, and he took care of his daughter entirely at weekends. He changed her, he made her bottle, he played with her and he put her to bed, leaving his wife with nothing she need do for the child at all. She got the impression that he enjoyed all this a great deal. She wondered if he would actually have let her take the child if she'd said she was leaving him for Christian Blome. She doubted it.

He loves her more than he loves me, she told herself as she came back into the living room, where her husband was helping her small daughter with her first attempts to walk. He was holding both the child's hands and moving slowly over the carpet with her.

And right, and left, and right and left, he said.

Lilo Besslein sat down on the sofa and watched them both for a while, smiling. Then she pointed out that it was the baby's bedtime. Her husband picked the child up at once and carried her into the nursery, where he changed her, put her down in her cot, and then sang her a lullaby to send her off to sleep.

Lilo Besslein much disliked his singing to the baby; she thought he was spoiling the child and had told him so, several times. Whether or not she meant well, he was not to be deterred. His own mother had sung him lullabies, so he was going to sing lullabies to his child. On this point he displayed the kind of stubbornness with which Lilo Besslein couldn't compete. When she heard him singing the child to sleep she felt hostility, as usual, a hostility whose violence was in no kind of ratio to its actual cause. She tried to fight against it. She thought of his bringing her a bunch of roses, but the recollection of the bunch of roses did not decrease her hostility at all, rather the opposite. When he handed her a bunch of roses once a week, she thought, he was actually demanding that she keep in line. She felt that the giving of this hackneyed gift, obtained without the expense of much thought or money, smacked of blackmail. She looked at the bunch of roses. It was hardly even a medium-sized bunch. She could guess at the part played in its purchase by his sense of thrift, which bordered on the miserly. She told herself he'd have been hard put to it to do any less to buy her willingness. She felt inclined to throw the bunch of roses out of the window, but she stopped herself. Bitterly, she rose, went into the bathroom, and took two more tranquillizer capsules. When she came back into the corridor her husband was just leaving the nursery. He went over to her, put his arms round her waist and hugged her in a way that told her he wanted to sleep with her.

But though the baby had been put to bed and there was nothing to stop them doing it here and now, he immediately let her go again. He was a creature of habit, and it would have upset his routine if he missed the television news at this point. He went into the living room, switched the TV set on and sat down on the sofa. Lilo Besslein sat down beside him and stared at the television screen, paying no attention to the news. Her mind was on other things. Close as she was sitting to her husband, she knew quite well he wasn't going to touch her until they had gone to bed and switched the light off. That was part of his routine too. She told herself she'd have liked it if he hadn't put off making love until they went to bed, if just for once he'd done it now. Suddenly she wanted to make him do it now. She moved even closer, she laid her arm round his shoulders, she put her face in front of his, kissed his lips and asked him if he loved her.

Yes, of course I love you, he replied, rather impatiently, moving away from her a little so that he could get a better view of the TV screen. She stayed where she was for a few minutes, discouraged. However, she told herself, she oughtn't to let one failure discourage her. For a split second, and out of a kind of obduracy, she was on the point of moving towards her husband again and expressing her intentions more clearly than by means of a kiss. But she was prevented by her upbringing, which had enjoined decorum on women in such matters. She couldn't go on sitting beside him being ignored until bedtime, so she rose and went into the kitchen. She put up the ironing board, switched on the iron, got the laundry basket out of the bathroom, and with the speed and the practised movements of a piece-worker she began to do the ironing.

*

When Lilo Besslein visited Christian Blome with her small daughter two days later he told her, beaming with delight and to her own horror, that he had taken the attic apartment in Malching. Quite contrary to her expectations, his parents had lent him the sum he needed for the agent's fee and the three months' advance rent as a deposit. Quite contrary to her expectations, he had got a job with a firm of builders.

They could move into the apartment in a month's time, he said, and he took her in his arms without noticing how his remark horrified her. She sat down on the mattress and told herself that now she must tell him the truth. She stared fixedly at him. She realized he was full of extraordinary confidence. He talked about his parents, and said they were very keen to meet her. They weren't very grand, he said, his father was assistant manager in a savings bank branch and his mother was a housewife. Neither of them had been at all pleased to hear he was planning to live with a married woman and her child, but they hadn't offered any further objections. His mother, he told Lilo Besslein, had said you can't choose where love will strike. And he smiled at her.

She was only half listening. While he talked, she was wondering how best to tell him that she and her small daughter were not going to move in with him. She told herself the baby was a good excuse for saying no. She decided to tell him she couldn't take the responsibility of leading such an insecure sort of life for the baby's sake. This was not, of course, true, but she thought she could use that sort of argument as a pretext to hide her own cowardice. She looked fixedly at him again. This time he did notice the way she was staring at him.

What's the matter with you, he asked, decidedly irritated.

I'm not going to move in with you, she said quietly, and a little hoarsely. Then she flinched involuntarily, as if she were afraid he might strike her.

He did nothing of that nature, however. He simply stared at her in silence, and then asked blankly what on earth she meant.

It's because of the baby, she said. I can't take the responsibility, letting myself in for such a risky, uncertain sort of life. She did not look at him. She was feeling

110

dreadfully ashamed of herself for taking refuge in such lies.

He paced up and down the room in silence for a little while. Then he asked if it was really that she wanted to stay with her husband.

It's a sacrifice, but I've got to make it because of my child, she said, still unable to look at him.

Why do you keep on about the child, he cried. You're not all that fond of her.

I mean, anyone can see she's more of a burden to you than anything, he added. Suddenly he burst into loud laughter.

Well, you've fooled me nicely, haven't you, he went on. You just sit back and let me go looking for an apartment, you just sit back and let me go looking for a job, and you never breathe a word about wanting to stay with your husband.

He roared with laughter again; next moment, however, his eyes were streaming with tears. He turned his back on Lilo Besslein, who did not know what to say in her own defence, took a handkerchief out of his trouser pocket and wiped his face with it. Then he turned back to her, visibly more composed, and asked if she wouldn't change her mind.

If only she'd trust him he'd make sure there was always enough money for her and the child, he said, and he sat down on the mattress with her and put his arms around her.

For a moment she almost let him persuade her. Then she thought of the insecurity of his job. She thought of the way he had failed his Finals, preferring to spend afternoons with her when he should have been working. She told herself he might well fail them again next year.

I'm not even up to coping with the kind of secure life my husband provides, she said. The sort of life you'd offer would be the end of me. And then she asked if they couldn't go on just as before.

He simply shook his head. Then he rose and began pacing up and down the room again.

He was quite unable to go on sharing her with her husband, he said. He'd never set eyes on the man, but he hated him from the bottom of his heart. The mere fact that she laid the table for her husband and shared his meals sickened him. He just dared not think of her spending all night in bed with him, because the idea of it sent him quite frantic. He kept on imagining her in her husband's arms, and the notion really hurt. Not just in the mind, either; it caused him actual physical suffering. When he thought of it he got violent shooting pains in the region of his heart. He had stuck with things the way they were up till now only in the hope that she'd leave her husband and come to live with him, and now, for the sake of his own peace of mind, he had to ask her to decide between the two of them.

If she was going to stay with her husband, he added, he didn't want to see her again. Then he stopped in front of her, looking at her expectantly.

I can't come and live with you. I just don't have the strength to begin all over again.

Instead of comforting her, he turned on his heel and left the room. A moment later she heard him slam the front door. She wiped the tears from her face and then went to fetch her daughter. The pregnant Ute was playing with her in the next room.

Had a quarrel, have you, she asked.

Worse than that, said Lilo Besslein. Unwilling to tell Ute any more about it, she nodded to Ute and left the apartment, feeling shaky at the knees. She drove home by the shortest route, and once home she took four tranquilizer capsules straight away. Then she sat down on the living-room sofa and waited for them to start working. When they did start working, she began to hope Christian Blome wouldn't break off their affair after all.

Next day she went to the Pizzeria Boccaccio in her lunch break, as she always did on her days at the pharmacy. She couldn't have said why she was so sure she would meet Christian Blome there, but she was. However, once she got inside the pizzeria she could not help seeing that the table where he always sat was unoccupied. Dismayed, in the grip of anxiety bordering on panic, she sat down at that table, ordered a glass of red wine and turned to stare at the restaurant doorway, hoping Christian Blome would appear in it after all. But he didn't turn up during the whole two hours she spent there. She was not going to lose heart entirely, though. She took four tranquilizer capsules and decided to go and see him at the commune's apartment tomorrow afternoon with her small daughter. But when she put this plan into practice and did go around to the apartment next day, Ute told her Christian Blome had gone away. Gone to visit his godmother in E, she said.

Lilo Besslein tried in vain to fight off the despair that suddenly swept over her. Did Ute know when he'd be back, she inquired.

In four weeks' time, said Ute.

That was when he was moving into the attic apartment in Malching, she added, to Lilo Besslein's astonishment.

But he didn't need a three-roomed apartment just for himself, she said.

Well, he was set on having it, said the student.

Why wasn't she moving in with him, she asked Lilo Besslein.

Because of her baby, said Lilo Besslein. She couldn't shoulder the responsibility of taking the baby to live such an insecure life.

It wouldn't be all that insecure, said the student. After all, Christian had a job. And if he lost that job he could always find another. He was young and strong and able to turn his hand to just about anything. And anyway, he'd be taking his exams again next year.

He might well fail them again too, Lilo Besslein pointed out, rather annoyed to have the student so boldly poking her nose into things that were none of her business.

She couldn't understand what she was so scared of, said Ute. Her own baby, she continued, indicating her belly, her own baby would grow up with a much less secure background. She and her boyfriend hadn't found an apartment yet, and the baby was due in three weeks' time, and her boyfriend didn't want to marry her because he was afraid that would turn both of them conventional, but all the same she wasn't worrying.

She always told herself things would work out somehow, she added.

Lilo Besslein did not reply. She could have told Ute how she, Lilo, had been carefully sheltered from her early childhood. She could have told her that she'd gone straight from the security of her father's house to the security her husband had to offer. She could have told her that all her life she'd never had a chance to armour herself against insecurity. But she was afraid the student would not understand. She shook hands and thanked her for looking after her little daughter so often, and then asked if she would ring her when Christian Blome was back. The student promised she would, and Lilo Besslein drove home feeling all was not yet lost.

Over the next four weeks she devoted herself to her little daughter, who was just taking her first steps alone, in a manner that surprised her husband. She kept buying new toys and new clothes for the child, and even made her two dresses. In the evenings, she painstakingly made a wall hanging of the Ten Little Indians for the nursery. Whenever it was fine enough she took the little girl out to play in the sand-box on the grass area in front of the building, and showed her how to shovel sand into a little plastic bucket and some small, coloured plastic moulds. She pointed out dogs and cats and said they were called bow-wows and pussies. She took her to the zoo and showed her monkeys, zebras, elephants, lions and tigers. She visited a nearby open-air swimming pool with the child, and splashed about with her in the children's pool, where the water was yellow with urine. It was only too plain, however, that there was something hectic and excessive about her concentration on the child, as if she wanted to make up for everything she had previously failed to do for her all at once. She was a good deal more equable in her attitude to her husband, too, and he appreciated this equability, unaware that it was the result of her daily overdose of tranquillizers. She cooked him a hot supper every evening these days, and made one of the puddings he liked, and laughed when he confessed to putting on another pound or two. She patted his paunch and said he was beginning to look quite imposing. Once she asked him if he was happy with her and their child. And when, after the briefest of hesitations, he said yes, and then in his turn asked her if she was happy with him and their child, she said yes too, after the briefest of hesitations, although in fact she was very far from happy. Her household chores and looking after her daughter were not really fulfilling, nor was her job at the pharmacy. Indeed, it was only the constant alternation of home and job that made them bearable. She missed her afternoons with Christian Blome far more than she had expected. She tried not to think of him too much, but she failed. She kept picturing him. She kept remembering his embraces and thinking of his whispered endearments while they made love. She rang the commune several times, but they always said Christian Blome wasn't back from E yet. Finally, one afternoon, one of the young men told her he had just moved into the attic apartment in Malching. She got him to give her the address again, to be on the safe side, for she was not quite sure now where the apartment was. Heart thudding, she replaced the receiver. She took four tranquillizers and then went straight to Christian Blome's building with her daughter. She was bursting with impatience as she drove there; she could hardly wait to see him again, and was annoyed when she couldn't find a parking place outside the pale yellow building. She had to leave the car in a nearby side street instead. Her daughter still walked very slowly, so she picked her up and hurried to the building in order to get there sooner. The door was open, and she took the lift up to the fifth floor. She put the child down on the floor before she rang Christian Blome's doorbell, leaving her arms free to go around him.

He opened the door at once, as if he had been standing near it. Plainly he had been told that Lilo Besslein had rung several times, asking where he was, for he did not seem particularly surprised to see her. Without embracing her, or even shaking hands, he stepped back and said she could come in. And when she was inside, he asked if she'd like to see around the apartment. Lilo Besslein nodded, and glanced into the first room. It contained Christian Blome's mattress and suitcase, and that was all. There was a naked light bulb hanging from the ceiling. The second room had nothing in it but his table and his chair and a bookcase in which he had already put his books and journals. The third room was empty. All Christian Blome had done in here was to fix several hooks to the walls and hang items of clothing on them. As for the kitchen, apart from the stove, which belonged to the proprietor of the building, it contained only two crates turned upside down. There were three glasses which had once held mustard and an opened bottle of red wine on the crates, along with a wooden tray, a knife, a fork and a spoon.

It would improve with time, Christian Blome remarked, before picking up the little girl, who had been clinging affectionately to his legs all this time. She patted his face with both hands, and he smiled at her.

He asked Lilo Besslein if she wouldn't like to sit down. She was having some difficulty in concealing her dismay at what she saw as the extreme poverty of

116

the apartment's furnishings. She nodded, went into the first room and sat down on the mattress. Christian Blome did not sit down beside her as he always used to, but remained on his feet, holding the child. He looked at her earnestly for some minutes, in silence, and then he asked her why she had come.

This simple question cast Lilo Besslein into great confusion. She thought it showed he didn't think it perfectly natural for her to visit him any more.

She told him that she had tried to reconcile herself to not seeing him again. She'd been devoting herself more than usual to her husband and daughter, to take her mind off it, she'd tried to forget him, but it was no good. She hadn't been able to help thinking of him all the time he was away.

She couldn't live without him, she added, and she looked pleadingly at him and then reached out her arms. But he did not move from the spot.

If she couldn't live without him, he said, she'd have to forget about being the daughter of a director of the Seitz Works and move in here, into this almost empty apartment. But he did promise her, he said, he'd do all he could to make it comfortable. However, he had to ask her to make her mind up quickly; he couldn't stand all this uncertainty.

Lilo Besslein did not know what to say. She almost used her daughter as a pretext again, saying she couldn't wish such an uncertain future on the child, but she suddenly found she dared not tell him any more lies, although she dared not confess her panic terror of insecurity either. She began to cry, hoping he would comfort her. However, he made no move to sit down beside her and put his arm around her shoulders.

Why couldn't they meet several times a week the way they used to, she asked, sobbing.

Because it was more than he could stand, having her deceive him with her husband and deceive her husband with him, turn and turn about, said Christian Blome.

It wasn't fair to either of them, he said, and it would get to her too in the long run.

Please wouldn't she trust him and move in with him, he added, and he put the child down on the floor, took her in his arms and kissed her. Suddenly she felt sure she would be risking her happiness if she didn't move in with him. Suddenly she felt she could cope with all the problems living with him would entail. She was overcome by a desire to undertake the first real adventure of her life.

All right, I will. I'll come and live with you, she said, with a certain solemnity.

For a moment he was speechless. Then he jumped up, pulling her up too, and danced across the room with her, much to her small daughter's surprise.

Hey, we must drink to this, he said, stopping abruptly. He went into the kitchen to fetch the bottle of red wine and two of the glasses that had once held mustard. They drank to their future, and when they had both sipped their wine Christian Blome gave the little girl a sip too. She pulled a face, making them both laugh. They soon sobered down again, however, and discussed the next steps to be taken. Christian Blome wanted Lilo Besslein to move in the very next morning, but she pointed out that she had to work in the pharmacy all next day, so they decided that she and the child would come the day after that, a Wednesday. Christian Blome said he'd go and buy the baby a cot. Lilo Besslein wondered how to tell her husband she was leaving him.

She could write him a letter, she said, and he'd find it when he got home.

Christian Blome thought this was cowardly, however.

No, he told her, she ought to face her husband openly and stand up for what she was doing. She'd been living with him for over three years, she couldn't just wriggle out of it with a letter.

It was only right for her to explain things in person,

he added, pouring more wine into their glasses.

Lilo Besslein assented, though she was already far from sure she would ever dare to face her husband openly and explain things in person. But her doubts about herself made very little difference to her high spirits. She felt there was something heroic about her decision to move into this almost empty apartment, with an unskilled labourer who might be sacked at any time. Full of euphoria, she got up and went from room to room again. The poverty of the furnishings, which had so dismayed her only a little while ago, didn't seem to matter now. She almost felt there was something symbolic about it. She saw managing without much comfort as a kind of test.

Why, you haven't even got a saucepan, she said, laughing, and promised to bring one with her.

But Christian Blome did not want her to bring any of her household goods. She was just to pack her own clothes and the little girl's, he said.

He didn't even have a wardrobe to put them in, said Lilo Besslein, laughing again.

He'd fix some more hooks to the walls and they could hang clothes on the hooks, Christian Blome promised. He wasn't quite happy about her sudden exuberance. He put his arm round her shoulders and tried to bring her down to earth again. His manner serious, he pointed out that life with him would inevitably be a great change for her. He said that of course he'd do all he could to help her cope, but he'd better remind her that she'd be left to her own devices during the day, when he had to be out at work.

For the time being, however, none of this could touch Lilo Besslein. Unwilling to think about future problems, she played around for a little longer, and then, glancing at her watch in alarm, set off for home so suddenly that Christian Blome almost forgot to give her the latchkey to the apartment. As she was going down to the ground floor in the lift, he quickly ran down the stairs, caught up with her in the street, and solemnly handed her the key. She put it in her handbag and drove home, feeling that the handing over of that key was an irrevocable step.

Her high spirits were only slightly dampened by her domestic surroundings and her husband's company. He had a good many mental reservations as he watched her singing as she worked in the kitchen, kissing and hugging her daughter over and over again. It wasn't just her cheerfulness that irritated him; he begrudged it her because he had no part in it himself. As soon as the child was in bed he began attacking her, right out of the blue, for overspending on the housekeeping. To his surprise, however, and most unusually for her, she refused to embark upon one of those discussions that regularly led to quarrels. She switched the television on instead and stared at the screen all evening, silent and lost in thought.

Her approaching separation from her husband pre-occupied her so much that she could not get to sleep, in spite of taking a large dose of tranquillizers. She lay awake until four in the morning, tossing and turning in bed as she tried to find a position in which she could sleep. At last she fell into an uneasy slumber. She was so tired and exhausted in the morning that she wondered whether to go to the pharmacy. Only the thought that her work would take her mind off the problem of how to let her husband know she was leaving him induced her to go after all, and then she was so busy all day that she hardly had time to smoke the occasional cigarette. As a result, she found herself quite unprepared to face her husband that evening. He had brought her a medium-sized bunch of roses again, which made things even more difficult. At supper, she decided to tell him her plans after supper. After supper, she decided to do it after the television news. After the television news, she decided to do it after they had gone to bed. But instead of telling him the

120

truth after they had gone to bed, she let him roll over towards her and make love to her. She felt no pleasure, her conscience smote her, and in addition she felt she was doing something shameful. Afterwards she lay awake until dawn again, tossing and turning. Before she fell asleep she decided to tell her husband in a letter after all.

She wrote the letter next morning, as soon as he had left. It was a short one, in spite of the serious nature of its contents. She told him she was in love with someone else and was moving in with him today, and she thanked him for all he had done for her. She put the letter in an envelope and wrote her new address on the back. Then she cleared away the breakfast things, washed the dishes, made the bed and hoovered the living room, the bedroom and the nursery. She wanted to leave the apartment neat and tidy. When she had watered the little orange tree and the little azalea, she brought four suitcases up from the basement. First she took her daughter's clothes out of the antique bureau and packed them in one case, then she set to work to pack her own clothes in the other three cases. As she was doing this, the telephone rang. It was her mother, wanting to know how she and her husband and the baby were. Lilo Besslein said they were all fine. Her mother moved on to discussion of her own high blood pressure, arthritis and domestic problems. Lilo Besslein listened patiently, wondering now and then how her mother would take what she was doing. She felt afraid of her reaction already. She knew her mother would come to M and stage a big dramatic scene in Christian Blome's apartment. When they had said goodbye she went on packing. She tried not to think of her mother as she packed, but it was no use. She kept wondering just what she would say when she heard her daughter had left her husband to go and live in an almost empty apartment with an unskilled labourer. She was sure her mother would view it as the end of the world and do all she could to get her to go back to her husband.

I oughtn't to be so scared of her, she told herself as she closed the three suitcases and carried them out into the corridor. Then she took four tranquillizer capsules and looked at the time. Half past ten. There was no real reason why she shouldn't leave the apartment now; the one thing that stopped her was the fact that Christian Blome did not get back from work until about four in the afternoon. She dreaded the thought of spending hours alone with her daughter in his apartment. She picked the child up out of her cot and took her into the living room. Then she poured herself a Martini and tried to picture her life with Christian Blome in that almost empty apartment. Suddenly it didn't seem such an adventure any more. He doesn't even have a wardrobe, she told herself, and all at once it was no laughing matter. In fact, his idea of herself and her child's moving in with him seemed downright irresponsible. She poured another Martini, drank it straight down, and refilled her glass. By noon she had finished the bottle. Unable to walk straight, she staggered into the kitchen and made her daughter some vegetable broth and potatoes. She fed the child and put her down in her cot. Then she took four more tranquillizer capsules and lay down the sofa. She fell asleep at once, and did not wake till nearly three in the afternoon, when her daughter's crying roused her. She immediately got up and set off for the nursery. When she saw the suitcases standing in the corridor her decision to leave her husband suddenly seemed quite crazy.

At least he looks after me and the child, she told herself, as she picked her daughter up out of her cot. Just for a moment she remembered that Christian Blome had probably bought the baby a cot too. She thought of his giving her the latchkey. She thought of him expecting to find her and the child there in his apartment when he got back. She told herself she must start now if she was going to be there on time. She glanced at the four suitcases in the corridor, undecided. Suddenly she was overcome by fear: fear that her husband might come home early and see the four packed suitcases. She pushed all thoughts of Christian Blome aside. Hands trembling, she dragged one of the four cases into the nursery and the other three into the bedroom and hastily began unpacking them. At four o'clock, all the clothes were back in their old places, and Lilo Besslein took the four empty suitcases down to the basement again. When she re-entered the apartment, the telephone was ringing. She took an involuntary step towards it, but she did not raise the receiver. Instead, she tore the letter she had written her husband into tiny shreds and flushed them down the lavatory. Then she took four more tranquillizers. She sat down on the sofa and gave way to increasing apathy as she stared at the grass area outside the window. The one thing that did temporarily rouse her from her artificially induced calm was the ringing of the telephone. Whenever it began to ring, which it did every ten minutes, she felt a violent pang of the heart. She briefly pictured Christian Blome, agitated and desperate, pacing up and down the almost empty apartment, stopping beside the cot he had just bought, hurrying to the nearest public phone and putting a couple of coins in the slot as he raised the receiver. She was desperately ashamed of her behaviour. Directly afterwards, however, her tranquillizer-induced calm would return, and she went on staring at the grass area outside the window, where the children from the housing block were noisily playing football. She took no notice of her small daughter, who was opening the bottom drawers of the wall unit and taking out table-cloths, napkins and cutlery. She even forgot to lay the table for supper. Not until her husband came home from work and stopped in surprise at the sight of her daughter, who was playing with the knives as well and the spoons and forks, did she summon up enough will-power to pull herself together. She apologized almost humbly for not having the supper table laid, and said she wasn't feeling well, before she went into the kitchen and made some supper out of leftovers.

✳

During her lunch hour next day, Lilo Besslein sent Christian Blome's latchkey back without any kind of note. Then she sat down at his usual table in the Pizzeria Boccaccio. She ordered herself first one glass of red wine, and quite soon afterwards another, and brooded gloomily. Her life seemed empty and pointless. She blamed her extremely conventional upbringing for the fact that she hadn't dared go and live with Christian Blome, but she couldn't manage to shake off the effects of it. She couldn't manage to free herself of it. She wondered whether to commit suicide. The idea did not in itself alarm her. She wondered coolly how to do it. She decided on an overdose of sleeping tablets. Hastily, she finished her wine, paid the bill, and went back to the pharmacy early. Once she got there she made sure Frau Högemann and Sabine Ickstett were not back yet, and then she took a packet of strong barbiturates out of a cupboard and put it in her handbag. She put a receipt for the barbiturates in the till before taking four of her tranquillizers. When Frau Högemann and Sabine Ickstett got back to the shop she was strangely calm. This calm mood lasted until evening. When evening came, she fetched her daughter from Frau Finsinger's and drove her home. Her husband had laid the supper table, as he usually did on her days at work. The three of them sat down to eat. Ernst Besslein talked about nothing in particu-lar, and Lilo Besslein marvelled at his lack of suspicion. Contemptuously, she observed the customary care with which he prepared his slices of bread. She wondered how he would react when he found her dead in bed beside him. She told herself that he wouldn't understand any of what had gone on in her mind; he never did. She glanced at her daughter, who looked very like him. She wondered if she loved the child, but she could not answer that question. After supper she played with the child for a little while. By now her daughter could say Mummy and Daddy. Then she and her husband put the little girl to bed. While he sang her to sleep, as he did every evening, she went into the bathroom and took four more tranquillizer capsules. Then she washed the dishes in the kitchen. After that she sat down on the sofa beside her husband and stared at the television set, which he had now switched on, lost in thought. When the news was over he switched the set off and started talking about their forthcoming holiday. He got out a brochure from a comparatively inexpensive hotel in a holiday resort in Carinthia, and they sat looking at photographs of the outside and inside of this hotel. It had a restaurant, a bar, a swimming pool and a sauna. There were also two tennis courts and several riding horses for the guests to use.

You'll be able to go riding again, said Ernst Besslein, and then stopped short. For his wife suddenly rushed out of the room in tears. Astonished, he followed her into the bathroom, to find her just stuffing a handful of sleeping tablets into her mouth. He snatched the packet away from her and yelled at her to spit the tablets out. But she swallowed them instead. For a moment he didn't know what to do, and stood there speechless, his hand cupped under her mouth. Then he thought of driving her to a hospital. He dragged her out of the bathroom and propelled her towards the front door. Much to his relief, she let him lead her down the path to the car. On the way to the hospital he asked her, several times, why she had taken the tablets, but she did not answer. She sat there beside him, withdrawn, staring down at her hands in her lap, and when they got to the hospital she left it to him to tell the doctor on duty what had happened. The doctor said she must have her stomach pumped out. He showed Ernst Besslein where the waiting room was, and disappeared with his wife into a room at the far end of the corridor.

Ernst Besslein sat down in the waiting room. He tried to read one of the magazines lying about, but he could not concentrate on the words. He kept seeing his wife standing there in the bathroom, stuffing tablets into her mouth. He wondered what on earth had made her so desperate, but he had no idea. The last few days had gone perfectly all right. They had not quarrelled. He did remember how absent his wife had seemed the day before, and wondered if she had some kind of secret, and if so what it might be, but he came to no conclusions. He just sat there helplessly, telling himself he had always behaved correctly, it was his wife who'd always been the awkward one. He thought it very irresponsible of her to take those tablets.

She's got the child to think of, after all, he told himself, suddenly indignant. He picked up one of the magazines again and leafed through it. The various articles in it did not interest him much, but he made himself read them to occupy his mind. Once, he left the waiting room and asked the nursing sister on duty if his wife was still in any danger. She told him not to worry. He went back to the waiting room and read another magazine. At eleven, a nurse finally came into the waiting room and told him he could see his wife now. She took him to the room at the far end of the corridor into which his wife had vanished a couple of hours previously with the doctor on duty. She was lying in bed, white as a sheet, and told him they were keeping her in hospital until twelve the next day. She asked him to drive home and fetch her tranquillizers and a pair of pyjamas. Ernst Besslein drove straight to

126

Lerchenau. When he got back to the hospital his wife had been moved to a ward which he was not allowed to enter at this time of night, so he gave the duty nurse his wife's bag, with the things she had asked for, and then went home and straight to bed. Next morning he rang up Frau Finsinger and took the little girl round to her before he drove to work. His wife was discharged from hospital at twelve noon. She still felt rather tired, but she was all right otherwise, and spent the rest of the day lying on the sofa. She could scarcely understand why she had tried to kill herself now, and when her husband came home with their child in the evening she promised him never to do it again. Then she asked him not to talk about her suicide attempt any more, and he changed the subject, reverting to their forthcoming holiday. They were going to leave the little girl with the Ohlbaums, in N, so that they could really relax. They had never left her for any length of time before, and Lilo Besslein was wondering whether her mother would be able to manage. Something else, however, worried her even more: whether she would succeed in weaning herself off tranquillizers during the holiday. She had come to a private decision to take two fewer capsules every day, and she was going to take only the number of capsules required for this plan away with her. Not that the plan stopped her taking her usual overdose up to the start of their holiday, but she put it into action the day they went away. She observed herself closely, and was delighted when she realized she actually could get by with a slightly smaller dose. Her husband, sitting at the wheel of the car, was surprised by her relaxed mood on the drive to the little Carinthian resort. They reached the hotel about four in the afternoon; their room was quite plain, but very neat and pleasant. They unpacked their cases, took out their bathing things and cover-ups, and went down to the swimming pool in the basement of the building. There were several youngish people splashing about playing water polo. Although the swimming pool was quite large, it was difficult to keep out of the way of the ball, which kept shooting off in the Bessleins' direction. They caught it and threw it back. In the end the young people asked if they'd like to join the game; pleased to have made friends so quickly, they said yes, and spent the next hour playing water polo. Then they went up to their room to change for dinner. Lilo Besslein took great pains with her appearance, and when she and her husband entered the dining room most of the men present looked admiringly at her. The young people of the water polo game waved and invited them to share a table. Two tables had already been pushed together; another one was brought up, and the Bessleins sat down. Ernst Besslein, always something of a stickler for formality, introduced himself and his wife, and the other men at the table reciprocated. The party consisted of a married couple called Schmude, a married couple called Nibler and a married couple called Ise. They came from three different towns and had met in the hotel. Herr Ise, a sandy, bespectacled man who was barely of medium height, bought a round of cognac before dinner, and they drank to a pleasant holiday. The second round was bought by Herr Schmude, who was tall and slightly puffy, with an accent which betrayed his Rhineland origins. To our lovely wives, he said, and he raised his glass, looking exclusively at Lilo Besslein, who was flattered and smiled at him. Ernst Besslein bought the third round of cognac, after a whispered request from his wife. The fourth round was bought by Herr Nibler, a slightly built man who was publicly bewailing the fact that they were sure to drink too much again tonight, just as they had for the last five nights. It was a long time since he'd gone off the rails like this, he said, feigning sorrow. He fell into bed full of drink at night, and resorted to the mini-bar in his room first thing in the morning. The party drank a good deal of white wine as well as the cognac, so they were all distinctly merry by the time dinner was over. As the dining room slowly emptied, they stayed sitting at the three adjoining tables. Herr Schmude, who was an economist, told jokes and winked at Lilo Besslein now and then. Abruptly, a feeling of anxiety overcame her. She stood up suddenly and went up to the bedroom to take four tranquillizer capsules. When she got back to the dining room the others had just decided to move on to the bar. The men paid for the drinks they had had. Lilo Besslein saw a slightly worried look come over her husband's face as he settled his bill, and expected him to warn her to go easy before they reached the bar. To her relief, however, he did no such thing; instead he put his arm around her shoulders as they walked from the dining room and asked if she was enjoying herself.

There was a three-piece band playing in the bar. Ernst Besslein immediately asked his wife to dance, and she agreed, not wanting to upset him in this good mood. She tried vainly to get him to keep in time as they danced. Then Herr Schmude asked her to dance too. She did not care for the way he pressed close to her. He asked if she'd like to go riding with him in the morning, and she said she'd have to discuss that with her husband. She then escaped from his clasp, saying she felt too tired to dance any more just now. When she sat down with the others, Herr Schmude, not to be shaken off so easily, sat down beside her. He kept fondling her arm when he wasn't actually holding her hand. She looked to her husband for aid, but he seemed to have no intention of doing anything about Herr Schmude's familiarities. Indeed, he noted the admiration his wife was attracting with obvious satisfaction. Even Frau Schmude, a brunette of about thirty wearing rather a lot of make-up, didn't object to her husband's behaviour. She was plainly used to seeing him make up to other women in front of her. With mingled affection and contempt she called him her roly-poly, and begged him not to drink his whisky and soda too fast. She'd had to put him to bed drunk as a lord last night, and the night before that, and she didn't want to be putting him to bed again tonight, she said, to everyone's amusement.

Herr Schmude, however, took no notice of her request. He said the whole point of this holiday, so far as he was concerned, was being able to get properly drunk for once. He was under severe stress all the year round; he needed a certain amount of alcohol to relieve it. He raised his glass to the others, emptied it, and ordered another whisky. When he had drunk this one he put his arm around Lilo Besslein's shoulders, kissed her cheek, although she shrank away, and asked he what her Christian name was. She said it was Lilo. He told her his was Georg, and offered to drink to friendship between them. Seeing no alternative, Lilo Besslein drank to friendship with him, and reluctantly let him kiss her on the lips. Then he put his arm round her shoulders again. She tried to evade him by moving a little way away, but he simply moved after her. Once more she glanced at her husband for aid. He had obviously been watching the whole scene, but he still did nothing to protect her from Herr Schmude's importunities. She wondered momentarily how Christian Blome would have acted in this sort of situation. She felt sure he wouldn't have let anyone make such crude advances to her.

He loved me, she told herself, and suddenly she felt very bleak. She wanted to be alone. She stood up, with an apologetic gesture, and said good night, taking no notice of the protests of the Ises, the Niblers and the Schmudes. Her husband, much surprised by her abrupt departure, said he'd be up in a minute, but she asked him to give her a little time. She had only just finished taking her make-up off, however, when he came into the bedroom and asked why she had come up so early.

It was very nice down there in the bar, he remarked.

She told him she didn't think Herr Schmude's advances were nice at all.

Why hadn't he, Ernst Besslein, told him where he got off, she inquired.

He looked at her for a moment, speechless, and then said well, he had no idea she'd suddenly turned so prudish.

She didn't call it prudish, not by a long way, not to fancy being pawed and kissed by anyone and everyone, she said, and she went for him with her clenched fists, hammering away at him until he caught her wrists.

If he loved her he wouldn't let people bother her like that, she cried, bursting into tears.

He let go of her wrists, but the way she went for him with her fists had hurt his feelings too much for him to feel like comforting her. He undressed, stony faced, and they went to bed without saying good night to each other.

They were roused by three knocks on their door in the morning. Herr Schmude was standing outside, freshly shaved and wearing riding breeches, calling them a couple of lazybones. To the vexation of his wife, who didn't want to be seen without her make-up, Ernst Besslein asked him into the room rather than leave him out in the corridor, and he also pulled back the curtains, allowing a flood of sunlight to fall into the room. Herr Schmude walked around the beds, kissed Lilo Besslein's hand, and then sat down in one of the two armchairs that stood to either side of the small round table by the window.

He'd only come to suggest all having breakfast together, he said, and when Ernst Besslein agreed, after an inquiring glance at his wife, he went on. He and his wife, the Ises and the Niblers, hadn't got to bed until four in the morning, said Herr Schmude, but he'd roused the lot of them. It would be a sin and a shame to lie in bed on a fine day like this, and on holiday too.

131

Would the Bessleins like to go riding with the rest of them after breakfast, he asked, addressing Ernst Besslein.

Better ask his wife, said Ernst Besslein; he didn't ride himself.

Lilo Besslein, thinking Herr Schmude was very pushy, said she'd rather sunbathe this morning. She swung her legs out of bed, fetched clean clothes and underclothes from the wardrobe, and went into the bathroom.

She expected Herr Schmude to leave the room while she was showering, dressing and making up her face, but he plainly had no such intention. He stayed there chatting to her husband instead, going on about the current economic situation, which he thought far from rosy. Much to her surprise, Ernst Besslein offered him a pre-breakfast schnapps from the mini-bar, and seemed to be drinking one himself. Herr Schmude did not rise to his feet until she emerged from the bathroom, when he linked arms with her and made as if to leave the room. Rather brusquely, she asked him to wait a moment. She picked up her handbag and went back into the bathroom, where she took two tranquillizer capsules. Only two. Then she set off for the breakfast room with him.

Frau Schmude, the Ises and the Niblers were already there. Unlike Herr Schmude, who was playing the part of cheerful extrovert, they not only looked as if they were hung over, but they were also all taking headache tablets generously distributed by Frau Schmude, who was lavishly made up again. Herr Nibler, once again, was bemoaning the fact that they had got so tight last night, just as they did on the nights before.

She'd been quite right to go to bed early, he told Lilo Besslein, and he swore he'd be more sensible this evening.

That was just what he said yesterday and the day before, and the day before that, remarked his wife, gesturing helplessly. She was a blonde, pretty in a rather doll-like way.

However, Herr Nibler seemed to take his good resolutions seriously, at least for the time being.

All this drinking and these late nights were doing him no good at all, he complained, and Herr Ise ordered a round of schnapps from the waitress serving breakfast, saying it was a surefire cure for a hangover.

They were just drinking to each other when Ernst Besslein came into the breakfast room too. Herr Schmude's presence had given Lilo Besslein no chance to make up their quarrel yet. She smiled at him, but he did not smile back, only looked at her rather grimly before he said a cheerful good morning to Frau Schmude, the Ises and the Niblers, and then sat down beside her. She was so upset by his behaviour that she rose to her feet again and went back up to the bedroom to take two more tranquillizers, in defiance of her good intentions.

The second round of schnapps was just being served as she came back into the breakfast room. She sat down beside her husband, who raised his glass to everyone except herself and then emptied it. She was already wishing she hadn't taken those two tranquillizers. It ruined her plan. She told herself she mustn't seize upon every excuse she got to take two or more capsules. She had come to consider the tranquillizers very dangerous, and she made up her mind not to take any at all during the day and wait until she went to bed that night before she had another four. She ate her breakfast without joining in the conversation. After breakfast, she was the first to leave the table. She went to the bedroom, put on her bikini and her cover-up, and went out to the sun terrace; it could be reached either from the back entrance of the hotel or from the swimming pool. She moved one of the many loungers into a good position, spread a towel on it, rubbed sun-tan cream into her face and body, and then lay down on the lounger. She tried not to think of anything at all. But she hadn't been sunbathing ten

133

minutes before her husband appeared beside her, thus inevitably causing her to think of him. She watched him move a lounger close to hers, spread a towel on it and take off his cover-up, revealing his little paunch and the roll of fat around his hips. She watched him unscrew a bottle of sun-tan oil and start oiling his face and body, thoroughly and with much ceremony. She watched him lie down on the lounger.

How much longer before he'd speak to her, she asked him, and when he didn't reply she told him crossly that he really was the end. Then she lay back on her lounger, trying to keep her temper.

She lay there in the sun until mid-day, turning now on her stomach and now on her back, and cooling off in the pool from time to time. At lunch time she stood up and set off for the bedroom. When she had gone a little way she realized her husband was following her, still in silence. She looked contemptuously at him. He stared grimly at her. Then they went on their way in single file. In the bedroom she stripped naked, but he did not deign to look at her; he merely stood beside his bed examining the sunburn he had acquired in the course of the morning with some concern.

As she dressed, she suddenly felt extremely restless. Her hands began trembling slightly. She felt she must, just must take at least one tranquillizer. She picked up her handbag, went into the bathroom and popped a capsule into her mouth. Then she thought of her plan and her good resolutions, and took it out again. As a result, she had difficulty in hiding the trembling of her hands at lunch, which she and her husband ate together with the Ises, the Niblers and the Schmudes. The restlessness got worse, too. She felt like jumping up and running off instead of sitting there waiting for course after course to be served. To her husband's obvious dismay, she drank no fewer than four glasses of red wine to calm herself. The alcohol did take the edge off her restlessness, and it even made her temporarily sleepy. While her husband stayed downstairs with the Ises, the Niblers and the Schmudes, she went back to the bedroom and lay down on the bed. She slept for an hour, but as soon as she woke she felt that restlessness again, mingled with feelings of anxiety. She didn't know how to fight them off. She paced up and down the hotel room for a few minutes. Then she took a cold shower, but the restlessness and anxiety got no better. They were becoming so bad that she was forced to take four tranquillizer capsules at once. Shivering, and miserable because she had lost control of herself again, she sat in one of the armchairs and waited for them to work. She wondered what to do. She could see she wasn't going to be able to stick to her plan any more successfully during the rest of their holiday. She could see the capsules she had brought with her to last the holiday were not going to be enough. She told herself that by next week at the latest she'd have to find a local doctor and get a prescription for tranquillizers. Suddenly she became aware that she was now, quite plainly, an addict. She thought it was practically criminal of Dr Gutt to have prescribed her the drug·so readily over a year ago in the gynaecological hospital. She wondered who could help her now. Feeling that there was no hope anyway, she reached for the packet of tranquillizers again and took two more capsules. She was just leaving the bathroom when her husband came into the bedroom. She could see at a glance that he was drunk. His face was evidently flushed with alcohol as well as his morning's sunbathing, his eyes looked even smaller than usual, and he was curling his upper lip in that way which, he believed, gave him a certain look of superiority. As always when drunk, he was ready to cast aside most of his inhibitions about marital behaviour. The rigidity of his bearing gave him away as he stalked up to her. Voice slurred, he suggested making up their quarrel.

How about a nice kiss, he inquired. Swaying

slightly, he put his arms around her waist, and before kissing her he pressed up against her in a manner that told her he wanted to make love.

She gave him a perfunctory kiss. She hated to think he had to be drunk before he wanted to make things up with her.

He'd better have a little rest, she said, and she escaped from his clasp and pushed him gently away. To her relief, he made no further advances. Instead, docility itself all of a sudden, he trotted over to his bed and lay down without taking his shoes off.

Rather amused, Lilo Besslein went over, knelt down at the foot of the bed and took them off for him. He thanked her effusively, saying she was the best wife in the world, and then closed his eyes and fell asleep at once. She stood by the bed for a moment, looking at him with mixed feelings. At heart, she rather liked it when he was drunk; then he would at least throw his strict principles overboard for hours at a time, and if he was never exactly generous, his behaviour became not quite so petty.

If only he'd get drunk more often, she said to herself, turning away. She wondered what to do now. She didn't want to hang around waiting for her husband to sober up. While he was sleeping it off, she decided, she'd go and look for a doctor without his knowledge. She left the room quietly, and went down to Reception to find out the addresses of the local doctors. The clerk at the reception desk told her there were two in the town, Dr Schlatter and Dr Uhl, both with surgeries in the so-called High Street. When she reached it, she found Dr Schlatter's surgery did not open for another hour. She hesitated for a moment outside the closed door, and then went to Dr Uhl's surgery, only one block along the street. His surgery hours had already begun. There were only two patients in the waiting room, obviously visiting tourists like herself, and Lilo Besslein did not have to wait long before she was called into Dr Uhl's room. He was a stout man of about fifty, and seemed kindly and easy-going. He waved her to a chair, inviting her to sit down, and then asked what he could do for her. She said she was sleeping badly, and asked him to give her a prescription for Tranxilium capsules.

Her own doctor sometimes prescribed her Tranxilium, she said, with a searching look at Dr Uhl. He shook his head several times, as if expressing doubts.

Tranxilium was a dangerous drug, he said at last, before picking up his prescription pad, you could get addicted to it.

I'll give you something else, just try this first, he said, to Lilo Besslein's dismay. As he wrote the prescription she wondered frantically how she could get him to change his mind.

Tranxilium had always helped her before, she said.

But Dr Uhl was not to be moved.

He wouldn't bring up the big guns to shoot sparrows, he said, giving her the prescription and then shaking hands.

Would she please pay his receptionist in the surgery, he added.

Lilo Besslein paid the receptionist and then left the surgery. Outside, she read the prescription. When she saw that Dr Uhl had prescribed her a sedative so mild you could even buy it over the counter, she tore it up and dropped it into the nearest litter bin. Still determined to get a prescription for Tranxilium, she set off for Dr Schlatter's surgery. His surgery hours still had not begun, but the receptionist let her in. There were no other patients in the waiting room yet. She waited for quarter of an hour, and then she was called in to see Dr Schlatter. He was younger than Dr Uhl, and not nearly so stout. After telling her to sit down, he asked her what the trouble was. Once again she said she was sleeping badly, and asked for a prescription for Tranxilium capsules. She felt desperate when Dr Schlatter also refused to prescribe her the drug. He advised her to go for a walk before bed instead, and finally gave her a prescription for valerian drops, which again she tore up once she had paid for the consultation and left the surgery. She went back to the hotel feeling utterly discouraged. Quietly, she opened the door of the hotel bedroom and went into the bathroom, being careful not to wake her sleeping husband, to count the tranquillizer capsules she still had in her handbag. She calculated that they would last her another week, if she didn't decrease her dosage, but not the remaining twelve days of the holiday for which she and her husband had booked the hotel room. Once again she decided to reduce her dose, and she took two fewer capsules next day. However, she took her usual dosage for the following six days. On the seventh day she went back to see Dr Schlatter and Dr Uhl, but they would neither of them prescribe her Tranxilium. She took her last two capsules on the morning of the eighth day. She had breakfast with her husband, the Ises, the Niblers and the Schmudes, and went riding with them for an hour after breakfast. Then she lay down on the sun terrace beside her husband and sunbathed until lunch time. At lunch her hands began to shake, first almost imperceptibly, then more and more violently, and she was gripped by restlessness mingled with feelings of anxiety. She drank four glasses of wine to calm herself down. Then she went up to the hotel bedroom, lay down on her bed and tried to sleep, but it was no use. Her restlessness and anxiety got worse instead of better. She stood up and walked up and down the room. She paused by the waste-paper basket, looking to see if the empty tranquillizer packet was still there. She would have given a lot to be able at least to hold the empty packet and look at it, but she saw that the chambermaid had already emptied the basket. She sat down on the edge of the bed, weeping. She wondered how she was going to get through the day. She told herself a long walk might do her good, but suddenly she dared not leave the hotel bedroom. She sat there on the bed, rigid with fear, waiting for her husband to come into the room.

He did not appear for another hour, and when he did he had obviously been drinking with the Ises, the Niblers and the Schmudes again, for he was in such a cheerful state that he entirely failed to notice her condition at first. He did sober down a little when she confessed, in tears, that she was addicted to her tranquillizers, but even then he didn't take the matter as seriously as it deserved. He thought it was all just one of his wife's exaggerations. Putting an arm around her shoulders, he suggested going for a nice walk together, but she stayed there on the bed, rigid, hands shaking, and she told him she dared not leave the bedroom. He asked what she was afraid of. She told him there was nothing she was *not* afraid of. He thought this was another of her exaggerations. Unable to comprehend her condition, he produced the canasta cards he had brought for rainy days, shuffled and dealt them. The very first game, however, showed that his wife could not concentrate. Weeping, she asked him to go out and try to get a packet of Tranxilium off prescription at one of the local pharmacies. He promised to do his best, and set off for the two pharmacies in the High Street. However, he had no luck. He tried to talk the pharmacists round, but they were not prepared to sell him any Tranxilium without a prescription. Discouraged, he went back to the hotel, where his wife was still sitting on her bed, rigid and with trembling hands. He asked if he should call a doctor. She did not want to see either Dr Schlatter or Dr Uhl now; she already knew they wouldn't help her, she said, before she crept into bed and pulled the bedclothes up to her chin. She stayed there all afternoon. At dinner time Ernst Besslein tried to persuade her to go down to the dining room with him. After much hesitation, she did get up and go into the bathroom to comb her hair, but then she dared not step outside the door. Finally Ernst Besslein went downstairs alone. He ate very fast, and made his wife two open sandwiches. Then he went back to the bedroom and found her still rigid with fear and still sitting on the bed. When he gave her the two open sandwiches, she asked him to take her home. She said she was in urgent need of medical treatment.

Unwilling to cut his holiday short, Ernst Besslein persuaded her to wait until next morning. She'd probably be feeling better by that time, he said. They spent the evening in their bedroom. Lilo Besslein did not sleep at all that night, even for short periods, and in the morning her anxiety feelings were worse than ever. Ernst Besslein realized he would have to cut the holiday short after all. While his wife lay motionless on her bed, staring at the ceiling, he packed their cases, took them down to the car and paid the hotel bill. Then he took his wife's hand and led her from the bedroom to Reception and then from Reception to the car. As they went along he realized that her hands were not just damp with fear, they were actually wet. He'd see she was all right, he told her, before he switched on the engine and set off in the direction of M.

✳

Back in M, Ernst Besslein immediately rang their family doctor, Dr Mörfelden. He said it was extremely urgent, so Dr Mörfelden was there within the hour. He examined Lilo Besslein, who admitted she had been taking sixteen tranquillizers a day, and said he wasn't able to treat addiction himself; she had better go to see Professor Püschel. The Professor was a psychiatrist with consulting rooms at the University Hospital, he added, before he shook hands and left the apartment.

When he had gone, Ernst Besslein looked up

Professor Püschel's number in the telephone book and then rang it. An assistant answered and told him he couldn't speak to Professor Püschel just now. Ernst Besslein again mentioned the urgency of the case, and she gave him an appointment for that afternoon. He was more than relieved, and tried to cheer his wife, who was huddled on the sofa with her knees drawn up, staring at the grass area outside the window. He told her he was sure Professor Püschel would help her, and she'd be quite all right, he added, in a few days' time. Then he asked her why she had been taking so many tranquillizers. She told him the drug had made her life more bearable. He couldn't see why on earth she found her life unbearable, but he did not say so. He began unpacking their suitcases instead. Once he had done that it was time to set off to see Professor Püschel. His wife's hands were wet with fear again as she left the apartment and walked down the path to the car with him. She did not say a word during the drive, just sat beside him, rigid and very upright, staring wide-eyed at the road. She was scared to leave the car when they got to the University Hospital, and would not get out until Ernst Besslein put both his hands out to her. They walked to the entrance of the psychiatric department together, and took the lift up to the first floor and Professor Püschel's consulting rooms. Ernst Besslein gave the Professor's assistant his wife's name and date of birth, and then they both went into the waiting room, where there were eight other patients. Smoking was permitted, and Lilo Besslein chainsmoked. After they had been waiting almost two hours they were finally called in to see Professor Püschel. He was a tall, grey-haired man, with a noticeably soft mouth and large bags under the eyes. He gestured wearily, inviting them to sit down, and asked what he could do for them. Ernst Besslein said his wife had been taking sixteen tranquillizer capsules a day for several months, and had been suffering from sleeplessness and severe anxiety since she stopped taking the drug. Professor Püschel made several notes. Then he glanced up and asked Lilo Besslein just when she had stopped. She told him the day before. Professor Püschel said the anxiety feelings might yet get a good deal worse, and she must come into hospital at once. Lilo Besslein made no objection. She asked her husband if she could have a room to herself, and he agreed. He asked Professor Püschel how long his wife would have to stay in hospital, but the Professor could not tell for certain when she would be cured. It might be one month or it might be three, he said, and then he rose, went into the outer room and asked his assistant to find out if there was a single room free. He waited while she telephoned. It seemed the only empty bed available was in a double room, but he promised Lilo Besslein to reserve her the next single room that came empty. Then he said goodbye and told his assistant to take her up to the open ward of the psychiatric department.

The open ward was on the second floor of the building. Lilo Besslein saw a few patients sitting in a corner seating area at one end of a long corridor. They were obviously on the road to recovery, for they were engaged in a loud conversation, punctuated occasionally by equally loud laughter. Other patients, silent and withdrawn, walked up and down the corridor. Professor Püschel's assistant took the Bessleins half-way down the corridor, and then asked them to wait a moment while she went into the nurses' room. As they stood there, Ernst Besslein took his wife's hand, which was wet again, promised to come and see her every day, and asked what clothes she wanted brought. She asked him to bring some pyjamas and underclothes, and a couple of sweaters and pairs of trousers, and she was just telling him which trousers and which sweaters when the assistant came out of the nurses' room with a sandy-haired woman of about fifty who was obviously

142

the ward sister. The ward sister went up to Lilo Besslein and shook hands. She was Sister Maria, she said, and then led her to a room opposite the seating area at the end of the corridor. There was another patient in it, a young woman of about twenty-five who was sitting up in bed and staring at the doorway, eyes wide with fear.

Oh, did we scare you, inquired Sister Maria.

I'd rather people knocked, she said. Nicer if they did.

Sister Maria did not seem inclined to go along with that.

Company for you, she said, turning down the cover of the other bed and gesturing in Lilo Besslein's direction.

Have a nice rest, now, and I'll bring you your medicine in a little while, she said, on her way out of the room already.

Lilo Besslein introduced herself to the other patient before she sat down on the bed.

Her own name was Vera Urfer, said the young woman, and they shook hands. Lilo Besslein suddenly felt glad not to be alone in a single room. She asked her husband to go and fetch her things, and when he had left she asked Vera Urfer how long she had been in the hospital.

Four weeks, said Vera Urfer. Dropping her voice to a whisper, she pointed at the intercom over the door, and said the nurses could use it to eavesdrop on their patients.

She was no better at all, she went on, but she told the nurses and doctors she was, so as to get discharged. All the doctors did was try out the latest drugs on the patients. They doped you with sedatives. The sedatives calmed your reflex actions down all right, but they didn't do a thing to help the fear all the patients felt.

No, they can't do a thing about the fear, she repeated in a whisper, and abruptly fell silent, for just then Sister Maria came back into the room. She gave Lilo Besslein three different sorts of tablets and waited for her to take them.

They might make her feel a bit dizzy, she said, before she left the room again.

Watching her go, Lilo Besslein noticed that there was neither key nor keyhole in the door. She glanced at the window, and saw that it had no handle. These observations increased her anxiety. She felt as if she had been delivered up to the mercy of the nurses and doctors.

You can't lock the doors and you can't open the windows, she said to Vera Urfer, who was crouching on her bed, knees drawn up, staring at a picture of a beach with palm trees and fishing boats.

And they locked the whole ward at night, said Vera Urfer; that was what upset her most. Not so long ago a patient did break out, all the same. They got the police searching for her, and then they put her in the closed psychiatric ward. It was easier to get put in the closed psychiatric ward than you might think. Some of the doctors here were inclined to think of psychiatric patients as mad, and once you were a psychiatric patient you faced the problem of proving you might be sick but you were completely normal otherwise.

How did she go about proving she was normal, asked Lilo Besslein.

Well, she got dressed in the mornings instead of just lying in bed, said Vera Urfer. And she made herself walk up and down the corridor. And when it came to meals, she threw everything she didn't want to eat down the lavatory so that the nurses would notice her empty plate and think she had a healthy appetite. And the other day, she said, she'd claimed to have slept for eight hours, because it upset the doctors if you couldn't get a wink of sleep all night in spite of the strong sedatives they gave you, and they made you pay for it.

That was the way to behave, and she'd advise Lilo

Besslein to do the same, said Vera Urfer, looking searchingly at her. Lilo Besslein was not sure what to think of these remarks. It all seemed a little excessive, and she wasn't going to worry how to act with the doctors and nurses at the moment. By now she was, in fact, feeling a little dizzy. She bent down, took her shoes off, lay down on the bed and closed her eyes, but then opened them again at once. As soon as she closed them she saw coloured patterns, nasty, tawdry patterns. She had seen them the night before as well. She glanced at the equally tawdry picture on the wall, the one of a beach with palm trees and fishing boats. Then she looked around the room. It was a perfectly ordinary hospital room, but she felt as if there was something strange, indeed hostile, about the various pieces of furniture and other objects it contained. She knew this was a totally subjective impression which wouldn't stand up to an outsider's scrutiny for a moment, yet she could not shake it off. She looked at her white iron bedstead and Vera Urfer's white iron bedstead. Vera Urfer was still crouching on it with her knees drawn up, staring straight ahead of her. She looked at the two white bedside tables, and the white wardrobe, and the square table by the window, which was covered with a green cloth and had a fading bunch of mauve tulips standing on it. She looked at the two green armchairs to the right and left of the table. She looked at the white radiator under the window, standing out sharply against the ochre paint of the walls, like everything else in the room. She looked at the white ceiling and the spherical lamp hanging from its centre. She felt she was at the mercy of these alien surroundings. The fear she felt still lurking just below the surface, in spite of the three tablets, swept over her again, fear such as she had never known before, much worse than ordinary fear, something for which the word *fear* was no longer really adequate. She lay there as if paralyzed. She could hear the patients in the seating area talking about one Professor Reizenstein, their conversation scarcely muted by the closed door of the room. Loud laughter interrupted their discussion several times, and she felt the laughter was hostile too. She had the impression that time was passing much more slowly than usual, that the minutes were stretching out into little eternities instead of flowing by. She wanted to raise her arm and look at her watch to see what the time was, but she was unable to do so.

She did not return to life a little until her husband appeared in the room, carrying a suitcase, and then she had difficulty in adjusting to the fact that he was there. She was isolated by her fear. Slowly, she sat up and looked at him. He too seemed like a stranger, standing there holding her suitcase in his ochre synthetic fibre suit, which matched the ochre of the walls. She asked him to put her clothes away in the wardrobe. As he was doing so a nurse came into the room with two trays. She told Lilo Besslein her name was Sister Monika, and put one of the two trays down on her bedside table. It held bread, butter and cold meat, and a pot of tea without milk. Lilo Besslein just poured herself a cup of tea and asked her husband to eat the food. He said this was a time she must be sure to eat plenty, but he picked up the tray, put it on the table, buttered himself several slices of bread, topped them with cold meat and ate with appetite. When he had eaten everything, Vera Urfer offered him the remains of her supper too, and far from refusing the offer he took her tray and made himself two more open sandwiches. Finally he asked his wife what to do about the child.

The best thing to do would be to leave her with her mother, she said, and then she lit a cigarette. She was feeling a little better; her fear had receded slightly, though it was lurking below the surface. She asked her husband if he would walk up and down the corridor with her. He assented, and they went out of the room

146

together and walked in the corridor. There were not many other patients there at the moment. A young woman with tousled hair and a strikingly pale face, wearing an expensive dark brown velour dressing gown, spoke to her and asked if she'd like to see her wedding photographs in the morning. A bearded young man with large, sweat-stained patches under his armpits showed them a teddy bear and said, proudly, that he had made it himself. A young girl offered them chocolates. Lilo Besslein was touched by the patients' friendliness. She wondered whether they suffered from the same sort of fear that had overwhelmed her just now. She wondered if they felt as much fear of the fear itself as she did. She tried to explain it to her husband: how the fear she had felt was so bad that that in itself made you fear it, but he couldn't really see what she was getting at, and she stopped trying to explain. She realized that he was becoming rather restless, and suspected he wanted to go home so as not to miss the evening news on television.

He could leave now, she'd be all right, she said, to his obvious relief. As if he had been waiting for some such remark, he fleetingly kissed her cheek, promised to come back next day, and then marched towards the lift.

The television's more important to him than I am, Lilo Besslein said to herself as she went back into her room. She found Vera Urfer still sitting on the bed with her knees drawn up, although she had put her pyjamas on in the meantime.

Did she want to go to bed now, asked Lilo Besslein.

Well, said Vera Urfer, since she'd stopped sleeping properly she really spent all day getting ready to go to bed. Before she came into the psychiatric hospital she didn't get a wink of sleep for a whole week, and ever since, her attitude to going to bed and getting to sleep had been quite different. Going to bed had become a major preoccupation. Even in the morning she would

147

wonder apprehensively if she'd get to sleep that night, and when she did manage to get four hours' sleep with the aid of a strong sedative, she would congratulate herself as if it were a tremendous achievement. Then she would note the physical position which had enabled her to sleep, and what she had been thinking of just before she fell asleep, and she tried to think of the same things next evening. If she couldn't get to sleep all the same, she would not allow herself to look at the time, because knowing that she had been lying awake for hours upset her so much it meant she had no chance of sleep at all. She was already terrified she wouldn't get any sleep tonight.

Wasn't she, Lilo Besslein, terrified of not getting any sleep too, she asked Lilo Besslein, who had taken a pair of pyjamas out of the wardrobe.

She tried not to think of it, said Lilo Besslein, and went into the bathroom. She had just put her pyjamas on when Sister Maria came into the room and gave her six tablets. She told her they were tranquillizers, something to make her drowsy and sleeping tablets. She was to take the tranquillizers and the pills to make her drowsy now, and the sleeping tablets in an hour's time. Lilo Besslein did as she was told, although she thought it was ridiculous for her to be taking tranquillizers again. She asked Vera Urfer if she thought the pills they had to take in this place were addictive.

Of course they're addictive, said Vera Urfer, and she laughed so mirthlessly that Lilo Besslein went over and stroked her hair to soothe her.

It's a vicious circle, but we'll get out of it somehow, she said, and she tried to fight against the hopelessness that abruptly swept over her. She suspected that they were already planning to cure her reliance on one drug with reliance on another, for she noticed that the tranquillizers she had been given had effects similar to those of Tranxilium, except that she really needed a higher dosage to make her feel all right. She found herself wondering how she could get Professor Püschel to prescribe that higher dosage. She decided to pretend her psychological condition was worse than it really was. Yawning, she picked up the two sleeping tablets and swallowed them. Then she slipped into bed. She lay awake for another quarter of an hour before she fell into a deep and dreamless sleep.

*

Lilo Besslein, much to her satisfaction, had done what she set out to do. Professor Püschel had taken her complaints seriously and increased her tranquillizer dosage, and ever since her psychological condition had been fine. Even if you couldn't open the windows or lock the doors, even if she too suspected the nurses eavesdropped on patients' rooms over the intercom, she liked it here in the psychiatric hospital. Most of all, she enjoyed not having to be responsible for anything. She took each day as it came, without worrying about the future. She couldn't understand Vera Urfer, who was trying so hard to get discharged. Unlike her, Lilo Besslein was so scared of life outside that she dared not think of the day she would be discharged from hospital.

She soon got used to the daily routine. She got used to a nurse coming to take her temperature and blood pressure at six in the morning. She got used to three nurses coming to make her bed at seven. She got used to having her breakfast and her tranquillizers at eight. She got used to seeing the two Turkish cleaning women who came to do the room at nine. She got used to Professor Püschel's visit at ten, to having lunch and more tranquillizers at twelve, to being brought coffee and cake at two-thirty, to having a visit from her husband at five, supper at six, and another dose of tranquillizers along with pills to make her drowsy and sleeping tablets at seven. She spent part of what time she had to herself doing a little painting. At her

149

request, her husband had brought her a sketching block and a box of watercolours. Now and then she read a few pages of the novel Irene Dülfer had sent her: Flaubert's *Madame Bovary*. Sometimes she walked in the grounds of the University Hospital with her husband. But she spent most of her time with the other patients in the seating area which, as mentioned already, lay directly opposite her room. She and they philosophized about the meaning of life. She heard the latest gossip about the various doctors and nurses and passed it on. They discussed depression and anxiety states. For the first time in her adult life she felt people understood her, and for the first time in her adult life she did not feel alone. She felt, instead, as if the patients here formed a community, and she belonged. This helped her bear her husband's incomprehension much better. Recently he had taken to asking both herself and Professor Püschel, with increasing frequency, when she was going to be discharged. She had been in the psychiatric hospital for over six weeks now, and he didn't see why she had to stay there any longer. She looked rather pale, from lack of fresh air, but apart from that he thought she seemed to be on far more of an even keel than before. He went to visit their little girl in N at weekends, and told her about the child at great length, thinking this would spur her on to take steps to hasten her discharge, and never noticing that he was achieving the opposite of his intentions. For Lilo Besslein was not pining to see her child, far from it; she did not miss her at all. Indeed, she was already dreading the days she would have to spend with the little girl when she got home. She dreaded the thought of going back to work in the pharmacy too. Most of all, she dreaded the thought of great stretches of time spent with her husband. She toyed with the idea of getting divorced from him, several times, and rejected it. There were times when she thought she would have the courage to begin all over again, and times when she doubted it. Once she actually told her husband she was wondering whether they ought to get divorced, and he left the hospital feeling mortally injured. However, he visited her again next day as if nothing had happened. He was pressing her hard to come home now. Looking after the child would be too much for her mother in the long term, he said, and he was talking of having a serious word with Professor Püschel about her discharge.

One afternoon he came into her room beaming, and told her she was to be discharged in a week's time. She was so horrified that she burst into tears. When Professor Püschel next came on his rounds she asked if she couldn't stay in hospital a little longer. Her question did not surprise him. He was evidently used to patients who wanted to withdraw prematurely from life, so to speak. He told her she must get used to the outside world again, but that was exactly what Lilo Besslein thought she couldn't do. In spite of the tranquillizers, her restlessness and anxiety increased during her last week in hospital. On the day of her discharge, she was troubled with violent nausea and a nervous cough first thing in the morning. The nausea and the cough meant she couldn't keep any food down; she threw up first her breakfast and then her lunch into the lavatory pan. Her husband came to fetch her in the car at about two o'clock, just before it was time for coffee and cake in the hospital. She said elaborate goodbyes to Vera Urfer and the other patients, and promised to come back and see them soon. On the way home her husband told her, in mysterious tones, that he had a surprise waiting for her. She wondered what sort of surprise it was, and suspected he meant her parents had brought her small daughter back to M. She was right. When she stepped inside the apartment her parents and the little girl came to meet her. She felt obliged to seem overjoyed. She hugged the child, who had grown taller and fatter and looked more like her father than ever, and then kissed her parents, who both told her she was looking awful. Her mother had laid the table for coffee in the living room. As soon as they sat down, she started talking about her daughter's job. It did neither herself nor her child any good, she said.

It was just too much for her, looking after the apartment and the child and working in the pharmacy too. That was why she'd ended up in a psychiatric hospital, and if she didn't want it to happen again she'd have to give notice.

Wouldn't she consider that, she inquired, looking hopefully at her daughter. Lilo Besslein, wishing to avoid an argument with her mother, promised to think it over, but this by no means satisfied Margot Ohlbaum. Having raised the subject of pharmaceuticals, she went on to the matter of all the drugs Lilo Besslein was still taking. She told her all those tablets would ruin her kidneys as well as her digestion, and advised her to break herself of the habit as quickly as possible. Lilo Besslein pretended she was going to take this advice. She had never dared contradict her hot-tempered mother, and she didn't dare now; she was afraid of Margot Ohlbaum's temper. There had always been something meek, even at times submissive, about her attitude to her mother. If she did ever stand up for herself she did it, as it were, from under cover. Just now she felt far too low to risk asking her mother to mind her own business. But though she was not particularly pleased to see her parents, she tried to delay their departure, for she was afraid of being left alone with her husband and her daughter. She would have given a good deal for things not to go on in the old way. And when her parents did finally go, she asked her husband not to watch the television news that evening, just for once. This request so surprised him that she felt she had to explain more fully. She told him she couldn't bear their daily routine, it made her suffer, she couldn't stand seeing him sit in front of that television set at the same time evening after evening, as if he had been condemned to do it. She told him she couldn't stand watching him top his bread with slices of ham, egg and pickled cucumber in the same way morning after morning. She told him she felt insulted by the way he approached her with pursed lips on coming home from work, asking for a nice kiss. She told him she felt injured by the way he brought her a bunch of roses whenever he wanted to sleep with her. She told him she could list thousands more little things that robbed her of all her zest for life. And then she stopped short. For she could see he was mortally offended, yet again. Sighing, she turned to her daughter, who had made great progress in learning to talk. The child put her hands on her mother's knees and kept saying bow-wow. Where did you see a bow-wow, then, she asked the child. Bye-bye bow-wow, said the child. And what does the bow-wow say, she asked the child. Woof, woof, said the child. Did you see a pussy-cat too, she asked the child. Bye-bye pussy-cat, said the child. And what does the pussy-cat say, she asked the child. Miaow, miaow, said the child. Did you see a moo-cow too, she asked the child. Bye-bye moo-cow, said the child. And what does the moo-cow say, she asked the child. Moo, moo, said the child. Did you see a cock-a-doodle-doo as well, she asked the child. Bye-bye, said the child. What does the cock-a-doodle-doo say, she asked the child. Moo, moo, said the child. Lilo Besslein picked her up, put her on her lap and stroked her hair. And where's Mummy, she asked. Bye-bye, said the child. No, you little silly, here's Mummy, she said, pointing to herself, but the child did not seem to understand. And where's Daddy, she asked. Da-da, said the child, pointing to her father. Feeling irritated, Lilo Besslein put the child down on the floor and cleared the table. Her daughter obviously didn't recognize her, which rankled. When she came back into the living room her husband had the little girl on his lap and was playing *This is the way the ladies ride*. The child squealed with glee as he let her slip down between his legs. Lilo Besslein sat down at the table with them, but she felt left out. She fancied her husband would manage very well with the child even if she weren't there herself. With a distinct impression of being superfluous, she went into the bedroom to unpack her suitcase. The watercolours she had painted in hospital lay on top. She looked at them, and decided all of a sudden that they were completely worthless from an artistic viewpoint. She wondered momentarily whether to keep them, all the same, but in the end she tore them up and threw them into the kitchen rubbish bucket. Then she looked at her watch. Time to take two of the tranquillizer capsules Professor Püschel had prescribed her. To her relief, he had not advised reducing the dosage. Indeed, he had told her she would need it for the time being. She had felt guilty about taking Tranxilium, but her conscience was clear over the new drug, which was called Nobrium. She would be going back to work in the pharmacy next day, which meant she had access to all kinds of tablets, but she was determined to stick scrupulously to her own prescription. This did not seem at all difficult for the first week after she came home from hospital. She was warmly welcomed back to the pharmacy. Frau Högemann was very sympathetic, and so was Sabine Ickstett, who had a steady boyfriend now. The wet, cold, autumn weather brought a great many customers stricken with flu into the pharmacy, and she very soon caught their germs, as did Frau Högemann and Sabine Ickstett, but she did not go to bed even on her days off work. She flung herself into her household chores with an almost neurotic concern for cleanliness. When the apartment came up to her standards, she would set off for the shopping street in the south of Lerchenau in the afternoons just as she

154

used to, with the child in her pushchair. She looked in the windows of the three boutiques and the jeans shop, and bought clothes indiscriminately: jeans, shirts, sweaters, blouses and skirts. Then she would go into one of the two self-service stores to buy what food she needed for supper and next day. After that she set off for home, and once home she would do some washing and ironing, or a little sewing, or else she just sat on the sofa drinking Martini after Martini, waiting until it was time to take two more tranquillizers and lay the table for supper.

Her Tuesdays, Thursdays and Saturdays in the pharmacy were equally monotonous. She would stand behind the counter from half past eight in the morning until noon, and again from two in the afternoon until half past six, selling medicaments; sometimes she made up ointments, suppositories or boric lotion in the laboratory. The day was broken only at lunch time. She still went to the Pizzeria Boccaccio in her lunch break, where she drank two or sometimes three glasses of red wine and thought of Christian Blome. She wondered how he was. She wondered if he was still angry with her. She wondered if he ever thought about her, and she wondered if he still loved her. She regretted not going to live with him, and had for a long time. She had a growing feeling that she would dare to do it now. She couldn't make out why she had shrunk from it at the last moment and unpacked those suitcases again. She tried to imagine the look on his face if she suddenly turned up at his apartment door, unannounced, with her child and a suitcase. The notion increasingly obsessed her. She could see him dancing round the almost empty apartment with her. She could see him kissing the little girl, showing her her new cot. She could see him fixing extra hooks to the walls so that she could hang her clothes up. And slowly, she came to a decision to leave her husband after all. Initially, the idea sent her to her tranquillizers for an increased dosage, but she put it into practice all the same.

One afternoon she brought the four suitcases up from the basement again, and packed her daughter's clothes and her own things. Then she wrote her husband another letter, telling him she was in love with another man and was going to take her daughter and live with him. She put the letter on the dining table and carried the cases out to her car. Last of all she fetched the little girl. Only when she was in the car, driving towards Malching, did she start to think Christian Blome might not be in. She told herself she ought to have rung him first, but she didn't have his number, she didn't even know if he had a telephone. And a telephone call would have ruined the surprise too, she thought. Once again she pictured him hugging her and beaming with joy. She drove faster, and reached the building where he lived fifteen minutes later. Luckily there was a parking place free outside. She parked the car, put the child on the pavement and took one of the suitcases out of the boot. She went to the door of the building, suitcase in one hand, child in the other. The door was not locked, but all the same she rang Christian Blome's bell before she took the lift up to the fifth floor. When she got out of the lift, Christian Blome was standing in his doorway. But instead of uttering exclamations of delight he stared at her in such dismay that at first she was at a loss for words.

We're a bit late, but here we are, she said at last, and she stepped towards him so that he could put his arms round her, but he did no such thing.

Well, come in, he said quietly, with an expression of extreme embarrassment on his face.

Bewildered by his embarrassment, Lilo Besslein went into the apartment with her daughter. There was a strong smell of frying about. She was just putting the suitcase down in the hall when a young girl appeared in the kitchen doorway. The girl went over to Lilo Besslein, glancing at the suitcase in surprise. Lilo Besslein's heart suddenly sank with foreboding.

This is Stephanie, said Christian Blome quietly, still with that extremely embarrassed expression.

We've been living together for the last couple of weeks, he added, and then introduced Lilo Besslein to his girlfriend Stephanie. Finding another woman installed in the apartment shook Lilo Besslein so much that she was left at a loss for words again. Intent only upon getting out of the apartment as fast as she possibly could, she picked up the suitcase and took the child's hand, but Christian Blome, guessing at the depth of her disappointment, barred her way.

Wouldn't she at least drink a glass of wine with them, he asked. She just shook her head and asked him to let her by, and he stepped hesitantly aside.

She must ring him up some time, he said, and he laid his hand on her upper arm. She merely nodded and went to the door, feeling weak at the knees. He was ready enough to open it for her. As she walked to the lift with the child and the suitcase he called something after her: living with him wouldn't really have been a good idea for her, he said. She did not answer. Speechless, she got into the lift and went down to the ground floor. Her disappointment was so great that it actually numbed her, and she was unable to think at all straight on the drive back to Lerchenau. Once she reached Lerchenau, and not before, it occurred to her that she must get the four suitcases unpacked before her husband came home, and destroy the letter she had written him. She parked her car in the Gluckgasse, took one of the cases out of the boot, and hurried up the path to the door of the building with the suitcase and the child. Rapidly, she unlocked the door and went up the six steps to the door of the apartment. When she had opened the door of the apartment she was horrified to see her husband's shoes in the corridor. Her husband himself was sitting at the dining table in the living room, white as a sheet, and her letter, opened, lay on the table before him. Stunned, he stared first at her and then at the suitcase she was still holding.

What's all this about, he asked, his voice rising sharply.

We've come back to you, she said, putting the case down on the floor.

Oh, did this fine lover of yours give you the brush-off, he inquired.

I can't talk to you if you're going to take that sort of tone, she said, and she put the suitcase in the bedroom and then fetched the other three cases from the boot of the car. Slowly, she began unpacking them. She was still numb with disappointment. She would never have expected Christian Blome to find another girlfriend so soon. She saw him standing there in his hall looking embarrassed, and it stabbed her to the heart. Her life seemed empty and meaningless, and yet again she wondered if she wouldn't be better off dead. She could tell that her husband was about to raise the roof. She didn't know what to say in her own defence. She wondered whether he would divorce her. It wasn't that she was particularly fond of him, but she was badly frightened of being on her own. She was afraid she just wouldn't be up to coping with life without a man. She smiled almost humbly at her husband, who kept appearing in the bedroom doorway while she unpacked the cases, as if he were checking up on her, before going away again to prowl round the apartment. When she had the cases unpacked she laid the table for supper. Her husband said he had no appetite, but he sat down at the dining table directly and topped his bread with slices of ham, egg and pickled cucumber with as much loving care as usual, just as if nothing had happened. After supper he put the little girl to bed and sang her to sleep, while Lilo Besslein cleared the supper table and washed the dishes. And then he watched the evening news on television as usual. When the news was over he switched the television set off and began prowling around the apartment again. As he did so he kept an eye on what his wife was doing in the kitchen, still as if he were checking up on her. Finally, he asked her what her lover's name was, how long their affair had lasted, and why she hadn't gone to live with him after all. She answered all his questions readily enough, if not always accurately. She did not, for instance, tell him that Christian Blome was living with another woman and had been for some time. She just said that at the last minute she hadn't been able to bring herself to do it, hoping this might win him over, and once again she smiled almost humbly at him. But neither her lies nor her smile could move him. To her horror, he said he would be taking steps to put things straight this very week. She asked if he wanted a divorce. He said yes, that was the idea, and watched expressionlessly as she burst into tears. She went into the bathroom and took four tranquillizer capsules to help her control the terror that suddenly seized upon her. Then she asked him to think it over, but he only said he had no need to think about it any more.

What was to become of the child, she said.

Well, he'd keep the child, he said. He was sure the courts would give him custody, seeing that she was psychologically unstable and had already spent seven weeks in a psychiatric hospital because of her addiction to tranquillizers. He was planning to stay in the apartment, too. Anyway, the rent would be too high for her on her own.

He'd advise her to start looking for a smaller place at once, he added, and then began pacing up and down again, not in the least affected by her sobs. When it was time for bed he got some bedclothes out of the wardrobe in the bedroom and took them into the living room, where his wife was sitting on the sofa brooding miserably. She got up immediately so that he could make himself up a bed on the sofa, and went into the bathroom to remove her make-up and take four more tranquillizers. But she lay awake for hours in the inflatable bed in the bedroom, thinking with dismay of her future.

✳

Ernst Besslein had carried out his threat. He had gone to his solicitor and petitioned for divorce, even though Lilo Besslein's parents came to M especially to dissuade him. When they had to face the fact that their efforts were in vain, they told their daughter she had better come home to them, but she would not go along with this suggestion. No, she said, she was going to stay in M and look for a small apartment, and she would need to work six days a week in a pharmacy now, not just three. She had already asked Frau Högemann if she could work for her full time, but Frau Högemann said no, so now she faced the problem of finding a new job as well as a new apartment. Her husband was no help whatsoever. Indeed, she had a feeling that her lack of success in finding either a job or an apartment was a source of satisfaction to him. She did her best to hide her failures from him, so as not to increase this satisfaction. She could keep going only with the help of an overdose of her new tranquillizers; she was taking sixteen capsules a day now. She didn't know whether looking for an apartment or looking for a job got her down most. She applied for jobs in pharmacies every day one came up, but most of her apartment-hunting was done on Tuesday and Thursday evenings: these were the times when the first editions of the Wednesday and Friday issues of the big M daily paper came out, the ones with the property ads. At 6 p.m. on the dot she took up a position outside the newspaper offices, where the apartment-hunters of M

160

regularly congregated. They regularly made a large crowd, too, all waiting for the newsboys to appear, with their correct money ready so as not to waste any time over change. Cars were parked by the kerb outside the newspaper offices and in the side streets nearby, and if you were hunting as a couple one partner sat in the car, ready to drive off as soon as the other had bought a paper. All the public telephones near the newspaper offices were occupied well in advance by people waiting with their small change ready, so as to ring the first numbers directly their partners rushed into the kiosk with the newspaper. These well-drilled apartment-hunters had an advantage over those who, like Lilo Besslein, had no partner. The moment the newsboys appeared the apartment-hunters rushed them. There was much scuffling. Everyone knew it really paid to be first on the spot or first to ring up for the more attractive places. Minutes counted, even seconds. As soon as the newsboys appeared, people who had previously been waiting quite amicably outside the newspaper offices would turn hostile. Their mutual problem did not endear them to one another; in fact, everyone tried to get a head start.

As soon as Lilo Besslein had her own copy of the paper she hurried to a nearby café which had a public telephone. The waiters soon came to know her. They knew she would never finish the cup of coffee she always ordered. She flitted through the ads for apartments, marked the possibles, and rushed to the telephone. The numbers she rang were usually engaged, or if they were estate agents' numbers there was nobody answering. After repeated attempts, however, she would usually manage to get at least one connection and fix a time to go and view an apartment. She often went round that very evening, but when she arrived it would be obvious that in spite of her haste she wasn't one of the first to look at the apartment, was more of a latecomer, and the place had usually gone already by the time she got there. If it hadn't yet gone, it was sure to be a squalid dump without any bathroom or heating. Then she would go home, discouraged, to study the ads at her leisure. She made lists. She put three crosses against the most hopeful ads, and went to bed early so as to be fit for her apartment-hunting again next day. In the morning she would ring estate agents. Again, the numbers of those agents whose advertisements particularly interested her were the ones that were always engaged. She might spend all morning trying to get through and never hearing anything but the engaged signal, and when she did at last speak to someone she had come to expect she would hear that the apartment in question was gone. Now and then she was lucky, and did get through to an agent and make a date to see an apartment; sometimes she saw up to four a day. It was always the same: there would be six or so people already standing outside the apartment building, all wanting to see the place too, and all early. They included married couples, single men and single women. They inspected each other as they waited for the agent to arrive in an aloof and derogatory manner, in fact with barely concealed hostility. By the time the agent finally turned up, usually late and in a flashy sports car, Lilo Besslein had lost heart, for she knew by now that agents and landlords would rather rent apartments to childless married couples or single men than to single and relatively young women. It got more and more discouraging: the moment she took a liking to an apartment she knew in advance she wouldn't get it, it would go to a childless couple or a single man or older single woman. After she had been intensively hunting for a month she became increasingly indifferent. She stopped going to the newspaper offices on Tuesday and Thursday evenings to get the Wednesday and Friday editions of the paper at the earliest possible moment.

She didn't study the ads for apartments until Wednesday and Friday mornings, by which time the cheaper places would already have found tenants. Sometimes she did arrange to view a place with an agent or landlord. She was looking at bed-sitters too, and once she had a chance to rent a bed-sitter, but used as she had been from childhood to living in a large villa, she couldn't bring herself to take it.

After her initial failures she neglected her job-hunting too. When she saw a job advertised in the paper she couldn't always rouse herself to ring the proprietor of the pharmacy concerned, or if she did ring and make an appointment to go and see the proprietor, she couldn't always bring herself to keep it. Instead, she often strolled aimlessly around the city, indulging a kind of neurotic craving to buy clothes or shoes. She spent the housekeeping money and the money from her savings account on these purchases, as well as her own earnings. She overdrew her current account by quite a large sum. When she had stocked up with clothes she would sit in one of the bars in the city centre and order glass after glass of wine, staying there until it was time to fetch her daughter from Frau Finsinger's. For although, as previously mentioned, she was doing less and less in the way of looking for apartments and jobs, she had begun taking the little girl around to Frau Finsinger on her three days off as well as on the three days she worked in the pharmacy. Dull despair, going hand in hand with an odd sort of lethargy from which only her frantic compulsion to spend could briefly rouse her, made her incapable of looking after the child and increasingly unable to make the necessary plans she ought to be making for her future. One day she just gave up looking for jobs or apartments. She even stopped looking at the ads in the paper, though the date for the hearing of the divorce petition was coming closer and closer. She waited for things to take their course with an unhealthy fatalism which might be ascribed, among other things, to the effects of her tranquillizer; she was still taking sixteen capsules a day. And while she lived each day as it came, no longer doing anything useful in the way of planning for the future, her husband was furiously active. It often sent her frantic. He paid frequent visits to his solicitor, to work out ways and means of getting custody of the child and not having to pay his wife any alimony after the divorce. As the furniture, crockery and linen were all her property, he drove into the centre of M several times a week to look at new furniture in the stores and buy new crockery and new linen. He stacked the crockery in the kitchen. He stacked the linen in the bedroom. And he stacked furnishing-store catalogues in the living room and studied them in the evening, after the television news. His parents had put a sizeable sum at his disposal, so he was able to make all these new and necessary purchases. They rang him up every evening to ask how he was, just as if he were seriously ill. Once they came to M for the weekend to demonstrate family feeling. The demonstration took the form of bringing their son a whole whipped-cream gateau and their granddaughter several bars of chocolate, while they neither shook hands with their daughter-in-law nor spoke to her. They made themselves at home in the apartment in a way that forced Lilo Besslein out of it. Feeling she had actually been hounded out, she got into her car and spent an hour driving around the city streets. She felt utterly forlorn. She was bewildered to find that the Dülfers, Einseles and Urzingers wanted nothing to do with her either. She had entertained them and fed them well countless times, but all three couples took her husband's side. They invited him and his daughter to coffee on Sunday afternoons, and made sure that he got back on Sunday evenings having been well plied with food and drink and bearing what amounted to a food parcel. The Rittmeiers were the same. Gitta

Rittmeier mothered Ernst Besslein, who had taken to displaying a melancholy world-weariness, again much like an invalid's. As for Eugen Rittmeier, who was an estate agent and could have been very helpful to Lilo Besslein in her search for an apartment, he wasn't going to lift a finger for her. The only people who stood by her were her parents, but they did so in an extremely trying way. Her mother in particular regarded the coming divorce as a tragedy. She begged her, daily, to do everything she could to get custody of the child. This, however, was the one thing Lilo Besslein really didn't mind about. Nor did she want to go home to her parents. She had married her husband largely to get away from her mother's influence, and now she foresaw, with dread, that unless some miracle happened she would have to go back, and she felt as if her parents' house were a trap. If she got into it she would never get out again. She could guess that even though she was twenty-nine, she would be condemned to the existence of a small child, with her Mummy and Daddy – particularly her Mummy – constantly finding fault. It wasn't just that: she was also sure that she would be deprived of those scraps of her personal freedom she'd managed to preserve through the years of her marriage. However, she went to N one weekend to discuss moving back to her parents' home and the steps that would have to be taken. All went well at first, apart from the fact that her mother was forever imploring her not to smoke so much. Her father said why didn't she have her old room back, the one she'd slept in as a girl. Nothing in it had been touched since her wedding day. Her mother said they could make the smaller of the two spare rooms into a nursery. Her father was going to get a removals firm to bring the furniture from the Lerchenau apartment back to N. It could be stored in the basement and the two attic rooms for the time being, along with the crockery and linen, and then, said her mother, she'd already have all her household goods if she got married again. And she patted her daughter's arm before going on to discuss her job at the pharmacy. She hoped, said her mother, that Lilo's misfortunes had brought her to see reason now and she wouldn't go looking for another job in N. After all, she wouldn't be paying a penny for board and lodging, and if she wanted any new clothes she had only to ask her father. She knew how generous he was. Moreover, the two of them had talked it over and decided that he would give her five hundred marks a month to spend as she liked.

Did she think she could manage on five hundred marks, she asked her daughter, who was having difficulty in hiding her growing desperation.

It wasn't a question of whether she could manage on that sum, it was a question of being financially independent, she replied, although she saw that her mother had suddenly gone very red in the face and the veins on her temples were swelling.

And she didn't know what she'd do all day, without a job, she added.

Why, look after her little girl, of course, supposing she got custody, and help her mother about the house, said her father, and he looked with concern at his wife, who had now clenched her fists.

You've been criminally negligent as a mother, she cried. You went and found a job and took a lover and got addicted to drugs instead of looking after your own child. It was thoroughly irresponsible of you, starting an affair when you were married and a mother. And you weren't the only one. It was irresponsible of that young man too, taking up with someone else's wife and mother. I'm sure he can't be worth much. But there, you've taken to painting your face like a tart, so I suppose that makes men think you're available. It's only yourself you've got to blame, you and your self-indulgence. Your divorce is coming up in a fortnight's time and you haven't found a new apartment or a new

166

job yet, have you. So what makes you so independent and emancipated, the way you're always trying to make out. You're too proud to be satisfied with being a housewife and mother, that's what it is. You want something better than that, don't you. But you haven't got the energy you'd need to make any real difference. You really just expect everything to drop into your lap, don't you, and when it doesn't you take refuge in depression. The fact is, you may be twenty-nine but you still don't know what you really want. If you actually had anything clear in mind you wouldn't be behaving like this. You aren't much bothered about anyone except yourself, and the way you let yourself drift along, well, it's enough to worry anyone. Sometimes I get the feeling you don't even want to take responsibility for yourself. But we're willing to help you all the same. We've offered you and your child two rooms. We've offered you both free board and lodging. In addition to which we've said we'll give you five hundred marks a month for pocket money. I don't see what more parents could do for their grown-up daughter. And we don't expect anything in return, or at least, all we expect is for you to look after your child and do a bit of housework.

Well, is that or is it not too much to expect, she asked her daughter, who did not answer. She could have told her mother she had no kind of real life, and never had. She could have told her that housework and looking after her child didn't make up for that. She could have told her that working at the pharmacy at least gave her more confidence. Finally, she could have told her that she had to work in a pharmacy anyway, because that meant she could get all the tranquillizers she took daily without a prescription. But she was afraid neither her mother nor her father would understand, and her mother's diatribe had so disheartened her that she had no strength left just now to stand up for her job at the pharmacy.

I'm tired, she said, and she rose, picked up her cigarettes and her lighter, and kissed first her father and then her mother, who begged her not to smoke any more before she went to bed. For the sake of a quiet life, she said she wouldn't, and then she left the lounge. Furnished as it was with Persian carpets and Persian rugs, a comfortable leather sofa, a solid oak cupboard and three oil paintings, this room showed that her parents had achieved prosperity. She went upstairs to her old bedroom on the first floor. When she got there she opened the window and looked down into the garden, which was lit by small, wrought-iron lanterns arranged about the place as usual. Summer was over long ago, although no snow had yet fallen, but this garden, with its round and semi-circular flower beds, its oval swimming pool, its shallow white stone urns about a metre high and planted with flowers in spring, and its cleverly landscaped group of trees, still made a very pretty picture. The small wrought-iron lanterns, moreover, were so imaginatively positioned that even on moonless nights you could just make out the tall trees in the nature reserve beyond the fence, and Lilo Besslein thought, with some reason, that this gave you an impression of the property's stretching on and on. She stepped back from the window and looked around her room. The white bed, the white wardrobe, the white bookcase and the white desk stood out clearly against the wallpaper, which had an abstract flower pattern in three shades of red. She had chosen the red wallpaper and white furniture at the age of fifteen, as well as the red carpet. She did not like the colour scheme and the furniture anywhere near as much now. She wondered if her parents would have the room redecorated if she came back here. She had no idea where else to go after the divorce, but she still couldn't reconcile herself to living in this house until further notice: a house that stood in a lifeless, high-class residential area on the northern side of N. Fierce dogs guarded the big houses around here. She hated the place; its streets were as empty as the streets of Lerchenau. She was afraid her parents would shelter her as over-protectively as before. She was afraid of leading the life of a prisoner in this luxuriously furnished house with its big garden, a prisoner who might just be let out for a few hours on parole. Sighing, she lit a cigarette. She was just beginning to inhale the smoke when she heard her mother coming upstairs in her high-heeled shoes. For a moment she almost threw the cigarette out of the window, the way she used to as a girl, and then she thought better of it. She told herself she'd been of age for years, and took her cigarette into the bathroom with her. A moment later her mother followed her in.

Oh, my dear, she said. Smoking again.

I'm feeling very edgy, said Lilo Besslein, and began removing her make-up.

You really must give up smoking if you come back here, said her mother, watching as Lilo Besslein removed the make-up first from her right eye and then from her left eye.

How nice you do look without those ugly black lines round your eyes, she said. You look much younger.

Won't you give up painting your eyes like that if you come back here, she asked her daughter, who was slowly losing her temper.

Why don't you tell me right away everything else I'm supposed to give up if I come back here, she said.

Now, my dear, said her mother, there's no need to be offensive, just because I'm telling you the truth. Those black lines round your eyes simply look cheap. No nice young man is going to take an interest in you if you look like that. As for myself, well, to be perfectly honest, I'm ashamed to introduce you to our friends with those black lines round your eyes.

Why don't you just put a little eye-shadow on the lids, like I do, she inquired.

Her daughter remained silent. She felt too low to start arguing over such details. They were not unimportant to her, but her mother had always gone in for inflating these things to the proportions of drama, and she knew very well that her life here would entail a running battle over them. She dreaded the thought of it. She already knew her mother would emerge the victor. Just at the moment she felt nothing but dislike for her; however, she kissed her cheek and said good night again before going back into her bedroom, where she took four tranquillizer capsules. But she could not get to sleep, all the same, and lay awake until dawn, wondering whether she really should come back here or not.

She had not come to any decision when she got up in the morning. She had breakfast with her parents, who seemed quite sure she would be coming back home the day after the divorce, and then returned to M. There was nobody in the apartment. Her husband had taken the little girl to Frau Finsinger's, as arranged, and then gone to work. Although the breakfast table was not yet cleared nor the bed made, she got the Martini bottle out of the built-in bar, and emptied half of it within a very short time before taking the dishes into the kitchen, washing them, and finally making the bed. She ought really to have dusted and hoovered next, but she didn't. She was soon leaving this apartment for good anyway, and felt no particular wish to keep it as clean as before. She sat on the sofa and slowly finished the other half of the Martini bottle. She realized she was getting steadily drunk. It was not a very pleasant kind of drunkenness; it merely gave her suppressed desperation a helping hand to the surface. She felt so desperate she couldn't even cry. She thought of her future with terror. She wished she could talk to someone about it, but she didn't know who there was to talk to. Frau Dülfer, Frau Einsele and Frau Urzinger, as previously mentioned, had all taken her husband's side, so they were as much out of the question as Gitta Rittmeier. She thought fleetingly of ringing a girlfriend in N at her office, but then she told herself she wouldn't be able to have a telephone conversation of any length with her during office hours. Suddenly she thought of Fred Meichelbeck. He was well known for his unconventional ways, and she could be sure that he for one wouldn't be shocked by her adultery. She dialled his number, and he lifted the receiver at once, as if he had been sitting by the telephone. He seemed rather surprised to hear her at first, but when she told him about her adultery and the divorce he put his mind to the matter at once. After all, he was an expert on love affairs, divorces and adultery. Why didn't she come and see him, he suggested, and they could talk it all over at their leisure. She agreed, and made herself another cup of coffee to sober herself up before she went to see him. Anxious not to cause an accident, she drove so slowly that other vehicles kept overtaking her. She was feeling slightly sick, and made up her mind not to drink anything else alcoholic at Fred Meichelbeck's, but she did not stick to this resolution, for Fred Meichelbeck, who welcomed her warmly, had put a bottle of champagne to chill so that they could, as he put it, celebrate the divorce.

Congratulations on leaving that square husband of yours at last, he said, and he raised his champagne glass and drank first to Lilo Besslein and then to the actress Beate Dötzel and the model Larissa Pretzfeld, who were there too. Like Fred Meichelbeck, they were both keen to hear the details. So Lilo Besslein told them about her affair with Christian Blome, and the events leading up to her divorce. She went on to tell them about her failure to find a new job and a new apartment.

She supposed she'd have to go home to her parents, she said, chiefly addressing Fred Meichelbeck, who strongly advised her against it.

She must be independent at last, he said. She'd better carry on with her present job for now, and get her husband to pay her alimony.

An apartment was sure to turn up soon, he added. Then he rose to his feet, got his address book and rang several women friends to ask if they'd heard of any empty apartments in Malching. None of them had, but he was still so confident that his confidence infected Lilo Besslein.

He'd ask around in the Daisy and the Ba-Ba-Lu, he said, and he was sure he'd hear of something.

What about a commune, he asked, would she go and live in a commune. Lilo Besslein said yes, she would. After a brief period of comparative sobriety, she was now getting even tipsier on champagne. Fred Meichelbeck had opened a second battle.

She was fed up to the teeth with conventional middle-class life, she said. She just wasn't made for it.

Then why had she married such a square, asked Beate Dötzel.

She married him just to get away from home, said Lilo Besslein, and if she didn't find an apartment within the next two weeks she'd have to go back home to her parents, and all her efforts would have come to nothing. She dreaded the mere thought of having to begin all over again where she left off three years ago, she said. But she couldn't find an apartment any more than she could bear to go home to her parents, who wanted her to give up work and devote herself to housework and her child. It was true that she was afraid of living alone, too. She wasn't used to relying on herself. She didn't think she could manage without help from anyone else. She only hoped she wouldn't get custody of her daughter, because she wasn't capable of bringing her up on her own. All the same, she knew that if she didn't she'd suffer from terrible feelings of guilt.

She was wondering if she hadn't better commit suicide, she added, and she picked up her champagne glass and drained it. Fred Meichelbeck poured her some more champagne. Lightly as he took everything, he did not much like the turn this conversation had taken. Beate Dötzel and Larissa Pretzfeld obviously couldn't think what to say either. There was a longish lull in the conversation, during which all present thoughtfully sipped champagne. Finally, Fred Meichelbeck turned to Lilo Besslein and said there was nothing to feel gloomy about. Why, she ought to be glad to think she'd be free of her square of a husband in a fortnight's time.

How was Ernst treating her, he asked.

He slept on the living-room sofa at night, she replied, and spoke to her only when he absolutely had to. He was acting as if he were seriously ill, talking in a very soft voice, and he'd recently taken to walking with a bit of a stoop. He was basking in the sympathy of his parents, friends and colleagues over his unfaithful wife. And he was making a fool of himself, acting the part of the perfect father. He spoiled the child and petted her as if he weren't her father at all but her grandmother. He kept bringing her new toys and sweets, he never tired of playing with her at weekends, he read her picture books and he took her out for long walks. He only had to put in an appearance for the child to ignore her mother completely.

In fact he was taking good care to make her look like a rotten mother, she added.

Did she love her daughter, Larissa Pretzfeld asked.

She really couldn't say for sure, said Lilo Besslein. All she knew was that she hated her when she rolled about on the floor, yelling. Sometimes she felt sorry for the child, when she'd hurt herself and come to her for comfort. And sometimes she felt moved when the child learned a new word and began to use it. But then again, she sometimes felt violent dislike when she saw

173

how much the child resembled her husband.

You obviously don't love her, then, said Beate Dötzel, a little reproachfully.

Is there any law saying a mother absolutely has to love her child, asked Fred Meichelbeck. Okay, bourgeois society considers it's very shocking, if not actually a crime, if she can't, he continued. Which means a lot of mothers pretend to have maternal feelings, and in the course of time they confuse them with the genuine article. At least Lilo isn't a hypocrite.

Here's to your love of truth, he cried, raising his glass and drinking to Lilo Besslein. She was getting increasingly drunk, and by now she felt so sick she couldn't smoke any more. She asked Fred Meichelbeck if he would make her a cup of tea. He rose at once and went to his small kitchen alcove, where he filled a kettle and put it on the stove. Meanwhile, Lilo Besslein was feeling even worse. Saliva gathered in her mouth, and she tried to control the nausea sweeping over her by breathing deeply, in and out. Then Beate Dötzel lit a cigarette, and the nausea got so much worse that she had to jump up and make a dash for the bathroom. She knelt in front of the lavatory, clinging to its sides, and threw up her breakfast as well as the Martini and champagne. Then she rinsed her mouth out and went back into the living room. Fred Meichelbeck had already put a cup of tea down on the table. She drank it in small, careful sips. When she had finished the cup of tea, she asked Fred Meichelbeck if she could lie down in his bedroom for a little while. The artist escorted her to the bedroom and drew the curtains. His bed was still unmade, so he made a move to smooth the sheets and shake out the quilt, but Lilo Besslein told him not to bother. As Fred Meichelbeck left the room, she took her shoes off and lay down. She meant to rest for only a short time, but after a few minutes she fell asleep. She dreamed of Christian Blome, and when she woke, some two hours later, she felt even more depressed than before. Sighing, she sat up, and then went into the living room. To her surprise, there was nobody there. She found a note from Fred Meichelbeck on the table, saying he had gone to the Ba-Ba-Lu with Beate Dötzel and Larissa Pretzfeld and urging her to come and join them. She took four tranquillizer capsules and drove off to the Ba-Ba-Lu. When she got there she went all round the bar, but she couldn't find Fred Meichelbeck, Beate Dötzel or Larissa Pretzfeld anywhere. Irritated by the artist's unreliability, she set off for the Daisy, but it turned out that Fred Meichelbeck and his two friends were not there either. She sat on one of the tall bar stools, ordered Serbian bean soup, and ate it ravenously. Then she paid her bill and went back to her car. It was only half past three in the afternoon and she didn't feel like sitting around at home staring at the grass area outside the window any more, so she drove into the city centre. She left the car in a multi-storey car park and wandered through the main shopping streets of M. She had her cheque book with her, but she made up her mind not to buy anything, for, as previously mentioned, she had already over-drawn her account. At first she just stood outside the windows of the clothes and shoe shops, looking at the displays. After a while, however, curiosity got the better of her, and she went inside to look at the things on the rails. She didn't try anything on to start with, and told the assistants who asked if they could help her that she was just looking. She wandered aimlessly from rail to rail, looking at dresses, skirts, blouses, blazers, trousers, trouser suits, coats and evening dresses, and left each shop feeling that she had herself well in hand today. It was not until she reached one of her favourite shops, a boutique called the Countdown, that the desire to buy something overwhelmed her. She tried on five dresses, three pairs of trousers and two trouser suits, one black and one white. They suited her so

175

much that she would have liked to buy them both, and it was only because she couldn't make up her mind whether to have the black one or the white one that she left the boutique, without making a purchase, but feeling she had been deprived of something vital. Badly frustrated, she hurried to another of her favourite boutiques, the Bajazzo, only fifty metres from the Countdown. She went in feeling as if she urgently needed something to wear, though she couldn't have said exactly what. Hands moving feverishly, she picked hanger after hanger off the rails, looking at the prices as well as the goods themselves, although she was more and more inclined to dismiss prices as a minor consideration. Then, indiscriminately, she tried on dresses, skirts, blouses, blazers, trousers, trouser suits and coats. She found herself less and less able to tell if something suited her or not; that didn't matter much now. Her power of judgement was increasingly suspended by an ever more urgent desire to buy, a positive compulsion. When she had tried on all kinds of things she went over to the rail of evening dresses, without letting the glances exchanged by the two assistants bother her. She picked out three evening dresses, a red one, a silver-grey one and a black one, and took them into the changing room. She put the red dress on first, and looked at herself in the mirror for a moment, undecided, before she took it off and slipped straight into the silver-grey dress. Once again she glanced in the mirror, perplexed. She saw that she looked exhausted and indeed haggard. Her hair was untidy from trying on all the clothes; there was sweat on her forehead and her upper lips and her armpits too were sweating profusely. Her whole body felt sticky and damp from the close atmosphere of the windowless changing rooms. She took the silver-grey evening dress off again and wiped the sweat from her forehead and armpits with her handkerchief. Then she slipped into the black evening dress. It was a very tight-fitting, sequinned dress, with spaghetti straps, and so deeply décolleté both back and front that you couldn't wear a bra under it. It was not just the deep décolletage that made it look daring, however, but the slit up the side of the skirt to thigh level. Before Lilo Besslein zipped the dress up she took her bra off, to get a better idea of the effect. Once again she looked at herself in the mirror, feeling unsure. She thought the dress was really too daring for her, with its deep décolletage and thigh-length slit. It would take a lot of courage to wear it; she wondered if she would ever summon up that amount of courage. She told herself she'd never be able to wear the dress either in the conservative circles where she was used to moving, or in the equally conservative circles where her parents moved. This in itself made her like the dress better and better. Her face assumed a defiant expression. She decided that once she was divorced she'd mix only with people who wouldn't be shocked by this kind of dress. All at once she felt that buying the dress amounted to a first step towards a better future. She left the changing room to display herself to the assistants. Both expressed their delight so credibly that Lilo Besslein's last scruples disappeared. One of the assistants showed her a sequinned black bag that might have been made for the evening dress, and she decided to have the bag too. Smiling radiantly, as if she had done something very clever, she went back into the changing room to take the dress off. Although it and the bag together came to nine hundred marks, she was not at all bothered about the money just now. She paid with three Eurocheques for three hundred marks each, and left the boutique in haste; she wanted to buy black evening shoes to match the outfit before the shops shut. She went to the most expensive shoe shop in M, and had very soon acquired a pair of beaded sandals with ten-centimetre stiletto heels. They cost two hundred and eighty marks. She paid with another

Eurocheque, and once again she felt as if she had done something very clever. Well satisfied, she left the shoe shop and set out for the car park where she had left her car. Half-way there, however, her mood began to swing. She thought of the money she had spent in both shops. Sobering down all of a sudden, she wondered what on earth had induced her to spend almost twelve hundred marks on things which were going to be of no conceivable use to her in the near future. She told herself that the evening dress would hang in her wardrobe unworn for months, maybe even years, for want of a festive occasion on which to wear it, and in the course of time it would get less and less fashionable. She wasn't even sure if she would ever venture to appear in such a daring dress in public. She couldn't understand how it was that she had felt, so recently, that buying the dress amounted to a first step towards a better future. All of a sudden she did not just see this notion as foolish; she actually feared for her reason. She felt that her desire for a spending spree, often enough degenerating into a neurotic compulsion, made her temporarily not responsible for her actions. She wondered what caused it. She told herself it regularly came over her when she was very unhappy. She reflected that it was always the same: her unhappiness caused her, almost forced her, to buy herself something, anything. It hardly mattered what; that depended on chance. All that mattered was buying something, because the act of making the purchase gave her a brief, deceptive thrill of happiness, which turned to its opposite almost as soon as she had left the shop.

And now, getting into her car, starting the engine and driving out of the car park, she was just as unhappy as she had been before she bought the dress, the bag and the shoes. She wondered whether to take them all back. But she couldn't quite bring herself to do that, not yet. She decided to try the dress and shoes

178

on again as soon as she got home, and she made herself stop thinking of the money she had spent today. Anyway, the streets were very busy just now and she had to concentrate on her driving. The road to Lerchenau was jammed with vehicles, and she could move only very slowly. It took her twenty minutes to reach the Gluckgasse and park her car.

It was nearly seven o'clock by now, but she walked up the path with her two carrier bags without particular haste. Her neighbour, Frau Deininger, was coming towards her carrying a rubbish bucket, and the hasty nod with which the usually loquacious woman responded to her greeting showed her, not for the first time, that Frau Deininger was on her husband's side, like the other tenants in the building. As she entered the building, went up the six steps to the apartment and unlocked the apartment door, she tried not to mind her neighbour's attitude. But it did hurt to think that apart from Fred Meichelbeck and his easy-going friends everyone she knew utterly condemned her. She felt excluded if not actually outlawed from society. She felt that it cost her husband's friends and colleagues and the tenants of this building an effort to observe common courtesy towards her, the adulteress. The same applied to her husband himself. When she entered the living room, where he had laid supper for himself and the child but not for her, it was a long time before he turned his head towards her. He then scrutinized her disapprovingly from head to toe, and finally, turning his head away again as if disgusted, wished her a scarcely audible good evening. She would not let his behaviour upset her; she went over to kiss the child. But the little girl turned her own head away as if disgusted too. She firmly took the child's face in both hands and looked at her, smiling. She saw that the little girl had her husband's small, grey-green eyes, and his slightly dilated nostrils, narrow-lipped mouth and thin, light brown hair as well. Her appearance, in short, was not calculated to arouse Lilo Besslein's maternal feelings. She glanced at the child's plate, which held a slice of bread and butter and some spiced sausage cut up small.

What's your nice supper, then, she asked the child.

B'ed, said the child.

And you're having spiced sausage too, aren't you, she asked the child.

Ice, said the child.

No, not ice, spiced sausage, that's what you're having, she told the child.

Spiced sausage, she repeated, loud and clear, so that the child could grasp it, and then pointed to the spiced sausage again and asked what it was.

B'ed, said the child.

No, you silly, that's not bread, she said, pointing to the sausage again. Suddenly feeling determined to teach her child something new, she picked up a piece of sausage in her fingers, held it in front of the little girl's face, and told her again, loud and clear, that it was spiced sausage.

Is that spiced sausage, she asked the child.

Ice, said the child, and she gave up her educational efforts and left the room to go and try on the evening dress and shoes again in the bedroom, where there was a large mirror. She undressed and slipped on the evening dress and evening sandals, which had little straps at the sides. An anxious expression on her face, she stood in front of the mirror. The sight of her reflection was more than reassuring: she thought she looked very good in the dress, and it suited her much better than the other, plainer clothes in her wardrobe. She wondered whether buying the dress hadn't amounted to a first step towards a better future after all.

The fact is, all I need is a place to wear it, she told herself, and she tried to imagine what kind of place that would be. But she could not get beyond very vague notions involving noisy parties. Lack of curiosity, and the timidity fostered by her upbringing which made her shrink from anything remotely resembling adventure, meant that her experience up till now was very limited. She just wanted to get out of her present, oppressive environment. As she took the dress off and hung it in the wardrobe, she decided to start looking for an apartment again. .

*

The next day was a Tuesday. Once again she took up her position outside the offices of the big M daily paper at 6 p.m. on the dot. A great many other apartment-hunters had already assembled there; she recognized some of them. A few nodded to her, and she nodded back. As she waited for the newsboys to appear, she fell into conversation with one of them, a woman of about thirty, who told her she'd been looking for a two-roomed apartment for the last six months.

She wasn't married, she said, and she had the utmost difficulty getting agents and landlords to accept her as a tenant, even though she had a job and a steady income. They always preferred single men or childless married couples to students and single women.

She was on the point of giving up the attempt, she added, smiling sadly at Lilo Besslein.

She herself was in much the same situation, said Lilo Besslein.

She was about to get divorced, and she had to find an apartment quickly, she continued. In less than a fortnight, to be precise.

I'm afraid you won't, said the young woman, and then she stopped short, for the newsboys had appeared. The apartment-hunters surged towards them. Lilo Besslein pressed forward so boldly that she soon had her copy of the paper. Clutching it, she ran to the nearby café with the telephone. She ordered a cup of coffee, and skimmed through the ads for apartments before she made a beeline for the telephone to ring several numbers. As usual, she found they were all engaged, but she was not going to give up. She kept ringing them again, in turn, and finally she did succeed in getting through to one landlord, a man called Seibold. Herr Seibold told her she could come and see the apartment straight away. She paid her bill and drove directly to the address he had given her in a street near the railway station, an area that had rather come down in the world. Driving past, Lilo Besslein saw shabby striptease joints, bars, amusement arcades, discount stores and sex shops. But none of this bothered her very much. Her dread of going home to her parents increased daily, and as a result she was nowhere near as choosy as she had been about where she lived and what an apartment was like. She drove slowly to the end of the street where the building in which the apartment had come vacant stood. The building itself looked very squalid, and was in urgent need of a new coat of paint. She saw a great many people walking about or standing in groups behind the two ground-floor windows to the right of the door of the building, and at first she had the impression there was a party going on. But when she pressed the doorbell under the name of Lobeck and went in, it seemed that this ground-floor apartment was the vacant one and the people were not, as she had supposed, party guests but people come to look at the place, like herself. One of them, who was just leaving, opened the door to her. She went into a corridor, which had a shiny, silvery metal cabinet with a door standing in the middle of it. If this cabinet had been a little wider it would almost have blocked the way to the back of the apartment, for it was about one square metre and reached nearly to the ceiling. Lilo Besslein opened its door until it hit the wall opposite and did in fact block the way. To her surprise, she saw that the cabinet contained a shower. She was still staring at

182

this shower when someone trying to get back up the corridor hammered impatiently on its door, and she quickly closed it again. The man who had been hammering, followed by his wife, squeezed through the space between the shower and the wall of the corridor and made for the front door, commenting that this apartment was a dump. Lilo Besslein did not let his remark put her off. She turned towards the first room, to the left of the front door. There were two more apartment-hunters standing in the doorway, a young man and a young woman, and they stepped out into the corridor when she asked them so that she could see into the room. It was so full of people, most of them holding tape measures, that she could not actually get inside. One glance told her that it was an extremely long and narrow room, with room for a narrow bed and a bedside table at the most along the shorter wall. There was a small iron stove in the corner by the door, with a rusty stove-pipe reaching almost to the ceiling, which was practically four metres up. She was just wondering if she would ever be able to light that stove when two more people wanting to see the room asked her to move. She stepped out into the corridor and wriggled through the space between the shower and the wall to see the other room. This room too was crammed with apartment-hunters armed with tape measures, some of them crouching down on the floor to measure walls so that she couldn't get in without causing a crush all round. She stayed in the doorway again, although she would have liked to go over to the window and see what the view was like. She saw that this was another long, narrow room, though at least twice the size of the first one. Another small iron stove with a pipe reaching almost to the remarkably high ceiling stood in a corner by the door of this room, too. A small, black-haired man was fiddling with the stove. You could tell at once that he was a Turkish immigrant worker, even if he hadn't been talking to his wife in a language Lilo Besslein did not understand, plainly pointing out something to do with the stove. The wife was a small, black-haired, black-eyed woman, holding two children by the hands. Lilo Besslein looked from the Turk to the other apartment-hunters, observing them more closely. They were mostly young people, perhaps students, wearing blue jeans and with hair worn either very long or very short. She saw several young women too, considerably better dressed and looking much more conventional than the other apartment-hunters. Finally she saw another Turkish family, over by the window. The sight of all these people, concentrated in the second room in particular, did more than soothe her fears: it actually left her hoping she might get this apartment. She couldn't say she liked it: it certainly wasn't just what she wanted, with its long and narrow rooms, probably so dark in the daytime that you would need the electric light on, and those stoves, and that shower cabinet in the corridor instead of a proper bathroom. But her failure to find an apartment at all yet, and her fear of going home to her parents' house, which she was coming to see as more and more like a trap, made her, as previously mentioned, a good deal less choosy than she had been.

Something could be made of this place, she told herself as she went out into the corridor again and opened a narrow door next to the second room. It was the door to the lavatory, which, grotesquely, was a room large enough to have taken a dining table and four chairs as well as the lavatory itself and the small wash-basin to the right of it. Shaking her head, Lilo Besslein closed the door again and went on into the kitchen, quite a pleasant, square room, with french windows to a small balcony. Near the wall with the balcony and sitting on a stool that might have been left behind by the previous tenants, there was a puffy, bald, elderly man wearing a much-mended woollen jacket and slippers and holding a notebook and a ballpoint pen. This must be Herr Seibold the landlord, for several people were crowding round him, expressing their wish to rent the apartment. Besides giving him their addresses, telephone numbers and occupations, they were feeding him sob stories about the desperate straits they were in, hoping to persuade him to rent them this apartment, which was only four hundred and fifty marks a month. As they pleaded with him, one of them, a thin young man with shoulder-length hair dyed red, actually burst into tears. Herr Seibold, taking no notice of their sad tales, just sat there on his stool looking bored, and even after they had told him their names, addresses, phone numbers and occupations he waited for quite a while, thrusting his right hand under his crumpled, shabby shirt and scratching his chest, before he noted down these particulars. Lilo Besslein made her way over to him and gave him her own name, address, phone number and occupation in a loud, clear voice. To her disappointment, he didn't even look at her, but just wrote the facts down. She was wondering höw to attract his attention when two more apartment-hunters pushed her aside. She took a couple of steps backwards, stopped by the kitchen door, and waited there for the others to leave the kitchen and the apartment itself; she was determined to have a proper word with the landlord once the place was empty. However, people were very slow to leave. More and more of them kept coming into the kitchen to give Herr Seibold their names, addresses and occupations, if they were in jobs at all, for most of them, as Lilo Besslein had suspected, were actually students, a good many of whom tried appealing to Herr Seibold's kind heart. Lilo Besslein got the impression that he was simply not listening to them at all. Leaning slightly forward, legs apart, he sat on the stool leafing through his notebook as though to estimate the large number of people after his apartment. His indifferent attitude did not change until the moment the Turkish family entered the kitchen. The woman stayed in the background with the children while the Turk himself came rather hesitantly up to the landlord, made a small bow and told him his name, address and occupation. Herr Seibold listened, but did not write anything down, not even the man's name.

Germany no good for you, you go back to Turkey, he finally said, waving dismissively so that the Turk had to take a couple of steps backwards. He stood there for a moment, irresolute, with his wife and two children, and then they left the apartment. There was only a handful of people left now, and Lilo Besslein felt they all wanted to wait and have a word with Herr Seibold. He suddenly rose and started out of the kitchen, but she stood in his way before he could get to the corridor.

Did he have a moment, she inquired.

He'd been sitting here for over two hours and he hadn't had his supper yet, said Herr Seibold, looking her over insolently.

She only wanted to know her chances of getting the apartment, she said, and she smiled ingratiatingly at Herr Seibold. Silently, he showed her the many scribbled pages of his notebook, listing name after name. Lilo Besslein thought he might easily have up to fifty names written down there. Some, she saw, were underlined.

Couldn't he underline her name too, she asked.

Herr Seibold looked her all over insolently again.

Was she married, he finally inquired.

Well, she was still married just at the moment, she said, but her divorce was coming through in thirteen days' time, and she had nowhere to go.

Wouldn't he give her a chance and underline her name, at least, she added.

Herr Seibold thrust out his fat lower lip and shook his head back and forth.

186

He liked to feel sure his tenants led blameless lives, he said pompously, and there wasn't any guarantee of that, not with a divorced woman.

However, he might turn a blind eye just for once. What was her name again, he asked.

Full of confidence all of a sudden, Lilo Besslein told him her name, address, phone number and occupation again. But all her confidence drained away at once when she saw that Herr Seibold was not actually underlining her name; he only put a dotted line under it, and added a large question mark in the margin to her particulars.

What's that question mark for, she asked him.

Like I said, it's because I'm not sure you'll be leading a blameless life, you being divorced and all, he said, looking her over again.

Specially in this sort of area, with all those striptease joints and bars and sex shops. I mean, it's easy for a woman on her own to go to the bad if she looks like you, he added.

Look, why not tell me straight out I've got no chance of the apartment at all, asked Lilo Besslein, her temper really roused now, because she had been so near crawling to this overbearing and seedy individual who obviously enjoyed being able to play Lord God Almighty, thanks to the apartment shortage.

Oh, I wouldn't say you've got no chance at all, he replied condescendingly. If all those people I've underlined decide to turn the place down, even with the rent so low, then you can have it, though mind you, I'm not under any illusions about your way of life.

You don't for a moment think all the others will turn it down, cried Lilo Besslein. She was near tears, and had to summon up all her will-power to keep from shedding them.

Well, let's be honest, I don't think it's very likely they'll all back out, said Herr Seibold, with a curt and guttural laugh.

Lilo Besslein gave him a glance of fury before she turned on her heel without another word and left the apartment. It was not until she got into her car that she began to cry, quietly and desperately. She cried all the way back to Lerchenau. Once home, she took six tranquillizers and went straight to bed. She had very little hope of finding an apartment within such a short time, but she made up her mind to go on looking before she went to sleep.

Next day she phoned all the agents she could think of, and along with other apartment-hunters she went viewing first apartments at six hundred marks a month or less and then more expensive places. She dressed in her best clothes, to make a good impression on the agents, and painted only the thinnest of lines round her eyes. But she met with one refusal after another, and a kind of dull despair came over her. It got worse when her father rang at the weekend, to tell her he'd arranged for a removals van to call for her furniture at seven in the morning on the day after the divorce and take it to N. She didn't intend to go home to her parents, but she dared not object. She thanked him for going to so much trouble instead. After his phone call, and despite the presence of her husband, who had now ordered new furniture, she drank a bottle of Martini, and when she was drunk she begged him tearfully not to divorce her. Couldn't he take pity on her, she asked. She was in an utterly hopeless situation. She hadn't found an apartment and she hadn't found a job. She'd really only gone looking for an apartment so that she needn't reproach herself, because even if she did find one it wouldn't solve her problems; she was terrified of living alone. She was nowhere near independent enough to cope without help from anyone else. On the other hand, she was independent enough to hate the thought of going back to her parents and having to do whatever they said. She'd never been able to stand up for herself, particularly with her mother, and she could see she wouldn't be able to stand up to her mother any better now.

Wouldn't he give the marriage another chance after all, she asked, and she looked imploringly at him.

But he was adamant.

There could be no question of any such thing, he said, and he rose to his feet and left the room to go and wake the little girl. He had put her down for her afternoon rest at mid-day. While he was dressing her, Lilo Besslein heard him saying they were invited to Auntie Dülfer's that afternoon. She told herself life went on for him just as if nothing much had happened. She felt sure he would soon marry again. Full of bitterness, she went into the bathroom, took four tranquillizer capsules and then lay down in bed. She heard him and the child leaving the apartment, and when they had gone she tried to sleep for a little, but she couldn't drop off in spite of all she had had to drink. She lay there, her arms folded behind her head, wondering what was to become of her. She felt she had no strength left to go on looking for an apartment, let alone a job. Come what might, she didn't want to go home to her parents. Suddenly she had an idea: she could go back to the psychiatric hospital. A long stay in hospital wouldn't actually solve her problems, of course, she told herself, but it would amount to postponing them. She felt she urgently needed a respite, a time when the doctors and nurses would relieve her to a great extent of responsibility for herself. She decided to go and see Professor Püschel next day.

✳

In the morning Lilo Besslein made an appointment with Professor Püschel's assistant for early afternoon. That done, her fears of the future began to recede. She was looking forward to being in the psychiatric hospital; she regarded it as a sanctuary. She was looking forward to talking to the other patients. She hoped to meet old acquaintances again. She was so sure they would admit her to hospital that very day that she spent most of the morning in preparation, getting out the pyjamas, clothes and underclothes she was planning to take with her. She left the apartment building about mid-day and went to the shopping street to the south of Lerchenau to buy herself a sketching block, a box of watercolours and a diary. Besides taking up painting again in hospital, she intended to keep a diary to help sort herself out. Back at home, she added the sketching block, the box of watercolours and the diary to the pile of clothes she planned to take. Then she went into the bathroom and got ready to go and see the Professor. She spent almost two hours in front of the mirror, and then set off late and in great haste. She was furious with herself for her unpunctuality all the way to the psychiatric hospital, and didn't calm down until she had reported to the receptionist and gone into the waiting room, for there were four more patients in there, all with appointments before her. She had to wait over an hour before she was called in. She rose at once and entered the consulting room, where Professor Püschel rose from his desk, beaming, to shake hands. He invited her to sit down and then asked how she was.

Lilo Besslein had worked out just what to say to him in advance. She told him about her imminent divorce, her search for an apartment and a job, and her dread of going home to her parents. When she realized he was getting impatient she stopped describing her present situation and told him she'd been taking sixteen capsules a day of the tranquillizer he had prescribed, to help her feel anywhere near able to cope with her circumstances.

She was obviously addicted to tranquillizers again, she added.

Professor Püschel seemed so unperturbed that she

was distinctly irritated. He noted down what she said in silence, and then looked keenly at her.

Yes, she ought really to come straight into hospital, he said at last, but he couldn't admit her just now. There wasn't a single empty bed.

When would there be an empty bed, asked Lilo Besslein.

Maybe in a fortnight's time, said the Professor, but maybe not for a month.

He'd make a note of it and let her know at once when they had a bed free, he added, and once again he looked keenly at Lilo Besslein. Just at the moment she was feeling too desperate to be able to weep. She simply sat there, stunned, and stared at Professor Püschel, who was shifting restlessly about in his chair. Obviously he was only waiting for her to rise and say goodbye.

When did she say her divorce was, he inquired, without much interest.

In a week's time, and she still didn't know where to go, said Lilo Besslein.

Well, he'd advise her to go to her parents for the time being, said Professor Püschel, and he half rose from his chair and shook hands.

Lilo Besslein left the consulting room without a word. She drove back to Lerchenau by the shortest route, and once home, she put the pile of things she had so prematurely got ready for hospital away in the wardrobe again. She was just closing the wardrobe door when the telephone began to ring. It was Fred Meichelbeck. He told her he'd heard of a bed-sitter coming vacant in a building in the middle of Malching. There was a girl art student in the bed-sitter at the moment, said Fred Meichelbeck, so it seemed quite likely that the agency concerned would let it to another single woman.

She'd better get in touch with the art student straight away and fix a time to see the bed-sitter, he added, and gave her the girl's name, address and telephone number, and the address and telephone number of the agency.

Lilo Besslein noted it all down and thanked him. Then she spent the next hour trying to ring the agency and the art student, but she couldn't get through to either. The agency number was permanently engaged, and nobody was answering the art student's phone. Disappointed, she temporarily gave up her attempts and went into the bathroom to take four tranquillizers. She was just popping them in her mouth when she heard her husband unlock the door and come down the corridor with her daughter, whom he had taken to fetching from Frau Finsinger's as a regular thing. She left the bathroom and said hello to the little girl. To her vexation, the child took no notice of her at all, but clung to her husband's legs and asked him to play with her.

No, he hadn't got time just now, he said, as he took off his coat.

His new furniture was about to be delivered, he added, much to the surprise of his wife, who wondered where on earth he was going to put new furniture in this already crammed apartment. Visibly annoyed, she went into the kitchen to make the little girl's supper. Some ten minutes later the furniture delivery men rang the bell. She closed the kitchen door, buttered herself a slice of bread, and tried to ignore what was going on. But now and then she did cast a glance at the pane of opaque glass in the door, beyond which she could see the shadowy outlines of the two delivery men and of the numerous pieces of furniture they seemed to be carrying into the apartment.

She waited until the delivery men had left before she came out of the kitchen and looked around the apartment. She saw another and very tasteless teak wardrobe standing in the corridor, along with a refrigerator and two kitchen cabinets. The kitchen cabinets were so wide that they left a gap of only about thirty centimetres for anyone to squeeze through to the rest of the apartment. She made her way through this gap and glanced into the nursery. Despite the lack of space, there ere two more kitchen cabinets standing in the middle of the room, with several saucepans and a frying pan on top of them. She went into the bedroom, shaking her head. The two box-shaped bedside tables and the inflatable bed, which had previously stood in the middle of the room, had been pushed against the window wall, leaving just enough space for a double bed covered with frightful purple-flowered fabric. Two teak bedside tables of conventional design and two armchairs upholstered in lime-green plush stood on this bed.

So he's got himself a double bed and two bedside tables already, Lilo Besslein said to herself, very bitterly, as she left the bedroom. She squeezed back through the narrow gap between the wall of the corridor and the two kitchen cabinets and refrigerator, and went into the living room. The two black and white armchairs now stood on the sofa, leaving space beside the dining table and its chairs for a second dining table with a circular plastic top on a sturdy chromium pedestal and four chairs made of chromium with bright yellow upholstery on their backs and seats. They and the table barred the way to the balcony, in the direction of which Ernst Besslein was gazing with obvious satisfaction as he sat on one of the new chairs with the little girl on his lap. Lilo Besslein saw a sofa upholstered in lime-green plush standing on the balcony.

Couldn't you have waited for me to move out, she inquired, shrill voiced.

Oh, come, it only means living in rather cramped conditions for another week, he replied, without so much as turning his head towards her, even briefly.

Rather cramped, did you say, she cried. Good heavens, it's almost impossible to move in this apartment any more, with all the rooms full of horrible furniture.

I suppose you don't actually expect me to disappear, just

like that, she inquired. But he did not reply. He sat there like a stuffed dummy, gazing at the lime-green sofa on the balcony. It cost her an effort not to go for him with both fists, and her knees were so weak with fury that she had trouble remaining on her feet. She had no doubt at all that he had arranged for early delivery of the furniture just to drive her out of this crammed and uninhabitable apartment in disgust. She wondered whether to go to a hotel. She had no money in her bank account or her savings book, of course, but there were still one hundred and fifty marks of the housekeeping money in her purse. On impulse, she fetched a suitcase up from the basement and packed it. She put in the daring black evening dress, the evening bag and the beaded sandals, as well as the clothes she thought she would need, and left the apartment without saying goodbye to her husband or her daughter. She drove to a small hotel in the shopping street to the north of Lerchenau, just one block away from the pharmacy where she worked. To her relief, they had rooms vacant. The woman at the reception desk, who was obviously the proprietress, asked her to fill in a registration form and then handed her a key with the number fifteen, saying the room was on the first floor. Lilo Besslein took the lift up to the first floor, and then went along a narrow and very dimly lit corridor. She found Number Fifteen at the end of the corridor. She unlocked the door and entered the room, carrying her case. It was an ugly, gloomy, double room, with green and yellow flowered wallpaper. The furniture was all stained dark brown and had narrow strips of brass around the edges; judging by its design it must have been made in the immediate post-war period. A picture of several snowcovered mountain peaks and an alpine hut, also covered with snow, hung over the twin beds. The floor was covered with a brown, stained carpet. The atmosphere thus created was one Lilo Besslein found instantly depressing. She put the case down on the luggage stand and went over to the window, which had a view of a back yard and six dustbins. Feeling that she couldn't stand it here, even for half an hour, she turned her back to the window and switched on the ceiling light and the two bedside lights, hoping they would make the room more pleasant. She was disappointed to find that they cast only the dimmest of light on the furniture, the walls and the other items. Sighing, she sat down on the edge of the bed. She told herself that at least she had a place to go for the time being. The room was sixty marks a night. She worked out that she could stay here two days, and after that she didn't know where she would go. To keep herself from becoming even more agitated, she picked up her handbag, took out her packet of tranquillizers, and went into the bathroom, where she took six capsules. Then she took her shoes off and lay down on the bed beside the window. She tried not to think of the future at all, but failed. However hard she attempted to concentrate on something pleasant, her unsolved problems kept surfacing. For a moment she wondered whether to ring the art student with the Malching bed-sitter that was going to be vacant once more. She had left her note of the girl's telephone number at home, but she could always ring Fred Meichelbeck and ask for it again. However, she did not. To be honest, she told herself, getting a bed-sitter would do her no good. She felt so terrified of being thrown upon her own resources. She had been sheltered from childhood, to the detriment of her own independence, and she just didn't think she could cope with life alone. She thought of Christian Blome. She wondered if she would have been happy with him. She told herself she had gambled away her very last chances of happiness with her dithering. She hated herself for her inability to throw overboard the conventional values she no longer believed in. As for her future, she had no more hope. She knew she would never be able to solve her problems. Her authoritarian upbringing, her mother's overbearing ways and last but not least her unhappy marriage had worn her out before her time, robbing her of all energy and confidence. She felt sure that at the vital moment she would give in and seek refuge with her parents, against her better judgement. She told herself she had failed all along the line and must now take the consequences. Quite calmly, she came to the decision to kill herself next day.

*

In the morning Lilo Besslein got up earlier than usual, so as to be at the pharmacy before Frau Högemann and Sabine Ickstett arrived. Then she could take her time over choosing one of the poisons kept in brown glass jars in the poison cupboard in the drugs room. But when she got to the pharmacy she found Frau Högemann already there, sitting at the desk in the dispensary checking accounts. She was obviously rather surprised to see her employee at work so early, for she looked keenly at Lilo Besslein, whose face was very white, and asked with some concern if she wasn't feeling well.

She'd better have a cup of coffee, she added, indicating the coffee pot standing on her desk.

Lilo Besslein had just had two cups of coffee at the hotel, but she did not want to refuse her employer's offer, so she fetched herself a cup from the laboratory, sat down opposite Frau Högemann and poured herself some coffee. As she did so Frau Högemann looked up from her accounts and cast her another keen glance.

She musn't take the divorce to heart so, she said.

Lilo Besslein did not know what to say to that. In silence, she reached into her handbag, took out a packet of cigarettes and lit herself one. She had just begun to smoke it when Sabine Ickstett came into the pharmacy. She hurried into the dispensary and said good morning to Frau Högemann and Lilo Besslein. She was obviously feeling cheerful.

She had something to tell them, she said. She'd been at a union meeting yesterday, her boyfriend had taken her, and afterwards she'd joined the union herself. They'd convinced her, at this meeting, that white-collar workers must get organized too and show solidarity with the working class if they ever wanted a change in the conditions of today.

Why didn't she join the union, she asked Lilo Besslein.

196

Lilo Besslein only shook her head and said she had other problems on her mind, and Sabine Ickstett pressed her no further but put on her white overall and then opened the pharmacy. There was already a customer waiting outside the door. While she served him, Lilo Besslein got up to put on her own white overall, which was hanging in the laboratory behind the drugs room. She stood there for a moment, listening. Then she found the little box hidden behind two bags of herbs, opened it and took out the key to the poison cupboard. She stood still for a moment again, listening. When she was sure there were no footsteps coming, she put the key into the keyhole of the poison cupboard and unlocked it. She saw that besides rat poison and insecticides it contained, among other items, a jar of arsenic, a jar of strychnine and a jar of cyanide. Without pausing to think it over, she took the jar of cyanide and put it in the pocket of her white overall. Then she locked the poison cupboard again, put the key in its box and put the box back in its hiding place. Feeling she had taken a great step forward, she went back to the dispensary, where she had left her handbag. Frau Högemann was still sitting at the desk, checking accounts. She smiled at Lilo Besslein, and Lilo Besslein smiled back before she picked up her bag, went round behind Frau Högemann's back and dropped the jar of cyanide into it. She had just closed the bag and put it in a corner on the floor when Sabine Ickstett called for her. She went straight into the shop. There were three customers waiting now; Sabine Ickstett served two of them and she served the third herself. He wanted a herbal laxative that would not irritate the intestine. Next she served a middle-aged woman who handed her a prescription for anti-depressants. After that an elderly man came in wanting a packet of contraceptives. Quarter of an hour passed before there were any more customers, and Lilo Besslein thought of the cyanide in her handbag. She wondered how long it would take her to die. She wondered if she would have to suffer a great deal of pain first. Sabine Ickstett, full of irritating optimism, distracted her thoughts. She told her, enthusiastically, all about the sense of comradeship prevalent among members of the union.

She'd felt accepted as part of a group at that union meeting for the first time in her life, she said, and she asked Lilo Besslein if she knew what she, Sabine Ickstett, meant.

Yes, she did, said Lilo Besslein, just so that Sabine Ickstett would leave her in peace. To her relief, two more customers came into the shop just then, both wanting a cold cure. Of the next five customers, four also wanted cold cures. Lilo Besslein told herself there was obviously flu around again. She saw Sabine Ickstett take a patent medicine to stave it off when she got a moment, swallowing three red tablets. She asked Lilo Besslein if she didn't think she'd better take some too. Not wishing to make her suspicious, Lilo Besslein did. Then more customers came into the shop, some of them with red noses, sneezing and coughing vigorously, and there was no time for Lilo Besslein even to smoke the occasional cigarette. It was not until Frau Högemann herself came into the shop at about eleven to serve the customers that she went to the dispensary, got a packet of cigarettes out of her handbag and lit one, and as she smoked it she looked at the brown glass jar in her handbag. It was about twelve centimetres high, and one-third full of cyanide. She told herself that amount of poison must be enough to make sure she died. Reassured, she closed her bag, put out her cigarette and went back into the shop. She served a number of customers before lunch time. She kept thinking of her approaching death, but she made no mistakes at all. When the lunch break came, she put her coat on, picked up her handbag, and looked long and thoughtfully at Frau Högemann and Sabine Ickstett before she left the pharmacy. They were rather puzzled. She went to the Pizzeria Boccaccio as she usually did at lunch time, sat down at the table where Christian Blome used to work, and ordered herself one glass of red wine and very soon afterwards another. She stayed in the pizzeria until it was time to go back to the pharmacy, but she didn't go back there as usual. Instead, she went into one of the two nearby self-service stores and bought a bottle of French cognac. With the bottle under her arm, she went back to the hotel and collected the key of her room. She took the lift up to the first floor, went down the long and dimly lit corridor, opened the door of her room, and locked it again behind her as soon as she was inside. Once again, she noticed the ugliness of the room, with its green and yellow flowered wallpaper, its dark brown furniture and its stained, brown carpet. She could have wished for pleasanter surroundings in which to die, and she was sorry there was no radio in the room; she would have liked to hear some music just now. She told herself that at least she had a bottle of French cognac to make death easier. She put the bottle of cognac and the jar of cyanide on the bedside table by the window, and then fetched the tooth glass from the bathroom. Hands steady, she opened the bottle of cognac, filled the glass, gulped down the cognac and filled the glass again. She wondered how her husband would react to her death. She wondered what her parents would say about it. Then she thought of Christian Blome.

I missed my chance of happiness, she told herself. She picked up the glass again, drained it quickly, and filled it once more. The alcohol was beginning to go to her head. She felt full of self-pity. She thought she hadn't deserved to die all alone in such an ugly hotel room. She glanced at her watch. Two-thirty in the afternoon. She wondered when she would be dead. She wanted to be cremated, and as she was not sure if her husband knew that, she tore a page out of her address book, wrote down that she would like to be cremated, and put the note on the bedside table. Then she drank another glass of cognac. She was getting increasingly intoxicated, and the more intoxicated she became the less she cared about dying. She felt quite sure life no longer had anything to offer her to make it worth living. She had given up all hope of a better future. She wondered when they would find her body: not until some time tomorrow morning, she supposed. Suddenly she thought of making herself beautiful for her death. She went to her suitcase and took out the daring black evening dress, the purchase of which she had thought amounted to the first step towards a better future, and the beaded, high-heeled sandals. Slowly, she undressed and then put on the evening dress and the sandals. Then she opened the wardrobe door, which had a large mirror just inside it, and inspected herself. She thought she looked very elegant. To heighten the effect, she went into the bathroom, combed her hair and made her eyes up for the last time, outlining them with careful brush strokes. Then she poured the rest of the cognac into her glass. This time she sipped it slowly, and as she emptied the glass she began to feel afraid of dying. She wondered if life really had nothing more to offer her, nothing to make living worth while. But she did not answer that question. Hands trembling, she picked up the glass jar of cyanide. She thought of her failure to find either an apartment or a job. She thought of her inability to cope with life on her own. She thought of having to go home to her parents.

I don't want to live any more, she whispered, and she opened the jar with shaking fingers, raised it to her lips, let the white powder that looked something like salt run into her mouth, and washed it down with the rest of the cognac in her glass. Then, panic-stricken, she concentrated on her feelings. But there were no effects just yet. She lay down on the bed and thought of Christian Blome. Suddenly she felt dizzy, and there was a violent rushing in her ears. She felt nausea. She tried to fight the nausea off by deep breathing, in and out, but that become more difficult every minute. She could scarcely breathe at all. Her chest felt tight. She sat up and put both feet on the floor, intending to open the window so that she could breathe more easily. Slowly, she stood up, ready to take a step towards the window, but no sooner was she on her feet, preparing to take that step, than she fell to the floor at the bedside, dead.

*

They found Lilo Besslein's corpse next morning. The chambermaid, coming to clean the room and make the bed, found the door locked on the inside. She knocked several times, and got no answer. Puzzled, she went to tell the hotel proprietress. The hotel proprietress took the lift up to the first floor. When she, in her turn, got no answer to her repeated knocks and requests to open the door, she called the police and told the officer on duty she thought there might have been a suicide in her hotel. The police arrived ten minutes later, along with a fire engine, an ambulance, and the cars of four doctors on emergency call. They broke down the door of the room and took charge of the brown glass jar which had contained the cyanide. The four doctors unanimously certified that death had occurred. The fact that the dead woman's passport and driving licence were in her handbag made it easier to identify her. Even before the police broke the news of his wife's death to Ernst Besslein, her corpse had been carried out of the hotel on a stretcher and taken to the Forensic Institute. By the time that Ernst Besslein, who had shown no emotion at all, got to the hotel, the police, the doctors and the firemen had left again. He simply collected his wife's suitcase and paid the hotel proprietress, who was extremely concerned for her hotel's reputation, for the two nights she had spent there. Then he drove home and broke the news first to his parents and then to his parents-in-law. Two hours later, his parents and his parents-in-law all arrived in M. Wilma Besslein and Max Besslein were as calm as their son, but Paul and Margot Ohlbaum were shattered. They kept crying quietly and asking Ernst Besslein exactly what had happened. Finally they all went to the Forensic Institute to see the body for the last time. This was the occasion of the final break between the families. Paul Ohlbaum accused Ernst

201

Besslein of hounding his daughter to her death with his divorce petition, and Margot Ohlbaum went so far as to call him a murderer. The two families did not even nod to each other at the funeral, which was on the day originally fixed for the divorce. Even before the ceremony the guests divided into two groups, the Ohlbaums being supported by a female cousin of Lilo Besslein's, one of her girlfriends from N, and two middle-aged married couples who were close friends of their own, while Ernst Besslein and his parents had the Dülfers, the Einseles, the Urzingers, the Rittmeiers and Frau Deininger. The two groups went to two different cafés after the funeral. The mourners in the Ohlbaums' party blamed Ernst Besslein for his wife's death. The mourners in the Bessleins' party said he was not at all to blame. Ernst Besslein went home feeling better. He was glad the funeral was over. He had been afraid it would upset him, but that had not been the case. He was surprised at his own indifference. In fact he was more bothered by all the furniture cluttering up his apartment than by his wife's death, but that problem was very soon solved. The removal men came to his door at seven on the dot next morning to take his wife's furniture away. The Ohlbaums arrived soon afterwards to make sure all their daughter's possessions were removed. As for Ernst Besslein, he was intent upon ensuring that the removal men didn't take any of his own new furniture. He looked in on the child now and then; he had not taken her to Frau Finsinger's that day. When his wife's furniture, linen, crockery and clothes had been taken away, and the removal men and the Ohlbaums had left, he arranged his new furniture. He moved the purple-flowered double bed into the middle of the longer wall of the bedroom and placed the two bedside tables to the right and left of the bedhead. He carried the refrigerator and the four kitchen cabinets into the kitchen and put them where his wife's kitchen cupboards and refrigerator used to stand. He arranged his new saucepans and frying pans, crockery and cutlery in the cabinets and put food away in the refrigerator. Then he went into the living room and moved the new white dining table on its chromium pedestal and the four new chairs to the spot where his wife's dining table used to stand. He put the lime-green sofa and the two new lime-green armchairs where his wife's black and white striped sofa and her black and white armchairs once stood. Then he walked from room to room, well satisfied. He thought the new furniture much nicer than the old. All he needed now was a cupboard for the nursery, a coffee table, a standard lamp and a wall storage unit, and he did not have to wait long for those. The nursery cupboard, the coffee table, the standard lamp and the wall unit were delivered late that afternoon. He asked the delivery man to put the coffee table beside the sofa, put the standard lamp between the armchairs, and put the nursery cupboard where his wife's antique bureau had previously stood. They assembled the new wall unit, which had built-in stereo equipment, a built-in television set and a built-in bar, and meanwhile he put his daughter's clothes away in the nursery cupboard and then watched them at work. It took them over an hour to assemble the wall unit, but he gave them only a five-mark tip. When they had left, he put his bottles of alcohol away in the bar and then arranged his books and records on the shelves of the unit. Then he walked from room to room again, very well satisfied indeed, before laying the table for supper for himself and the little girl. He gave the child some bread and spiced sausage, and arranged slices of ham, egg and pickled cucumber carefully on his own bread and butter. After supper he put the little girl to bed and sang her to sleep as usual. Then he switched on the new television set and watched the news, sitting on the new sofa. When the news was over, he fetched a bottle of beer and the sports section of the daily paper and sat down on the sofa again. Suddenly he thought of his wife. He pictured her with her mahogany-coloured hair, her big blue eyes, her soft mouth, her slender waist and her long legs. He remembered the way she used to smile and laugh. He remembered the way she used to burst into tears. He remembered the way she used to get herself up to look pretty. He told himself her body was probably burnt by now, and something akin to grief stirred within him. But it was immediately dispelled by the thought of her infidelity. He could never forgive her for that. He wondered why she had not gone to live with her lover. He wondered why she had killed herself. He thought fleetingly that the approaching divorce might have been one of the causes of her suicide, but then he suppressed that idea. He considered he had acted perfectly correctly in petitioning for divorce. He was sure he was in the right.

I have nothing at all to reproach myself with, he told himself, before he leaned back on the sofa and began to devote himself, with the requisite peace of mind, to the sports section of the paper.